The Last Outrageous Woman

A Novel

The Last Outrageous Woman

A Novel

Jessica H. Stone

PENCHANT PRESS INTERNATIONAL

New South Wales, Australia
Washington, United States of America

Penchant Press International

New South Wales, Australia
Washington, United States of America

www.penchantpressinternational.com

Publisher's Note: This is a work of fiction. Names, characters,
places, and incidents are a product of the author's imagination.
Locales and public names are sometimes used for atmospheric
purposes. Any resemblance to actual people, living or dead, or
to businesses, companies, events, institutions, or locales is
completely coincidental.

Cover Design: William L. Rink
Cover Model: Laura Rink www.LauraRink.com
Cover Photography: James Imhoff
Editor: Denise Winkler, Ph.D.

The Last Outrageous Woman/ Jessica H. Stone 1st ed.
ISBN 978-0-9724960-8-7

For my mother

The choice is ours, in every moment.

M. J. Ryan

Chapter One

A L i t t l e   H e l p   f r o m   t h e   P r e s i d e n t
T a m p a ,   F l o r i d a

"Now, I know you're the President, Mr. Roosevelt, but you have got to come down off of there."

Caroline stood with arms upstretched, pleading with the resident who balanced on top of the recreation room's piano. He wore only his pajama bottoms and a shiny purple party hat. He waved a small American flag and grinned. Then he stuck his tongue out at Caroline.

Mattie leaned against the door and watched the mini-drama unfold. At eighty-six, she thought she'd seen it all. But nope, even after five years as a resident of the Restful Palms Retirement Home she'd never seen anything quite like this. She started to laugh then immediately clapped her hand over her mouth. It shouldn't be funny. Wasn't funny. Not at all. Tobias Tarpin had been a U.S. Senator at one time. A powerful man. Now his brain played tricks, let reality sift through holes in memory and logic. Lately, he'd taken on the persona of his favorite politician. It can happen to any of us, she thought. Probably will.

Mattie looked away from the piano for a moment and scanned the room. Tables covered with checkers board games and partially completed jigsaw puzzles crowded together to make space for a circle of folding chairs, wheelchairs, and walkers. Almost time for the afternoon sing-along. Another inane activity designed to keep the elderly busy. A bitter taste filled her mouth, and she pressed her lips in a thin, flat line.

To shake the feeling, Mattie slid her hand into the pocket of her dress and rubbed her wrist across the paper she'd carried for over two weeks. She'd touched the folded edge of the *Notice to Leave* form so often she worried she'd worn it thin. The paper was a ticket to freedom if she could get someone in authority to sign it and sign it soon. For Mattie and her friends, time was running out.

The other women had put her in charge of the document because, after all, the whole crazy scheme had been her idea. And, she suspected, they probably figured she was the sneakiest of the group because she'd never been caught pulling a prank. Not the time she slipped bubble bath into the entryway fountain, and not even the time she spiked the orange juice dispenser with an entire bottle of vodka at the Mother's Day brunch. They probably figured if anyone could pull the wool over, it was her. Mattie bit her lower lip. They were counting on her; she couldn't let them down.

A sharp clap jarred her thoughts. She looked back to the piano and to the heavyset woman who strained to reach the wobbly gentleman now marching on the piano's lid. Sweat glistened on Caroline's brown skin; wet rings stained the short sleeves of her uniform. Mattie could hear the frustration in the younger woman's voice.

"Mr. Roosevelt, you can make your speech down here, where you won't get hurt. Where are those orderlies?"

This is it, Mattie thought. This is the right time. *The perfect time.* Caroline was the Assistant Director of Restful Palms—her signature on the line would do.

Mattie inhaled, held her breath a moment, exhaled, and pulled the form and a pen from her pocket. Her feet hurt more than usual today, but she ignored the pain, took another deep breath, and crabbed across the long room. Her slippers flapped with each step. When she reached the piano, she extended the paper. "Sorry to bother you but would you sign this please?"

"Not now, sugar." Caroline shot a look at Mattie, glanced at the form, and turned her attention back to the man. He now balanced on his left foot and held his right leg straight out. "I'm a little busy here."

Mattie moved closer and touched Caroline's arm. She struggled to keep panic from her voice. *This has to work.* "A quick signature," she said. "Then I'll go get the orderlies for you."

"Put your leg down, Mr. Roosevelt." Caroline smacked the side of the piano. "Gimme that." She snatched the paper from Mattie, skimmed it, scribbled her name, and thrust it back. "Now go find me those lazy boys." She looked up and slapped the piano top. "Mr. Roosevelt! No!"

Mattie gripped the paper and bolted. She didn't want to give the Assistant Director time to rethink anything, and she certainly did not want to watch President Roosevelt urinate on the retirement home's piano.

Clutching the paper between crimped fingers, Mattie hobbled as fast as she could toward the elevator that would take her to the fourth floor and to her friends who waited—probably holding their collective breath. She knew she had to appear normal; not attract attention. But it was all she could do to keep from bursting out in laughter or maybe even song. Yes! She and her four best friends—Edna, Helen, Rose, and Dolores—were about to escape this endless boredom and embark on the most amazing journey any of them had ever imagined. Like all residents in the independent living wing of the retirement home, they could, of course, come and go anytime they wanted. However, Restful Palm's policy required residents to sign a *Notice to Leave* form to let management know where they planned to go and for how long. More often than not, the management tried to talk residents—especially the elderly women—out of extended visits away from the campus, citing concerns for their health and safety. Mattie always figured the real concern was for the cash Restful Palms would not collect for meals and other incidentals while residents were away. But now, no one would try to convince them that they weren't smart enough, or healthy enough, or strong enough, to go on this adventure. No one would attempt to frighten them out of their plans, or tell them they were too old to make this trip. This was really happening and she, Margaret Lynn Snorgenson, had the paper to prove it.

She reached the elevator and pressed the button with her knuckle. Normally that simple action caused her pain, but if it did today, she was too excited to notice. As she waited for the doors to open Mattie grinned and thought back to that lovely spring afternoon, just a few months ago, when Edna told her circus story and shared her dream to ride a camel; the dream that launched their outrageous adventure.

Chapter Two

The Dream that Launched a Journey

"More tea, Miss Rose?" Caroline Franklin smiled at the petite woman who dressed, as she always did, in pale pink. Today Rose wore a satin suit with a collar of cream-colored lace. Her ever-present strand of pearls matched the soft white curls that framed her heart-shaped face. A pink patent leather handbag hung from a hook on the wall behind her chair. Rose offered a weak smile and shook her head no.

Caroline hadn't expected more. As far as she knew, Rose rarely spoke or did much of anything except buy pink accessories for her room and attend these luncheons. Caroline turned her attention to the others. "Ladies? Edna? Helen?" She held the teapot high.

Caroline knew all the residents by name, and she never forgot a birthday. She knew the dates when their families had dropped them off with promises to visit, and she knew how easily, and how often, promises were broken. She remembered the dates when one by one, their friends had rested in the retirement home's chapel for the last time. "Anyone? More tea?"

Helen looked up at Caroline, shook her head no, but offered a wide, reassuring smile. At eighty-eight, Helen—the only other black woman at Restful Palms—did Caroline proud. She decked out to the nines—every day—in pressed pantsuits and heavy gold-toned jewelry, and she wore her gray-and-silver-streaked hair pulled in a tight French knot. She stood tall and straight like someone who'd spent a lifetime as a swimmer or long-distance runner. Helen smelled of lilacs and her slow southern drawl never failed to calm even the most agitated resident or frazzled member of the staff.

Caroline smiled back and shifted her gaze from Helen to Josephine. She tilted her head, lifted the teapot a little higher. Josephine sniffed once, then turned her face away as if, Caroline thought, in disdain.

For the most part, Caroline liked the residents of Restful Palms. Mattie, the spunkiest and certainly most cantankerous of the ladies, amused her. Her wiry hair swirled in a perpetual frizz; she wore a snarl much of the time, and she was so fiercely independent that she'd rather starve than let someone cut a piece of meat for her. Her entire wardrobe consisted of one pair of nasty old bedroom slippers and the half-dozen housedresses Caroline's cousin had fixed up for her. Caroline suppressed a chuckle. She suspected that Mattie was behind several of the fraternity-type pranks that kept the residents entertained and pushed the already overworked staff. Roger Simpson, the retirement home's Director, vowed to get to the bottom of things. He even put Caroline in charge of hunting down the perpetrator, but somehow Caroline never had enough time to investigate the offenses. She smiled softly and turned her attention to Edna.

Muddled and confused much of the time, Edna reminded Caroline of a confused little dog who'd been scolded, or worse. She couldn't remember names most of the time, and couldn't decide between chocolate or vanilla ice cream, or if she wanted a second cup of coffee at breakfast. But Edna was kind and loving and never had a mean thing to say. She was the complete opposite of her late husband—a man everyone on the staff had called "Captain Control" behind his back.

Caroline even liked Dolores, who whined and complained both to and about the retirement home staff. Yes, even Dolores, with her vast selection of sparkling sweatshirts, her lumbering gait, and her taste for sugary treats had a certain charm. But Josephine was hard to like.

Although time had taken her perfect posture, Josephine carried herself with the precision of someone who'd learned to walk with a Bible balanced on her head. Her brow furrowed into deep lines; her mouth puckered—a caricature of a librarian with lips pinched in a perpetual shush. Despite the Florida heat, she dressed in tweeds and on Sunday mornings, she wore beige cotton gloves to the chapel. She did meet with the other ladies each month, but it seemed to Caroline that Josephine was cool and distant, not genuinely part of the group. Caroline thought of the woman's husband; he would go first, and Josephine would be left behind, widowed and lonely.

Yes, Caroline knew a great deal about these ladies and their lives since they'd come to the retirement home. She knew they had, or would, outlive their spouses and that except for a few aches and pains now and again—over-the-counter pain tablets were the strongest drugs any of them used—they were all still in excellent health.

But other than being aware that they'd lived through the Great Depression, WWII, and a series of presidential administrations, Caroline didn't know anything about who they were, or what they'd done before they arrived at Restful Palms. For some reason, this bothered her. Sometimes, when she was close to them, she felt subtle, but visceral feelings of grief. Unspoken sadness around unfulfilled goals and disappointed dreams. Debilitating boredom. Her cousin told her to forget it—don't let it bother her—collect her paycheck and leave it alone. They'd be dead soon anyway.

But Caroline *was* bothered, and she couldn't leave things alone. Maybe that's why she volunteered to work an extra shift, to serve them, once a month when they reserved the private dining room for their "Ladies Only Luncheon." She sure didn't do it for the money. Lord knows, she barely made bus fare in those two extra hours. Besides, her cousin was right about one thing; they wouldn't be around much longer. There were six for lunch today. Last month there had been seven. And two months before that, nine.

"I'll take another slice of cake," Dolores interrupted thoughts.

"Now, sugar." Caroline set the teapot down and rested her hands on her broad hips. "You know your doctor don't want you eatin' so many sweets. You are eatin' yourself to Heaven."

Dolores waved her off. "Better eat my way to Heaven than starve my way to the other place."

Caroline clicked her tongue and shook her head as she collected the empty plate from in front of Dolores. "I'll be right back, ladies." Balancing her load on a tray, she left the private dining room.

"You can have mine," Edna said. She pushed her plate, cake untouched, toward Dolores.

"No," Dolores said. "You're already too thin. If you lose any more weight, you'll be as skinny as that old stick, Mattie."

Mattie growled low in her throat, but she didn't say anything because she knew Dolores was right. She had become stick thin, had dropped pounds—*too many pounds*—in a very short time. Certainly not something she tried to do. But her fingers twisted so tight that some days it was just easier to skip meals than to try and grip a fork. And there was no way, *no way* she'd let some young pup spoon-feed her. She thrust her fists under the napkin on her lap and scowled at Dolores.

In Mattie's opinion, Dolores was an embarrassment and gave senior women a bad name. She was food-obsessed, self-absorbed, and loud. Although she would celebrate her eighty-first birthday in October, she still slopped food like a child. A few days earlier, Mattie overheard two nurses joking that they could tell the day's menu by looking at the food dribbles on Dolores's shirt. If Mattie had been in charge, Dolores would not have been allowed to join their group. But everyone, except men and members of the Restful Palms Retirement Home staff, was invited to participate in the Ladies Luncheons providing, of course, they could contribute five dollars a month to the room reservation fee.

Dolores ignored the scowl and continued. "Don't you worry. Caroline will get me another piece. Besides, she's such a buttinski. She's here to serve us, not to monitor our behavior. In fact, I have half a mind to . . ."

Helen interrupted her. They'd heard this rant before and today was Edna's day. She leaned forward and looked past Dolores. "So now, darlin'," Helen said, "It's been one month since Louis left us. God rest his soul." She reached across Dolores and patted Edna's hand. "I'm sure you've made some plans. Will you be staying here? With us?" The women all turned toward their most recently widowed.

Edna managed a smile. "I don't think so." Her voice wavered. "My daughters, you met them at Christmas—Joan and Suzanne—they think I should leave Restful Palms. They think I should move to a home in Atlanta."

"Atlanta!" Mattie said. "Why, that's not even in Florida. You'd never get to visit any of us." She leaned forward, brought one hand to the table top. "Edna Fisher, you've lived in this state forty-some years. Why that's . . ." Mattie paused, did the math. "That's almost half of your life. This is your home."

Edna looked at her plate for a moment and then pushed it away. "They think it would be better for me."

"Better for them to get their greedy mitts on your money." Mattie snapped her words. She looked around the table. "There is nothing wrong with Edna," she said. "There is no reason for her to move. We've all met those girls. They're out for one thing. Nobody says it, but we all know it." Mattie narrowed her gaze and focused on Helen.

Helen swallowed and glanced down for a moment. She and Mattie had shared a table at the Christmas dinner the year they'd met Edna's daughters.

Joan and Suzanne had taken charge of things before they even slipped out of their coats. The two barked commands to the retirement home staff, shouted out instructions to the residents, and even tried to direct Louis. Helen had found it almost amusing to watch how the two sisters and their father had competed to control every moment of the evening. Almost, but not completely, amusing.

"That's a little harsh," Josephine said. She peered over the top of her reading glasses—her dressy reading glasses, the ones with the mock tortoise-shell frames, the ones she wore to church, and to these luncheons. "If my girls ever want anything, I'll be happy to give it to them. I'm sure Edna feels the same way." She sat back and crossed her arms. "Tobias has always wanted our girls to be happy." As the only one with a living husband, Josephine felt obliged to inject him into every conversation lest he, like the other men, simply faded away.

Helen nodded to Josephine. She and Mattie agreed about most things, but on this point, she wasn't entirely in Mattie's camp. True enough, Edna's daughters would probably want control of the money now that their father had passed. And for sure, they didn't seem cordial. Still, Helen liked to give folks the benefit of the doubt. She looked at Edna, studied her face a moment, and wondered about Edna's relationship with her daughters. Helen sighed. No matter what issues festered between Edna and her girls, Helen knew the pain that comes from losing a child, whatever form the loss took. Helen also knew the sorrow of laying a spouse to rest, and so she tried to smooth the waters.

"Edna, darlin' your girls love you. They maybe they seem a little bit . . . you know . . . abrupt at times, but they're just busy people. That's all. And for sure, they know you love them and want them to be happy."

"Of course I want them to be happy. It doesn't matter, you know. Not really. I'll do whatever they say." Edna folded her hands and rested them in her lap. The fingers of her right hand covered her wedding band. Her voice so soft now, Rose asked for a repeat.

"All I meant was I'm used to it. I always did what Louis and the girls wanted."

The women fell silent. The clatter of trays and silverware from the main dining room served as rhythm, background music, for the retirement home. The whirr of a motorized wheelchair passing by the open door provided the melody.

Mattie cleared her throat. "Edna, if you could do anything, anything at all, no matter how . . . you know . . . how unlikely. Just once. What would it be?"

Edna looked up. Her answer, offered so quickly, surprised the others. "I'd like to ride a camel." She hesitated, looked across the room to a Currier and Ives print nailed to the far wall. In the winter scene, a man in a plaid coat lugged a Christmas tree through deep snow, while women in flowing skirts skated over a frozen lake. But Edna didn't see the snow-covered village or the horse-drawn sleigh. She saw shifting sands and towering pyramids. "Ever since I was a young woman, I've dreamed of riding a camel. In Egypt."

"A camel?" Rose tilted her head to one side. She knew what a camel was. But ride a camel? Who rode camels? Did ladies ride camels?

"What a great wish! You have a story. I know you have a story." Mattie's face lit up and flushed. The idea of something new sparked her, made her sit up straight and lean forward. "Edna, tell us why you want to ride a camel!"

Caroline waddled into the room and positioned a plate with two slices of strawberry sponge cake in front of Dolores. "I'm headin' out now, but no rush. You ladies, take your time." Dolores licked her lips and reached for her fork.

"Yes, yes." Mattie made a dismissive gesture. "We'll take care of ourselves." She glanced up at Caroline. "Oh, and would you close the door on your way out?"

"That was a bit rude," Josephine said.

Mattie ignored her. "Come on now, Edna." She smiled at her friend and raised one eyebrow. "Tell us the story about your camel."

Edna flushed and cleared her throat. "I, I um . . ."

"Yes, tell us." Helen burst in. She, too, leaned forward, her bracelets jingled as she rested her arms on the table.

And so, while dishwashers hosed apple sauce and gravy from plates, and nurses propped patients like rag dolls, and orderlies lined wheelchairs against the lobby walls, and while Dolores worked her way through mounds of sponge cake and sugared strawberries, Edna shared her story.

Chapter Three

We were married, Louis and me, two days after my high-school graduation ceremony. I skipped a year, and I was shorter than most of the other girls in my class, so I guess I looked a little fragile to Louis. He decided to be my guardian. My protector. That's what he called himself; my protector. He used to tell his friends that he was the head of the household, the one in charge of things, and that would never change. Naturally, I was impressed with Louis. Everyone was. After all, he went to a year of junior college and was the assistant manager of the only bank in our town.

My girlfriends all approved of Louis. They all said I had such an easy life. I didn't have to drive. Louis wouldn't hear of his wife driving a car. And I never had to buy the groceries or even pick out the furniture for our home. Louis made all the decisions. I didn't have to do anything except care for our children and follow his directions.

Louis was a good Christian man. We took our children—the girls, Joan and Suzanne, and our son Randall—to church for

Sunday morning and Wednesday evening services. We sat third row back from the altar, on the right side of the aisle, twice a week, every week. We never missed.

On Wednesdays, I made a tuna casserole with green beans for the potluck dinner after services. I tried, once, to make that dish with an onion ring topping. I found the recipe in *Redbook Magazine*. They have such good recipes, you know. But Louis said, "No."

"Good to follow routines," he said. "Routines will keep us in line, make things run smooth. No need to fix things that are not broken."

Louis wanted the children to have exposure—that's what he called it—exposure, to the world. So every Friday night he took us all out to dinner. I made sure the children were scrubbed and dressed proper, and we went to the Big Boy Restaurant twenty miles away in Ubly. It was our routine.

Louis ate the roast beef and new potatoes, the girls had lasagna, Randall and I split fish and French fries. We ordered the same meals so often that the waitress didn't even need to bring us menus.

"See," Louis would say, "routines create efficiency."

But the year that Mr. Barnum and Mr. Bailey wanted a permit to set up their circus inside the town limits, Louis did something completely out of the routine. The only time in fifty-one years of marriage.

Louis led the town council, and usually he opposed such things but he knew the circus would bring in a lot of money and that would be good for the bank. So he convinced the council to let the circus have their permit.

Louis and his two tellers, and the three other members of the council encouraged everyone in town to attend. My heavens weren't we surprised when word spread to the neighboring towns! So, the year our children were seven, nine, and ten, Louis took us, the whole family, to the circus.

Louis knew there would be huge crowds. Crowds of people he did not know, and I could tell this worried him. He was worried about me. Worried that because I was so thin, and pale, and not at all crowd-wise, I might be an easy target for someone up to no good. He worried that the children might get lost or kidnapped in the fracas that was bound to occur.

For our protection, Louis tied the family together with a long length of rope. He looped belts of cord around our waists and left a couple of feet between each of us. If any one of us strayed farther than those few feet, the rope pulled at our waist and tightened around the waists of the others. This reminded us to return to the fold.

Louis put me in the middle with our daughters on either side. He and Randall took the end positions. When he first came up with the plan, I was upset. I thought that, as the mother, I should be on the outside to protect our children. But Louis was firm. The end position would be too dangerous for me. Even though our son was only ten at the time, Louis said *the men* would protect the family.

He told us everything he knew about circuses, but there was no way Louis could have prepared us for all the sights and sounds of that day.

There was music from a calliope, and bells, and whistles, and elephants trumpeting. Oh, they made a loud racket. Men whooped for you to come by and let them guess your weight. Others called out for you to stop and pop balloons with darts. There was a game where men hit an anvil with a hammer; if they made a big brass bell ring, they won stuffed bears to give to their girlfriends. All the young men in our town lined up for that game. They hollered to each other, made bets, and bragged until it was their turn. Their girlfriends giggled and blushed.

And the fancy food . . . my goodness, you wouldn't believe it . . . the air was sweet with cotton candy. There were fried corn dogs and hot popcorn in three different colors.

Moving five people, tied together, through a crowd proved more difficult than Louis had expected. People kept trying to walk between us and of course, they got caught. That made folks upset, and they let him know what they thought about his rope idea. Some of them weren't all that polite about it, either. But Louis stuck with his plan; once he made a plan, Louis stuck to it.

At one point, we stopped in front of a tent painted with pictures of midgets, and women with beards, and one really, really fat lady. The crowd thickened, and the rope pulled tight around my waist. Happened so fast the wind went right out of me with a whoosh. I had never been in a crowd before and, at first, when I was out of sight of my children and Louis, I panicked. But only for a second.

I remember people crushed up against me. Men, tall men, pressed on me. One man's metal belt buckle pushed into my arm and left the faint imprint of a truck on my skin. Another man squashed between Joan and me. His body was rock hard, and he smelled of old sweat and manure. I wrinkled my nose and tried to breathe through my mouth. His smell disgusted me. But later . . . later, when I remembered his smell, I would have feelings that I considered inappropriate for a married Christian lady.

When we were finally through the crowd, when we were finally safe inside the big tent, we settled in our seats. We were a bit uncomfortable because the rope between us was a few inches too short to loop over the sides of the chairs. But we made do by sitting sidesaddle on one thigh.

Can't you imagine our excitement when the lights dimmed, and the show commenced? Clowns tumbled and rolled in barrels and bounced on trampolines. One man swallowed a burning stick, and jugglers tossed plates and knives in circles around their heads; one even balanced a bicycle and a bowling ball. A handsome young man walked on a wire way up high. That scared me because there wasn't a net to catch him if he fell.

An animal tamer, from a real African safari, cracked a whip and made lions and tigers roar and claw the air with their huge paws. You could barely hear the circus music over all that cracking and roaring. And there were bears and, oh my. I can't even remember all of it. Everything was so strange and exciting and so different. But what I do remember . . . the most thrilling of all for me . . . were the camels.

I'd seen pictures of elephants in a magazine at the doctor's office. And the farmers around our town had plenty of white horses, although none that could count or dance, but the camels were beyond anything I ever dreamed of. They were taller and twice the size of any horse and their huge faces filled with expression. They snarled and sneered. They even laughed. When they laughed, they showed their thick ivory teeth. Why, I could hardly catch my breath. I stared at their brown eyes bulging out like chestnuts. Their lips looked so soft. So silky.

Dark-skinned men dressed in long white robes walked beside the camels. They carried colored ropes with tasseled ends and called commands to the beasts.

Louis leaned over Suzanne and told me that the men were called camel drivers. "They are," he said, "most likely Egyptians. From Egypt."

I covered my mouth with my hand. I could not think of what to say; I was just that amazed. Then, a beautiful young woman dressed in a pink ballerina skirt and pink ballerina shoes ran on her pointed toes into the ring with the camels and the men. She tiptoed up to the biggest animal and reached for the driver's hand. He shouted something and that great creature kneeled down, all steady and stately. The girl climbed onto a golden chair high on the camel's back. She let go of the driver's hand and held her arm in the air and tossed her head back as the animal unfolded its knees and stood up. I could barely believe how high up that girl was and how grand that animal was.

The ringmaster wore a bright red suit and tall, shiny black boots, and a top hat, and he called into his megaphone.

"Laaadies and Gentlemen. This is a royal camel. This camel is a gift to the people of the United States of America. A gift from the Sheik of Egypt himself. This camel is the smartest, and the most regal, and the most majestic camel in the whole world!"

The crowd clapped and cheered, and I believed every word.

When the show ended, Louis directed us out of the tent and through the crowds to the gate. As we passed by an arcade, I spotted something I'd missed earlier, a ring off to one side. I probably missed it because of the crush of the crowd. There, in that ring, were three huge camels. They stood still and calm and watched the people go by. I stopped, which caused the rope to tighten on the children and Louis.

"Look!" I pointed to a sign posted near the ring.

CAMEL RIDES—FIVE CENTS

"Oh, Louis, *please.*"

I begged and whined and pouted, but Louis was so appalled that a good, clean, married lady would even think of such a shocking act that he was, for the first time in our marriage, speechless. He remained so upset and repelled by the thought of his wife on one of those filthy animals—he called them filthy animals—that a full three weeks went by before he climbed into my bed to perform his duties.

Edna stopped speaking. She stared, unfocused, at the far wall.

"Did you go to the circus the next year?" Helen's eyes were wide and bright. Her voice startled Edna—brought her back to Restful Palms.

"No." She shook her head and sighed. "The circus never returned to our town, but for years, while washing the dishes or scrubbing the floors, I would think about that camel. The most majestic, the most regal, and the smartest camel on earth. I remember when I hung the laundry on the line I would watch the bed sheets billow out and I would daydream about the camel drivers and their long robes whirling in the wind."

She smiled. Her face flushed with memory. "I used to pretend, for a minute, that I was the Queen of Egypt, the wife of the Great Sheik. Yes, Edna, Queen of the Desert who rode her camel to . . . I didn't know exactly where to . . . but I would ride my camel there."

She stopped and searched the faces of her friends. The others sat motionless. No one poked at sponge cake or licked strawberry from the tip of a fork. They stared at her, mouths open, eyes wide. Edna's cheeks flushed with color, a perfect match to the frosting. She lowered her eyes and stared at her hands on her lap. "I guess such thoughts are, you know, sinful."

Josephine cleared her throat. "Not exactly sinful," she said. She leaned toward the table and brushed at a crumb. "But your husband was correct." She picked the crumb up between her forefinger and thumb and placed it on the edge of her saucer. "Riding a camel would be outrageous behavior. And we," she cleared her throat again, "are certainly not *that sort of women.*"

Again, the circle went quiet. The ladies avoided eye contact. They stared at their hands or at slices of untouched sponge cake. From the hallway came the clump, clump, clump of someone moving along with a walker.

An orderly pushed the door open, stepped into the room, and stopped. This silence was not normal in a group of old women. It made him nervous. He backed out of the room and closed the door without a sound.

Finally, Mattie lifted her head. "Well," she said, "I want to be *that sort of woman.*" She looked around the table, gathered her courage. "I want, one time . . . once in my life . . . before I meet my maker . . . to be an outrageous woman."

She made a fist and pounded on the table. Not too hard, but hard enough to startle the others. They jerked upright, turned their full attention to her. She looked from one wrinkled expression to the next. Her friends appeared confused and maybe a little frightened. Dolores tapped her right hearing aid, not certain she'd heard correctly. Edna pressed two bone-thin fingers to her lips. Helen scrunched her brow into a furrow. Rose rolled her pearls like rosary beads.

"I'm serious," Mattie said. She pounded her fist on the table again, this time with more force. "For once in my life I want to do something shocking." She cast a look at Edna, then jutted her chin out. "Something like ride a camel." She looked around the table again, her gaze confident. Defiant. "In Egypt."

"Don't be ridiculous." Josephine slapped her napkin onto the table. "That's plain foolishness and . . ."

"Wait." Helen interrupted her. She raised her hand, insistent as if she knew she had the right answer in class. "I always wanted to go to Australia." She lowered her hand and leaned forward. She put both palms on the edge of the table and gripped it hard. "I want to see a kangaroo. A live kangaroo. A real kangaroo." She looked at Edna.

Edna's eyes grew wide. "My, my," she whispered.

"Good," Mattie said. "Camels and kangaroos. Excellent."

"What about you—you troublemaker?" Dolores tilted her head and tapped her left hearing aid. "What would you do?"

Mattie's face softened. She closed her eyes and held her breath. Then she opened her eyes and exhaled. She looked around the table; the others, each of them, leaned forward, waited. "I would sail a ship somewhere. I would stand on the bow with my legs spread wide for balance. I would feel the salt spray on my face and the pull of a fierce wind in my hair. I would sail a ship. Anywhere. Any ship. A ship bounding over shimmering waves." She smiled, wistful.

"Why Margaret Lynn Snorgenson, I cannot believe you." Drops of spit flew from Josephine's mouth, and her jowls quivered as she spoke. "You should be ashamed of yourself for even thinking these things. And, and . . ." she shook her finger at Mattie, "for goading these others on." She snatched up her napkin and wiped her mouth.

Rose either missed Josephine's outburst or ignored it. "I don't know if this is so adventurous as ships and kangaroos and camels," she said, "but I'd like to visit my brother's grave in Wisconsin. I've never seen it and . . ." She looked down. Her hands trembled as she smoothed imaginary crinkles from the table cloth.

When Rose looked back up her eyes appeared watery and clouded. "There's something I never got to say. To do . . ." Her voice was so soft the others had to lean close to hear, "when he was alive."

"That works, dear." Mattie reached over and patted her friend's arm. She turned to Dolores. "What about you? Any unfulfilled dreams?"

"Now that you ask." Dolores straightened, took a deep breath, and pushed her chest forward. "As you all know, I've had a very full, busy life as the secretary to Mr. William T. Broughton who was the head attorney at . . ."

Mattie blurted out, "Yes, yes. We all know about your important job with Mr. William T. Broughton. Typing papers and all that. But you? What about you? Any wishes before you eat your last slice of cake?"

Helen kicked Mattie, a soft kick, under the table. But Dolores was unperturbed. She stuffed a chunk of dessert into her mouth and gulped it down. She slurped her tea then wiped her lips. She held court.

"As you know, my people are Irish." She placed her hand over her heart and rolled her eyes to the ceiling. "I am Irish. Actually, my grandfather . . ."

Again, Mattie interrupted. They knew this story as well as they knew about the important papers and all the typing. "Ireland. That's good. What would you do in Ireland?"

Dolores let the interruption slide, refocused on the group, and beamed. The others, she felt, hung on her words. She pictured a spotlight glittering on the rhinestone cat curled on her lavender sweatshirt. "I'd kiss the Blarney Stone."

"This has gone too far!" Josephine pushed back and snatched at the cane that hung from her chair. "I've seen that on the television. That fellow . . . that fellow, *Rick Steves* goes to Ireland." She gripped the cane and pulled it around next to her. "There are a million stairs to climb to that stone. You could never make it up there with all that weig . . ." She stopped, tried to stand, grabbed at the edge of the table to steady herself. "You have to lean backward over some hole and a man," she shuddered, "a total stranger, puts his arms around you to keep you from falling and you have to kiss a dirty old rock that thousands of people have kissed. Filthy thing—crawling with germs." She straightened. "If you ladies want to talk about such behavior, that's just fine. But I don't want any part of it." She started for the door. The others stared at her, slack-jawed. She twisted around, pointed her cane toward the table and waved it back and forth in a woozy motion.

"And furthermore, I don't believe I'll be joining you ladies for lunch in the future. Good-bye."

Josephine turned and did her best to stomp away, indignant. She could only muster a shuffle, but the others understood. Stunned, they watched her go. This sort of thing did not happen at Restful Palms.

"That's that." Rose broke the silence.

"Wait," Mattie said. "Forget her. She still has a husband to babysit. The rest of us are free. And . . ." she took a deep breath and continued in a rush of words. "We have money." She glanced around the table. They were watching. Waiting. "We have pensions and Social Security. And, we have our health!" Her words tumbled over each other. "We could go together. We could go to Ireland and Australia and, and . . ."

"Egypt?" Edna said.

"Yes. Egypt." Mattie raised her fist in the air. A crumpled tissue fell from her sleeve.

"And Wisconsin?" Rose asked.

Mattie nodded. "Definitely. Wisconsin." She paused and looked at each of her friends. Their eyes sparkled. Something had happened. Mattie knew it. They all knew it. Mattie pushed herself back and clutched the edge of the table for support. She stood. Again she raised and circled her fist high above her head. "Ladies," she said. "We can be, no, *we are,* outrageous women!"

Chapter Four

The Secret

They had decided to meet in Helen's room for two reasons. First, her room was the largest and provided enough space for five chairs if they squished in close, and second, the private dining room was not all that private. They were sure that Caroline, and even the young orderlies, listened in on their conversations. Most certainly, if word of their plans reached the director of Restful Palms, or worse, Edna's daughters, the five of them would be locked away forever. Best to keep things hush hush. Plus, the very idea of keeping a secret from Edna's daughters, from the other residents, and from the staff of the Restful Palms Retirement Home, gave them tingles.

The five friends moved a little faster and smiled a little wider than they had the week before but the truth was, none of the staff or the other residents paid the least attention to them. Only Josephine noticed a slight difference in their demeanors, but she took this as a jealous snubbing of her since she still had a husband and they were reduced to talking nonsense about preposterous, and in her opinion, foolish behavior.

Although Helen kept her room spotless at all times, and her decor resembled a feature on the cover of *Home and Lifestyle Magazine*, she spent the week in a full-out attack on any specks of dust that might have the nerve to linger in her home. She even paid the cleaning staff a little something on the side to help her do the heavy work like scouring the tub and vacuuming the tops of the drapes. She used vinegar and newspaper to wipe each glass surface including the table top that served as a display case for her extensive collection of framed family photos.

One particular photograph, a single instant captured in black and white, caused her to pause in her work. She held the oval frame to her heart, closed her eyes, let her body sway to a silent rhythm. She didn't have to look at the face of the man in the military uniform, or at the bundles of babies he held, one under each arm, to feel the rumble of the train as it pulled into the station on that autumn morning, 1942.

"You alright, Miss Helen?" She jumped at the touch of the cleaning lady's hand on her shoulder.

"Yes. Yes. Just taking a break." She skimmed the room. "You certainly have done a great job. Let me go get my checkbook."

When the cleaning lady turned, Helen swallowed, brushed her hand, a soft caress, over the photo and returned it to the table with the others.

An hour before the meeting she smoothed clean doilies on the back of each chair, covered her table with a white linen cloth, and laid out her best china and flatware. When finished, Helen stepped back and surveyed her handiwork. She decided to give the spoons one more polish before her friends arrived.

Helen wasn't the only one who made an extra effort or shelled out extra money for the cause. Rose suggested that she order lunch and have it delivered to Helen's room. She spent much of the week in the dining hall discussing possible luncheon menus with the kitchen staff. Although there wasn't much choice—tomato soup or clam chowder, chicken or beef—Rose took her job so seriously that the head cook offered to come in early to prepare something special for her and the other ladies. He told his wife that the old gal was polite, sent compliments to him, "the chef," and that she dressed up every evening for dinner. This was the least he could do.

He baked a chicken with rosemary and fried new potatoes in butter and dill. He grilled asparagus in sea salt and added a scoop of peach chutney for color. Even the prep cook participated by carving what he hoped looked like blossoms from plump radishes. Rose was so pleased that she gave each of the kitchen staff a five-dollar bill, an amount that, when totaled, added up to her discretionary spending for a full month.

The others, too, had volunteered to help with the preparation and organization of this special luncheon. While Helen polished her spoons and Rose triple-checked the menu with the kitchen staff, Edna, Mattie, and Dolores selected their dressiest attire and thought about their contributions to the event.

Given her background as the secretary for Mr. William T. Broughton, Dolores insisted that she be the one to take notes. When the Ladies Only Luncheons had started up a few years earlier, she'd been afraid they wouldn't let her join. No husband or children or grandchildren to talk about. But none of them gave the impression they cared about her background—or anyone's background for that matter—and besides, she knew about the law. A little bit about the law. Enough to get them pointed in the right direction whenever the subject of wills or insurance policies came up. And although they never needed a typist, *she would be ready* if the opportunity presented itself.

She stood in the kitchen of her studio apartment, slathered a slice of toast with peanut butter, and thought about her outfit. She still owned several suits from her years as a secretary at the law firm, but they would be too dressy for a luncheon meeting. Even for an important meeting like this one. Probably make the other women feel underdressed if she wore a suit. No, today, a skirt and fancy top would be best.

The bottom half would be an easy choice. She owned five skirts, all of them light blue denim, all of them with elastic waistbands, and all of them knee length. Picking out the best top, that was another story. Dolores had a penchant for glitter. Tasteful glitter. She owned two chests of drawers crammed full with rhinestone-studded tops. Some spelled out messages, like *Party Girl* and *Drama Queen*, others outlined animals, cats and puppies mostly, and several twinkled with holiday symbols— Christmas trees, Easter eggs, shamrocks, and pumpkins.

She finished the toast, then inspected, and rejected, at least a dozen different shirts before selecting a navy blue tee with a sparkling American flag sewn across the front. She gave it a shake and looked closely at what might be chocolate on one of the white stripes. Still another month before the Fourth of July, plenty of time to soak the shirt before then. Besides, with all the excitement, no one would notice that stain today.

Edna volunteered at the Restful Palms library for two hours a week, not because she liked books, or even liked to read. She volunteered at the library because it was one of the few times in her adult life when Louis did not direct her every move. In fact, the retirement home staff let her run the one-room library, let her be in charge for those two hours every week. They even let her arrange the brochures and flyers left by pharmaceutical reps, estate planning agents, and funeral homes.

Edna smiled as she thought about the library. She slipped into a pair of pastel blue capris and a matching cotton blouse. She'd been so thrilled with the freedom, and the responsibility, that she continued in the position after Louis passed. And now, because her work in the library gave her access to travel magazines, it was obvious to all of the ladies that she would be in charge of maps and guidebooks.

She pulled two white cotton socks from her drawer, each with a blue puff ball sewn on the back edge. The sales girl at Walmart had called the socks "footies," and she had explained how the puff balls kept them from sliding down into tennis shoes. Then that girl helped Edna pick out several pairs of footies with puff balls in colors to match the rest of her capris and blouses. Edna sat on the edge of her bed and laced up her shoes.

"Aren't you quite the fashion plate, Edna Fisher." She stuck her feet straight out, turned her ankles this way and that, and admired the small round ball at each heel.

Because she started the whole thing, the ladies elected Mattie to run the meeting. She wasn't worried about that; years ago she'd wanted to be a teacher, so the idea of getting up in front of groups didn't bother her in the least. What did bother her was the decision of what to wear.

She paced in front of her closet and stared at her wardrobe. Today was the second day for her green dress, the one with the small orange squares and orange buttons. She owned six housedresses and wore each one for three days in a row before she dropped the soiled garment into her hamper. This meant she only had to send her laundry out twice a month. She frowned. "I am so sick of these dresses," she said aloud.

She selected a fresh one, a pale yellow shift with a white collar and white cuffs on short sleeves. Buttons, the size of quarters, the color of lemons, filed down the front, fixed permanently in place with bright blond thread. The front panels of the dress stayed pressed together by a long strip of Velcro. The problem wasn't that she couldn't afford anything else; the problem was that she couldn't get in, or out of, anything else without help. And *that* was out of the question.

Mattie called the meeting to order by pointing toward the two world maps Helen taped to her wall. The first, a glossy full-color National Geographic pullout from the Restful Palms library, featured strange animals and exotic foreign people around its borders. Lovely to look at, but small and hard to read.

The second map had remained pinned to the wall at the insurance agency where Helen's husband had worked for over forty years. When he retired, he took it down, folded the paper twice, and handed the map to her. Although she couldn't remember why, she'd kept it in the top drawer of her desk since that day. The map was large and easy to read, but the paper had yellowed with age and curled at the edges. The ladies debated the wisdom of planning with an outdated map, but eventually, they reasoned that the continents probably remained pretty much where they'd been when Clarence was alive. An old map would do.

"All right now," Mattie said, "I listed the places where we want to go, and I think we should draw our route on the map."

Edna raised her hand. "I have a marker in my purse," she said.

The others watched as she rummaged through the contents of her bag—a roll of pennies, a package of *Juicy Fruit* gum, her change purse, a recipe for peanut butter brownies. "Look!" She waved a pamphlet and let it drop to the floor. "That's what those nice young men from the witness program gave me."

"Witness program?" Rose glanced at the paper and frowned.

"She means the Jehovah's Witnesses." Dolores nodded toward Edna and twirled one finger at her temple.

Edna continued her search—a comb, toenail clippers and three folded hankies. She found the marker, pushed out of her chair and shuffled to the map.

"Right then." Mattie tapped her finger on the state of Florida. "We are here." Edna marked an X on the spot and circled it.

"And we want to go here." Mattie pointed to Wisconsin and waited while Edna drew a line between the two states. "And then, to here." She moved her hand across the Atlantic to Ireland.

Edna followed the course with the marker. Her line meandered a bit, but no one took notice.

"Onward to Australia." Mattie's hand fluttered across the continents.

Edna accidently placed an X on New Zealand but scribbled it out and moved to the correct country.

"Now to Egypt."

Edna followed Mattie's finger with the marker and then drew a small triangle on Egypt. "This is a pyramid," she said.

Rose leaned forward and squinted at the map. Dolores scratched something out on her pad and started a new sentence.

"Now, up to this point, I think we should take airplanes." Mattie rapped one knuckle on the pyramid. "Flying makes sense." She waited then added, "Questions?"

"I've never been on an airplane." Helen frowned.

"I flew here from Wisconsin," Rose said. "But that was a long time ago and those other places, they seem so far away." She pointed to Australia.

Mattie sighed. "Don't worry. It won't matter if our destinations are far away or our flights are long. We can sleep on the plane and when we wake up, we'll be in another country. Heaven knows, we all take plenty of naps right here, and we never get anywhere."

Edna, Helen, and even Rose laughed and made jokes about all the snoozing and all the snoring in Restful Palms until Dolores wailed.

"Wait!" She held up her pencil. "I can't get all of this."

Mattie rolled her eyes. "Just get the highlights. Now, we have to move on because the next place we go, we go by ship." She pointed to a small dot in the middle of the Mediterranean.

Edna strained to see the spot on the map then drew a wonky line from her pyramid to the dot.

"What country is that?" Rose asked. The others strained to see the spot under Edna's mark.

"Malta, ladies. Malta." Mattie crossed her arms and waited for the word to sink in.

Rose raised her hand. "I've never heard of Mal Ta. Are you sure that's a country?"

"Yes. It's a country. I did some reading and found out that Malta is not too far away from Egypt. A small country, true, but ships sail from Egypt, back and forth, three days a week. Plus, Malta has an international airport with flights to the United States." She glanced back at the map. "We can ride Edna's camel, sail a ship to Malta, and then fly home to Florida."

"Mattie-Girl," Helen said. "How long do you expect this trip will take?"

Mattie grinned at Helen. "Excellent question. I figure the whole adventure, from start to finish, will take us three months." She waited a beat, then added, "we can leave right after Labor Day and be home before Christmas."

Mattie took her seat and watched as Edna completed her task. A thick, black, somewhat wobbly line began in Florida, traveled the world, and returned, in a magnificent circle, to the Restful Palms Retirement Home. Edna had added a few thousand miles to the trip by going first to Brazil, but the final result of her drawing was nothing short of spectacular. She sat down, breathless.

The ladies might have remained longer, staring, awestruck, at that great circle, if it hadn't been for the knock on the door.

"It's the lunch." Rose pushed up from her chair. "Quick! Cover the map! They'll see."

Dolores, Mattie, and Edna lined up, shoulder to shoulder, in front of the map while Helen and Rose answered the door. They opened it a crack and peeked out.

"Lunch for, uh . . ." The orderly checked a sheet on his clipboard. "Five. You want me to set up?" He pulled one bud from his ear and let it dangle on its thin cord.

"No, no. But thank you, just the same. Leave the cart here. We'll take it in." Helen forced a smile. "Don't bother coming back to check. We have what we need."

The orderly yawned, grabbed at his ear bud and jammed the thing into place.

Helen watched as he hitched his sagging pants up enough to cover his boxers, checked his clipboard again, and slouched on down the hall. She frowned, made a clicking sound with her tongue, then stepped into the room and closed the door.

Except for Dolores, who wolfed her food when excited, the ladies barely touched their meal. They chattered non-stop, interrupted each other, pointed at the map, and shook their heads. Jell-O melted, gravy gelled, and tea cooled while the ladies planned their adventure. They made lists and took note of questions to research: what to wear in Ireland, how to approach a camel, where to buy motion sickness pills for the sailing trip. For the most part, everything seemed reasonable. But there were two daunting problems.

First, what to do regarding arrangements. They'd need tickets, flights, passports, reservations and rides to places like Blarney Castle and wherever kangaroos live. None of them had ever traveled. They had no idea how to make the arrangements.

Second, *what if something should happen* to one of them along the way? Something like a broken hip, or a stroke, or something even worse. What would they do? No one wanted to think about this, but, as Helen noted, "Stuff does happen, usually when you least expect it."

"Usually in threes," Dolores added.

They sat quietly for several minutes. Rose focused on her hands resting on her lap. Edna carefully placed the roll of pennies back into her purse. Helen stared at her shoes. Her clock ticked the time.

"We can't do it." Helen sighed. "We just can't do it."

"She's right," Dolores said. She lifted a dinner roll from Helen's plate. "You plan to eat this?" Helen looked up, shook her head no.

"But there must be some way . . ." Mattie clenched and unclenched her fists. Her lower lip quivered, her nose grew puffy and red.

Rose watched her friend's face. She'd never seen Mattie at such a loss. Mattie was the strong one in the group, the one who always had an answer. Sometimes Mattie's shenanigans frightened Rose, especially when she tried to tease Rose and the others into going along. But now, Rose's heart broke to see her friend this way. She closed her eyes, took a deep breath, exhaled long and slow. Her eyes snapped open. She waved her hand at them. "Wait. Wait. I have an idea."

The others turned to her, stunned. Rose hardly ever offered a suggestion, and she never, ever raised her voice.

"We need a helper. We need someone who can work a computer and call airlines and, and . . ." she caught her breath. "We need someone who will stay here and handle things. Someone we can trust. We need someone who will keep our secret." Rose lowered her hand and looked around at the others. "Right?"

Helen and Mattie stared at her. Dolores swallowed the last of the roll and nodded.

"I know! I know!" Edna waved her hands, clapped once. The others turned their attention to her. "Katie! My granddaughter, Katie. She's in school, some college. Art psychology, or philosophy of art, or something like that. She has one of those computer things with her all the time. Always. Everywhere she goes. She will help us."

Mattie frowned. "I don't know about that, Edna." She made a face and bit her lower lip. "Young people today . . . they're so different from when we were girls. I'm not sure she would understand what we want to do."

"More important," Helen said, "she might not understand *why*."

"No, no. You'll see." Edna leaned in toward them, "Katie is different. She has funny hair and she smells a little odd." She wrinkled her nose then hurried on. "Not a bad smell, more . . . you'll see. And," Edna straightened, stretched her arm up and pointed toward the ceiling. She waggled one finger and proclaimed, "Katie has a tattoo!" Exhausted from the effort, she slumped back in her chair, her smile plastered in place.

Dolores held up her hand. "How do we know we can trust her not to tell your daughters? Isn't one of them her mother?"

Edna moved her head from side to side. "No, my daughters are her aunts, and they don't get along with Katie."

"Jesus could not get along with either of those girls." Mattie gave a snort.

Edna pouted a moment, and then went on. "It's true. My daughters aren't all that kind."

"Witches," Mattie said.

Helen slapped Mattie's arm and scowled.

"But they did take Katie in when Randall and Elton passed away. Katie isn't blood, you see. Randall and Elton adopted her when she was three. Raised her as if she were their own. Better than any mother. They were great parents."

"Wait a minute." Dolores interrupted. "I missed something. Isn't Elton a man's name? How could . . ."

Helen shot Dolores a look that stopped her cold. Edna ignored the interruption.

"When Randall and Elton passed, Katie was only fifteen, so my daughters and their husbands took her in and shuttled her back and forth until she turned eighteen." She reached out for her cup of now cold tea. "Honestly, I don't think it was a good situation for anyone. But bottom line, Katie turned out fine. A good girl. She's been kind to me." She sipped the tea, made a face and placed the cup in a saucer. "Trust me. Katie is our friend. She's our . . ." Edna fished around for the word.

Mattie finished the thought. "Our secret."

"Yes. Our secret," Rose said.

Mattie stood up and threw her arms around Edna. Dolores made a note on her writing pad. Helen and Rose grinned at each other. Then Rose jolted forward.

"Oh. Oh." She rapped on the table for silence. "I got so excited by the map and our secret and all, I nearly forgot. I brought some cheese for our lunch." She looked up at the clock and quipped, "Better late than never."

Again, the others watched in amazement. What had come over their Rose?

She pulled a wax-covered round from her handbag. "It's supposed to be fancy. Dessert cheese, the box said. I can't have any dairy, but my son doesn't remember that. We lived in Wisconsin when he was young, so I guess that's why he thinks I like cheese. Cheese is the only thing he ever sends me. I get cheese for my birthday and cheese for Christmas. And, once every few years or so, he remembers Mother's Day. I get cheese then, too."

Dolores reached over and took the round. "I'm sorry, dear." She broke the wax cover with the end of her spoon. "I didn't even know you had a son."

Rose swallowed. She looked beyond her circle of friends to the window and to the lace curtains that swayed, ever so slightly, in the balmy breeze. Helen's room, high on the fourth floor, faced north, the cool side of the building. A stand of areca palms and a cluster of sand pines provided shade from the Florida sun. Lucky Helen, she could keep the window open all year round and feel safe. Rose watched the gardener yank weeds from around the base of a young tree. She wondered if the others kept their windows open and if they felt safe all year round.

Rose pushed the thought away, pulled her gaze from the window and turned to her friends. "My son lives in California. In Hollywood, California. He's a big-time movie director from what I heard." She paused, glanced down, and mumbled something.

"Sorry, didn't hear you. Could you say that again?" Dolores fiddled with her hearing aids.

Rose looked up and searched Mattie's face. Mattie smiled and nodded encouragement. The others held their breath; the day had been so perfect. Rose cleared her throat.

"I said he doesn't visit very often." She smiled, soft. "Which is a good thing because he won't even know I've gone away."

The ladies exhaled.

"Now that," Mattie held up her teacup, "is worth a toast."

Dolores sat the spoon and cheese on the table and with the others, she raised a cup. "Here's to us, ladies."

Rose said, "To our trip around the world."

"To our secret," Edna added.

"To *the outrageous women*," Helen grinned.

Teacups clinked.

Chapter Five

Dreadlocks and Patchouli

Edna made the call. Katie agreed to stop by after her classes the following Tuesday afternoon. On the appointed day the ladies sat in a circle in Helen's room and waited. They sipped cups of tea, nibbled on pecan cookies, made small talk. Every few minutes, one of them checked her watch.

Helen stood closest to the door when the knock came. Katie bounded into the room, dropped a backpack on the floor and engulfed her in a bear hug. Taken by surprise Helen almost toppled over. "Good heavens." She grasped the doorknob for balance.

"Grannies." Katie stood before them, pressed her palms together as if in prayer, and bowed. "Namaste, oh great, wise ones. I come to serve."

The ladies sat dumbstruck. Nothing Edna said had prepared them for Katie. At five-eleven, she stood two inches taller than Helen and towered over the others. Military camouflage pants drooped from her bone thin hips. A baggy sweatshirt, with the arms cut out and the bottom third cut off, exposed her belly button with its winking ring of silver. She stepped out of her sandals—footwear made of what the ladies would later decide had to be car tires—and left them by the door. Dark green polish colored her toenails; bracelets of bells, beads, and braided string circled her ankles. Edna had been wrong. Katie didn't have *a tattoo*; tattoos *covered* Katie. Snakes slithered through vines; butterflies drank nectar from brilliant ruby hibiscus; stars danced around a grinning quarter moon. And that was only her left arm.

A gold ring threaded through her right nostril; something that frightened Rose, but intrigued Mattie. And Katie smelled musky, sweet, ancient.

Dolores spoke first. She grunted, pushed out of her chair and rumbled over to the girl. She lifted one of the thick, rope-like strands that hung from Katie's head. "Dear, *what on earth* has happened to your hair?"

Despite their initial shock, the ladies took to Katie. She let them touch her dreadlocks, explained the meaning of at least some of her tattoos, and gave each of them a squirt of patchouli.

Before long, she sat in a lotus position on the floor in the middle of their circle of chairs with her laptop balanced on her legs. As the ladies went over their plans, she listened, observed, and typed. Dolores watched, fascinated at how fast this young person typed without looking, not once, at the keys. But she did stop, occasionally, to run one finger across her computer's screen. Dolores wondered if Mr. William T. Broughton would have purchased one of those machines for her to use if he were still alive today.

When the ladies finally exhausted all of their thoughts about their adventure, Katie took over. She handed her computer to

Dolores. "Don't type," she said, "but let me know if you hear a 'pinging' sound."

Dolores glowed. This was an important job, and Katie could obviously tell she had more than a little experience in *that* department. She hunkered down, stayed still, and listened hard for any sounds that might come from the small machine.

"So, grannies." Katie paced in front of the world map. She traced their line with her finger. "This is a lot of traveling. You're right. You are going to need some help along the way." She stopped, looked at each one in turn. The ladies stared at her, hung on every word, except for Dolores who remained fixated on the computer screen. Katie smiled. "Lucky for you guys, we have Facebook." The ladies sat wide-eyed, waiting. Katie had expected more.

"Facebook," she said again. "I made a profile page for you guys. It's called *"The Outrageous Grannies."* She beamed. Still no response. They didn't get this. How could they not know about Facebook? She continued. "So, how it works, see, is we get lots of friends. Friends from around the whole world." She pinwheeled her arms and spun.

Helen mumbled something about seeing something about "a face book" on the news but said she didn't pay much attention. From the other women, only open admiration and complete incomprehension. Katie hurried on. "We ask them for help. You know, somebody to pick you up from the airport. Someone to help you find a place to stay . . . or maybe," she brightened, "you can even stay with them. Yeah, cool."

She glanced at Dolores and the computer. Nothing yet. "So, I'll keep track of things from this end. We can stay in touch by email. We can use this." She bent down and sloshed through her backpack. She straightened and held out a cell phone. "Here. I got this at the student co-op. For cheap. Sort of old-school. Last year's model." She examined the phone, turned it over for a quick check and then looked up. "But no biggie. We'll sign you up for an international plan. You can get my emails everywhere you go."

Katie tried to hand the phone to Edna, but Edna stepped back and thrust her hands into the pockets of her capris and shook her head.

"Not me," she said.

Katie bit her lip. She turned toward Helen.

"No way, child." Helen made a brushing motion with one hand. "I can't barely use the regular telephone. And besides, I wouldn't be able to see those little numbers."

Frustrated, Katie turned to Rose, but Rose's lower lip trembled, and she looked as if she were about to cry.

"For Pete's sake," Mattie reached for the phone. "It's a telephone, ladies. Surely we can figure out how to use a telephone." She squinted at the keyboard and small screen. "But I might need to get my glasses adjusted before we go." She jabbed at the tiny raised keys with her knuckle. The screen clicked to black.

Katie sighed. "I can see we have some work to do."

Her laptop pinged. Dolores jerked, squealed, and threw her hands in the air. Katie grabbed the computer before it hit the floor.

"Ah ha! Grannies, it has begun. You have a place to stay. In Wisconsin!"

Chapter Six

Katie's summer vacation zipped by as she prepped her grandmother and four adopted grannies for their adventure. She helped them apply for passports, arranged for auto payment of bills, booked flights, drove them to a clinic for shots and health certificates, and taught Mattie how to use the cell phone.

Mattie followed the basic concept of emails and texts, but she could not get her fingers to uncurl enough to push the right keys, in the right order, to spell out words or to load and send photos. Eventually, she and Edna worked out a system. Edna couldn't remember any of Katie's instructions, but she could wield the eraser end of a pencil with ease. So, with heads bent over the palm-sized machine, Mattie gave the directions and Edna pushed the raised rubber buttons. Katie shook her head and grinned.

"Go, grannies, go."

Time flew for the ladies too. They didn't notice when Caroline pulled the months of June and July from the pages of the community calendar. They didn't observe the shifting colors in the garden or take note of the summer fruit cups next to their dinner plates. They were too busy packing and repacking, reading the travel articles Edna found in the Restful Palms library—even the ones that had nothing to do with the countries they planned to visit—and cleaning clutter from their rooms; good to leave everything in tip-top shape. They spent the majority of their time with Katie because they were eager to learn everything she could teach them about travel, and because they loved her. However, while they trusted her completely, there was one issue the ladies did not share with Katie: What to do *if something should happen.*

"I think it's too morbid, you know, for young people to worry about these things," Rose said. She contemplated the marble cake Dolores had ordered for their meeting. "Maybe we should decide what to do and leave a note somewhere." She dipped one tine of her fork in the maple cream frosting and touched it to her tongue. Rose scrunched her face, placed her fork on the edge of the plate and pushed it away.

"It says here that moving a body across international borders can be extremely expensive." Mattie read from a pamphlet she'd picked up at the travel clinic. "It also says that family members must get permission from both governments to transport bodies between countries." She frowned. "Maybe we should put enough money in the fund to cover . . . you know."

"We could scatter the ashes in an attractive spot. Maybe a garden or some other lovely place, wherever we are at the time." Helen ventured a test bite, and then she too pushed the plate to one side.

"Fine by me," Dolores said. She pointed to Rose's plate. "Do you want that?"

"Sounds good to me, too," Rose said. She edged her plate across the table to Dolores. "But I think I'd like my son to have my ashes. *If something…*"

Helen reached over and rested her hand on Rose's arm. "Darlin', nothing is going to happen. But if something does happen, we'll make sure your boy gets his mama's ashes." She patted Rose's arm. Rose swallowed and nodded once to Helen.

"So, we agree?" Dolores dragged the plate closer and dug in. They all nodded. All but Edna.

"My daughters would have a fit if I died and you scattered my ashes." She smoothed the tablecloth with one hand and avoided eye contact with her friends. "I'm sure they have elaborate plans for what they want to do with me once I'm gone."

"They want your money, darlin'." Helen waved one hand in the air. Her bangles jingled together. "The rest is just show. Fluff." As soon as the words were out Helen dropped her hand to her lap and looked down. Her face burned as she silently chastised herself. What a mean-spirited thing to say, even if what she said was true, which of course it probably was . . . but it might not be.

Edna pouted but stood her ground. "You don't know my daughters. They would . . . they would be so angry."

"Who gives a rip?" Mattie said.

"Oh Mattie, your language," Rose said. "Just because you wear those boots doesn't mean . . ." her voice trailed off.

Mattie had taken to using terms like "rip, friggin, cool, and sweeeet," ever since the day Katie gave her a pair of weathered combat boots. Together, they'd removed the laces to make it easy for her to slip in and out of the boots, and then, with great ceremony, the two of them threw Mattie's bedroom slippers in the trash. Mattie treasured those boots. She ignored Rose's comment. "You'll be dead. So, like I said, who gives a friggin rip?"

Edna snuffled. A single tear surfed down a wrinkle and plopped onto her collar. Rose reached over and wrapped her arm around her friend's shoulders. She glared at Mattie.

Dolores swallowed a bite of cake, held her fork poised over her plate, and weighed in with a suggestion. "Look, if something happens to you, we'll email Katie. She'll call your daughters, and they can decide what to do from there. The rest of us can put some extra money in the fund and be done with it." She eyed her plate, then speared and inhaled the last bite of cake.

Edna blew her nose, dabbed her eyes with a hankie. Then she, too, nodded yes.

One afternoon Katie arrived with five Halloween-type masks. "Grannies. So far I only put your story and some maps and pictures of the countries where you are going on your Facebook page. But people want to see you. So we are going to post your photos." She dropped her backpack to the floor. "To spice things up a bit, and to confuse the aunties if they ever happen to see your home page, I brought disguises. Your friends will love it."

Katie plopped down next to her pack and shuffled through the contents. She pulled out a couple of library books, her computer, a bottle of patchouli oil, a wounded apple, and finally, a crumpled paper bag. "Here they are." She held the bag over her head. "Oh, forgot to tell you—I'm so stoked. You already have over a hundred Facebook friends. Totally sweeet."

"Sweeet." Mattie echoed Katie's enthusiasm although she and the others had absolutely no idea what Katie was talking about. Even though she'd tried to explain it to them several times, they remained baffled by the whole Facebook thing, and they were not at all clear about who these friends were. But they trusted Katie, and so, they agreed to line up in front of the map and pose while she snapped their photos.

Edna wore a clown mask as it reminded her of the circus she'd attended so long ago. For fun, and to fit with Edna's choice, Katie programmed the cell phone's ringer to play circus music.

Helen chose an elephant nose and ears because they looked so real and because she thought the animal's dark ashy color coordinated with her pale gray pantsuit.

Rose rejected the gorilla mask but cut eyeholes in a paper bag and popped that over her head.

Because her people were Irish, Dolores chose to wear a leprechaun mask that came with a jaunty, green felt hat. A hat that later she would find reasons to wear to the dining hall several times a week.

Mattie selected a Steve Jobs mask, which she wore with her housedress and her combat boots. Her boots, like Dolores's hat, caused a bit of confusion among the residents of the retirement home, but the staff had seen stranger things, and as long as the ladies were happy, and not harming themselves or others, well, best to let things be.

Chapter Seven

First Flight

Mattie wanted some sort of dramatic leave-taking, some sort of flamboyant farewell, but Helen convinced her it would be prudent to downplay the whole thing lest the Restful Palms' Director, Roger Simpson, decided to recheck their paperwork. So, the week before their departure, Katie casually carried a couple of their bags out to her car each time she visited. During her last visit, she crammed all five of their handbags into her backpack and took those to the car as well.

On the final morning, the ladies individually ambled out the front door as if to take a moment of fresh air. They timed their departure from the Restful Palms to coincide with breakfast when most of the residents were pushed up to tables in the dining room, and the hallways were clear.

They stayed silent, didn't say a word until Katie flipped on her blinker and eased onto State Highway 275. Then high-pitched giggles and clapping and "Oh my," and "Can you believe this?" and "Lordy, Lordy," filled the air. No aviary had ever warbled as loud or as fluttery as Katie's car that morning.

Katie stopped in front of the airport security checkpoint. "I can't go through without a boarding pass so you ladies are on your own now. But don't worry, you can reach me on the cell, day or night. I'll never turn it off." She stepped back and looked at each them.

Helen stood tall and straight, her burgundy satchel a perfect match to her pantsuit. Her calm demeanor and gracious poise gave no indication that an hour earlier she'd been so nervous she'd thrown up in the gas station restroom when they'd stopped for fuel. Katie knew, but she promised not to tell the others.

Rose fingered the pink silk chrysanthemum sewn on her white patent leather purse. Her cotton bag, gardened with peonies and butterflies, slumped on the floor by her feet. Every couple of moments she reached up, touched her pearls, exhaled, and dropped her hand back to the flower.

Dolores, or "Granny D," as Katie called her, wore a new top, one she bought at the outlet mall specifically for this journey. A silver rhinestone airplane flew through white sequined clouds. Katie smiled and wondered how Dolores had managed to stain the shirt so soon.

Mattie held her boots ready to place in the X-ray machine even though the TSA agent said she was old enough to leave them on. "Don't need to," she said. "No laces. No trouble."

Katie grinned and shook her head. She didn't have to worry about Mattie.

Then there was her grandmother. Katie chewed her lower lip
and hoped, for the millionth time, she was doing the right thing.
For sure, the aunts would be pissed when they found out what
she'd done. She watched Edna stoop and tug at her sock. Today,
her footies glowed fluorescent orange and sported oversized
black puff balls shot through with silver threads—Katie's travel
gift to her grandmother. Katie sighed. There might be hell to pay,
but *at least she's having fun.*

"Please have your boarding passes ready and . . ."
The airport announcement looped around again. Katie swal-
lowed and forced a cheerful look. "Okay, grannies, this is it."
They held up the line. Some behind them frowned and
checked their watches, others smiled and waited with patience
while the ladies hugged Katie and then hugged her again. Tears
flowed, bags were dropped, picked up, dropped again. Kisses
were blown, hands waved, and final instructions about emails
and photos repeated. Voices blended.
"Please be careful."
"I love you."
"I love you, too."
"Thank you."
"Thank you so much."
"I love you."
"Bye-bye."
"Bye-bye."

"Here, young man." Mattie tried to hand the flight attendant a dollar bill. "I don't know how we'd reach those compartments without your help."

The flight attendant smiled and patted Mattie's shoulder. "No need to pay me. It was my pleasure, miss."

Mattie blushed and looked away as he helped each of the ladies secure their seatbelts and pull their seats forward. It had been forever since someone had called her "miss."

"Now ladies, relax and enjoy the flight. We'll be in Wisconsin before you know it. Oh yes, and if you need anything, push this button." He pointed overhead.

"Oh, I don't think we could reach that high." Edna eyed the panel above her seat.

"Don't worry." Helen stretched one arm up. Her fingertips grazed the button. "Tell me if you need anything, and I'll call." She smiled at Edna. Edna reached over and squeezed Helen's hand.

The takeoff was smooth; the ladies settled in. After careful attention to the flight safety demonstration, Edna and Rose went over the Safety Card several times together. They read the instructions for water landings out loud, helped each other locate the strips of emergency lighting along the aisle, and quizzed each other on the location of the nearest exit rows. Helen and Mattie huddled close and chatted about their plans the way they'd done a hundred times in the weeks leading to this moment. Dolores stared, open-mouthed, at the brilliance of the sunlit clouds below the plane. They reminded her of something from her childhood, but she couldn't quite place the memory. All five of them were taken aback when the flight attendants brought small bags of mixed nuts and cups of tea and did not charge them. How wonderful, this flying thing!

Chapter Eight

Three months earlier, the Methodist minister Reverend T. Clarenbach and his wife Rebecca, had laughed when they read the Facebook request:

Five senior ladies want to take a break from retirement-home living and travel the world. They'll need a little help with transportation and housing along the way. Mostly, they'll need hugs.

The post came with contact information for a girl named Katie, and a photo of five elderly women, standing shoulder to shoulder, wearing a rather bizarre assortment of Halloween masks. Without further discussion, the reverend and Rebecca opened their home to the ladies.

Reverend Clarenbach was busy in his roles of shepherd and chaperone to twenty-two preteens at the State Youth Jamboree that weekend, which meant that the tasks of chauffeur and hostess fell to Rebecca.

She stood in baggage claim next to carousel number four, with a square of cardboard. One side, hand-printed with a blue marker, read *All cookies are 25¢ each*; the other side read, *Welcome Ladies*.

Rebecca flipped her ponytail over her shoulder and glanced down at her sweatshirt and jeans. She dusted a patch of dried mud from one leg. Mud from an earlier project. She checked her watch. There hadn't been enough time to change or clean up. She hoped her guests would understand.

The Clarenbachs hauled everything from folding chairs to floral arrangements in their twelve-year-old Chevy Suburban. Their running joke was that someday the Lord's work would require a shiny red two-seater sports car. Someday, but not today. Today, in addition to picking up five seniors and their luggage, she'd collected six bags of fresh fertilizer meant for the flower beds around the church, a donation from the farmer's co-op. The bags filled the entire back of the vehicle. The farmer had stepped back from the vehicle and closed the rear hatch. He and Rebecca eyed the car. A thin film of damp fog already hazed the glass. "You might wanna open them windows."

Rebecca nodded. "Yes, I think I will."

"I thought you might like a tour of the town before we head to the house." Rebecca clicked her seatbelt and exhaled. It was a challenge, but with a bit of arranging she'd managed to stuff the ladies and all their bags into the car. She looked in the rearview mirror. They appeared a tad snug, but she figured they'd survive. "We all buckled up?"

Lynden, Wisconsin, proud home of the "Little Beavers All Stars," hosted three antique shops, two nail salons, a tack and feed store, Wicker's Furniture Emporium, four taverns and the Blue Bird Café.

"This seems like a sweet, clean, little town," Mattie said. She reached from the back seat and touched Rebecca's shoulder.

"Thanks. It is a great little town," Rebecca said. "We have two churches in Lynden. Methodist and Baptist. And two cemeteries, one on each end of town. And a library."

She drove the length of Main Street, made a U-turn, and retraced their route. At the end of Main, she made a right turn onto Maple, drove for one block, and then made another right onto Cypress.

Edna peered at the thick trunks of ancient oaks lining the street. She watched a girl, five maybe six, ride a lavender bicycle along the sidewalk. The bike sprouted purple and white fringe at the end of each handle. A straw basket decorated with plastic flowers balanced on the fender. The flowers jerked up and down as the front tire rolled over each crack. Despite training wheels, the bike wobbled, and the little girl stopped frequently. She braced with her feet on the ground, adjusted her pink helmet, and started up again.

A few houses farther on, a woman stood at her front door and chatted with the mailman. He still wore his summer shorts even though autumn was just around the next block.

"This reminds me of our town in Michigan," Edna said. "Where Louis and I grew up and where we raised our children. That was in the fifties. Such a lovely time." She mellowed with the memory.

Helen looked over the back seat and smiled at her friend.

Edna continued. "I remember when that nice young man used to sing. Elvis, I think. Elvis Paisley. Yes, that was his name."

"Presley, you ninny."

Mattie shot a look at Dolores.

"What? Why are you staring at me like that? Everybody knows his name was Presley. Besides," Dolores glared first at Mattie and then at Edna, "knowing what I do about Louis and all, I'm surprised he would let you listen to *that* kind of music."

No one spoke for a moment. Then, Edna looked across Dolores at Mattie—a flash of mischief in her smile.

"He didn't," she said. "Not really. But he worked. The children went to school. And . . . we had a radio."

Mattie laughed and slapped her thigh.

Dolores sniffed, crossed her arms, upped her chin, and stared straight ahead.

Rebecca slowed at the end of Cypress. "There you have it, ladies, that's our town. Does anybody want to visit a church? Stop at the library?"

"I need to use a bathroom," Mattie said. She tried to cross her legs, but Dolores held her pinned against the door.

Rebecca nodded. "Home it is." She made two more right turns and drove down Main Street again.

Much like their old Chevy, the Clarenbachs' home served the community. To accommodate members of the flock who'd fallen on hard times, Todd and Rebecca converted their basement into a mini-dormitory. The dorm hosted three twin beds and a rollaway cot along with a pool table, mini-fridge, TV, and a take-one-leave-one library of paperback books. The guest room, upstairs and across the hall from the bathroom, did not resemble the basement. In fact, it didn't resemble any other room in the stark, utilitarian home.

Twin feather beds covered with pink-and-cream lace spreads pushed against walls papered with ivy leaves and morning glories that wound up and around a whitewashed trellis. Twin nightstands, each with crocheted doilies, offered copies of an inspirational pamphlet titled *The Upper Room*, a bottle of spring water, and a small crystal dish for jewelry, coins, or dentures. Rose walked to the window. It was only open a couple of inches, but she closed it and slipped the lock into place. Then she moved to one of the beds and touched the edge of a lace pillow sham.

"So, that's the house," Rebecca said. "You gals decide who bunks in the dorm and who shares the guest room. I have a few emails to answer before dinner, so I'll let you get settled. Make yourselves comfortable, use whatever you need. Consider our home, your home."

Following a brief discussion, the ladies decided to draw straws. Longest two straws would get the guest room. Not wanting to bother Rebecca for a broom, Edna tore five strips of more or less the right lengths from her boarding pass.

Mattie and Helen won the draw. Mattie was about to twirl in a victory dance when she glanced over at the others. Rose slumped against the bedroom door. She clutched her satchel in her arms.

"You know," Mattie said. "The pink room is pleasant, I guess. But I used to think it would be fun to go to college. I sure would like to switch places with someone and give the dormitory a try." Dolores shot her hand in the air. Mattie ignored her. "Rose?"

Over a dinner of leftover tuna casserole and green beans, Rebecca shared her plans for the next day. "We'll have breakfast, and then I'll drive you to the cemetery where your folks are buried."

Rose gave a shy smile.

"After that, I'll take you across town to the other graveyard. Your brother? Right?"

Rose nodded and lowered her eyes.

Rebecca continued. "My husband is coming home tomorrow night, he should be here in time for supper, so you'll get to meet him." She looked up at the kitchen clock. "Oh gosh, I have to run. Choir practice." She pushed her chair back and stood. "Now, don't worry about these dishes. Rest. Rest and make yourselves at home. I'll be back around nine, but no need to wait up. See you in the morning."

The five travelers should have been exhausted, but they were still too excited to sleep.

Rose washed the dishes. Helen dried. Edna took a shower. Mattie nosed around and discovered a deck of cards. Dolores rummaged through her bags until she found a stash of peanuts, a package of cookies, and two chocolate bars. She assembled the snacks on a tray table in the dorm, and then she, Mattie, and Edna settled in for an evening of Old Maid and munchies. Helen and Rose climbed the stairs and retired to the guest room.

Helen fluffed her pillow, eased back, and arranged her knitting project on her lap. She pulled a length of yarn from a ball and looped it around one of her needles.

"Rose," she said. "You've never talked much about your family. Come to think about it, before we started this whole adventure, I didn't even know you had a brother. Tell me about him."

Rose pulled a sock over her foot. For the past couple of years, her legs had been bothering her. The doctor suggested she wear support hose to bed, but she thought they were too tight and didn't allow her skin to breathe so she substituted them for wool knee socks. "I don't talk about him." She turned her foot one way, then the other, and silently approved of the fit; these were new. She pulled the other sock from her bag. "It's one of those things."

Helen frowned at a knot in her yarn. She was about to change the subject—after all, most people had family they didn't like to talk about. So she was a bit surprised when Rose continued.

"I guess I never talked about Wayne—that was my brother's name—Wayne, because I guess I'm ashamed." She pulled on the other sock. She knew the socks didn't help. Her legs still hurt, but she'd grown accustomed to wearing them.

Helen stopped moving her needles. She looked up at her friend. Rose sat on the edge of her bed. Her thin fingers clutched the hem of her blanket. Her legs, now covered in chocolate brown stockings, didn't quite reach the floor. She sat motionless, eyes closed. Wisps of white curls framed her face.

"My goodness," Helen said. She lowered the needles to her lap. She spoke in the soft, tranquil voice she'd used to quiet her boys when they were hurt or frightened. "We're grown women now. Each one of us has done something we wish we didn't. But it doesn't matter. We're good people. You're a good person, I know that, Rose. Maybe talking about it, even some, might help." She picked up her needles and tapped them together. Rose looked up and watched Helen for a moment. Helen's fingers moved with calm control; her needles clicked a faint and steady rhythm. Rose sighed. Then she spoke. Her voice cracked, but her eyes were dry.

Chapter Nine

Rose's Story

Wayne was fifteen when I was born. Daddy called me God's little surprise. I guess he and Mama weren't planning any more children after Wayne. But they loved me, and Wayne was happy to have a kid sister. I don't remember a lot from the early years, but I do remember that Wayne helped Daddy mow the lawn and trim our hedges. And, I remember that he gave me rides on his shoulders. He'd carry me over to the apple tree in our backyard and hold me up high so I could grab at the apples. I remember how he smiled and laughed. My brother laughed a lot. I remember that. But all that was before the accident.

When the Depression came, Wayne went away. I was three then and didn't understand why my brother left. Later, I found out that Wayne went to work in the coal mines a long, long way from Wisconsin. He sent some letters and money to Mama and Daddy and once he sent a postcard to me. It had a picture of a striped cat on the front and a note on the back. Mama read Wayne's message to me. "Be a good girl," it said. "I'll be home soon."

After that, I pestered Mama and Daddy until they finally let me have a kitten. She was black and white. I named her Cookie.

I was six and could already spell and print, and I was learning to do the times tables when Wayne came home. I was so excited when Daddy said he was going to pick Wayne up at the train station. I couldn't wait for my big brother to come home.

But Wayne was different when he came back. He was more like a stranger than a brother. Mama made up his old room at the top of the stairs, and he stayed in there a lot of the time. Sometimes he made groaning noises or screamed. And sometimes he yelled out bad words. Mama told me not to listen. She said to go outside and play with Cookie.

Daddy told me that Wayne had an accident in the coal mine and hurt his head, but that he might get better if he took some medicine. So Mama drove Wayne to the city, and they went to a doctor. I guess the doctor gave him some medicine because after a while Wayne did get better. He didn't scream or yell out those words anymore, and he spent more time downstairs with us. But he didn't laugh or help Daddy mow the lawn. He liked to do things like clean the silver set or polish the brass door handles. He could take all morning to shine one spoon. Sometimes he sat on the floor and rocked back and forth.

Mama and Daddy tried taking him to church with us a few times, but he didn't like church. One Sunday, right in the middle of Mama's favorite hymn, *The Old Rugged Cross*, Wayne stepped into the aisle and threw a hymnal at the choir. It hit the altar and knocked over a big vase of calla lilies. That vase crashed into the altar candles, and one of them landed on the Bible and caught the pages on fire. I think the pastor poured wine on the Bible, but I'm not sure. There was so much commotion.

Daddy and a bunch of other men jumped up and tried to grab him, but they couldn't catch Wayne. He ran toward the back of the church, ran so fast that I thought he'd keep running until he disappeared, but Mrs. Fritz, the Sunday school teacher, stuck her foot out and tripped him. Wayne fell, and Daddy and the other men jumped on him.

The sheriff came to the church and put handcuffs on my brother and then put him in the back of the police car. All the men stood around Daddy and the sheriff, and the sheriff was talking, but I couldn't hear what he said.

Mama cried and held my hand tight. We stood on the church steps with Mrs. Fritz and the other ladies. I think maybe some of them cried too, but I don't remember for sure.

The sheriff took Wayne away for a bit. When they came back, Wayne was quiet and calm. Maybe the sheriff knew the doctor and got Wayne more medicine. I don't know. But Mama and Daddy never made Wayne go to church again; they left him at home. And they left me at home, too. To keep Wayne company.

On Sundays, after they left for church, Wayne took his boots out of the closet. The ones he wore in the coal mine. He took off all of his clothes except his underpants and sat on the kitchen floor. He made me stay in the kitchen with him, and he made me take off all of my clothes and he made me stand in front of him while he polished those boots.

Sometimes he looked down at his boots, but sometimes he looked up at me and smiled at me in a strange way. I was embarrassed, standing there without my clothes on. But I was scared whenever Wayne smiled at me that way.

When he got done polishing, he'd touch one of my nipples with the flat part of his finger, and he pressed hard. When he pulled his finger away, it left a waxy black mark. The smell of that shoe polish stayed on my skin, even after a bath, even after I rubbed the spot with a washrag.

The first time he made me take my clothes off in front of him, I cried and tried to run outside, but he grabbed me and punched me . . . hard. In the stomach. He told me that if I cried anymore, or if I told *anyone*, especially Mama or Daddy, he would kill my cat. And he told me *how* he would kill Cookie. Wayne said he would twist Cookie's head and then give a big tug and pull it off her body.

"Blood and guts everywhere," he said. "'Wring that cat's head clean off if you say anything." Then he made a twisting motion with his hands and laughed—a mean laugh. This scared me even more than standing naked in front of him. Nothing Wayne did to me was as bad as imagining Cookie's bloody head, twisted off.

Sometimes at Sunday dinner, when we were all around the table, Daddy would ask me what we did that day. Wayne would look at me and make a quick wringing motion with his hands, too fast for Mama or Daddy to notice.

"Nothing," I'd say. "We didn't do anything today."

Wayne kept taking his medicine but slowly, over time, he changed. He stopped rocking back and forth and started pacing or stomping across our living room. He got mad at things, all sorts of things. Sometimes he got mad, and none of us could figure out what he was mad at. He threw things; Mama's best china teapot, a vase of flowers Daddy brought home to help her feel better about the teapot, books, plates, even the birthday cake Mama baked for him. He threw that birthday cake right in her face. We never knew what he was going to do next.

One time I heard Mama talking about Wayne. She told Daddy she was afraid of him. "He's so big," she said.

She said she didn't think I should stay with Wayne on Sundays, but Daddy said it would be all right because Wayne wouldn't actually hurt anybody; he was only confused.

I was ten when Wayne killed Cookie. It was a bright sunny day. I remember that because Cookie was curled in a pool of sunlight at the end of the living room sofa. Wayne stomped around the house. He wore the greasy jeans and the white undershirt he always wore, and that day he had on his black boots, all shiny. He stomped around and around from one room to the next, and then he saw Cookie.

"No!"

I ran over to grab her, but Wayne had that awful Sunday smile. He pushed me out of the way and picked up Cookie, gentle, and cradled her in his arms. Cookie yawned and stretched, and I think she purred. Wayne took her outside and walked around toward the back of the house.

"No! No!" I ran after him. "I didn't tell, Wayne." I was crying and running.

Wayne kept walking. Big, long steps.

"Wayne, please give me Cookie. I didn't tell. I promise. I didn't tell."

At the back of our house, he stopped. Now he held Cookie up in the air. She squirmed and tried to get away, but she couldn't. Wayne held her too tight.

"Didn't tell what?" It was Daddy. He came around the corner of the house.

"Pleaaassse, Wayne." I stretched up toward Cookie.

"Didn't tell what, Wayne?" Daddy tried to grab Wayne's shoulder but Wayne slipped out of his reach.

Wayne didn't even look at me. He said a bunch of bad words, lifted Cookie high, above his head, and then, he dropped her. She spread her paws to land on her feet, but right before she hit the ground, Wayne swung his boot out and kicked her in her belly. She slammed against the back of the house.

I screamed and ran over to Cookie. She was lying there, at the edge of Mama's flower bed. Blood and something white slid out of her mouth. I picked her up and hugged her. Pink foam bubbled out of her nose.

Wayne laughed. A mean laugh. He dusted his hands together and walked around to the front of the house.

Daddy kneeled down beside me. He pried my fingers open and took Cookie. "Cookie has gone to Heaven," he said. Then he looked up, toward the front yard. "God have mercy on us," he said.

Mama came outside and put her arms around me. She held me close. "Shhh. Shhhh," she said.

Daddy carried Cookie away to bury her. He promised me that she would have a beautiful grave and that he would take me to see it. He promised that she would go to Heaven and be with Jesus and the angel cats.

Mama took me into the house and up to my room. I peeked at Wayne's room when we went past, but the door was closed, and there were no sounds coming from in there. She helped me change out of my T-shirt because it was covered in blood. Then she helped me put my pajamas on and, even though it was the middle of the day, she put me to bed.

Mama brought me orange Jell-O cubes and a glass of milk, but I didn't eat. I cried and cried thinking about Cookie until I finally fell asleep.

The next morning, the house was quiet and still. I tiptoed downstairs, went fast past Wayne's room, but the door was open, the bed was made, and the room looked like he was never even there. Mama and Daddy's room was empty, too. There was a bowl and spoon on the kitchen table. There was a note under the big Tupperware box where we kept the corn flakes.

We went to town. Wayne too. Please eat breakfast and play.
There is a sandwich for you in the ice box. We will be back
before dinner. We will have spaghetti. Your favorite.
We love you.

When Mama and Daddy returned, they were alone. Wayne was gone. They never said anything about him, and I didn't ask. But I jumped whenever I heard a knock on the door. I kept my bedroom window closed and locked all the time after that, even in the summers when it got hot. I put a chair under the doorknob in my bedroom in case he came home. But he never did.

Rose slid off the bed and shuffled across the hall to the bathroom, careful not to slip in her new socks. She pulled two tissues from the box behind the toilet and shuffled back to the guest room.

Helen stopped knitting. She had been afraid to before, afraid that if she did, Rose would freeze and not be able to get her story out. But Rose appeared stable, no tears, no trembling. Helen stuffed her yarn and needles into her bag and dropped it to the floor by her bed. "So, darlin'," she said. "What finally happened to your brother?"

Rose climbed onto her bed. She slid beneath the covers, pulled the sheet up to her chin. "It was years later," she said. "I was in the hospital having my son." She gazed at a watercolor on the wall by her bed—a pastoral scene with a young Jesus, a child, and two white lambs. "He was such a sweet baby, easy delivery. It was all easy with that one." She smiled.

"Your brother?" Helen nudged her back on track.

"Yes, about my brother," Rose said. "The attending nurse looked at my chart and saw my maiden name. The hospital made us list our maiden names and our married names back in those days."

"And?"

"She told me she recognized my name from when she worked at a hospital the next town over. She said she worked in the asylum, the mental hospital. She told me there was a guy there with the same last name as mine. First name a Shane or Dwaine or something like that. She wanted to know if he was any relation to me. Of course, I shook my head no."

Helen nodded. "Of course."

"That nurse said that the fellow was one piece of work. Real crazy. She said they had to lock him up, day and night."

Rose stopped and lowered the sheet. She pushed a tissue up the sleeve of her nightgown.

Helen barely moved. "What happened to him?"

"Oh, you know." Rose reached up to the light switch. "Ready?"

"Sure," Helen said.

Rose flipped the switch. She listened to Helen arrange her bedding.

"Night, darlin'," Helen said.

Rose didn't answer right away. She lay still, in the dark, until the only sounds from the other side of the room were low breaths and an occasional soft snort. She knew Helen was asleep.

"The nurse told me he hung himself," Rose said. "With his boot laces." She sighed. "I found out they buried him in a grave on the far side of town. I've never been there. And I thought I'd go. Sometime. If I could."

Chapter Ten

Graves

Rebecca woke to a timid knock on her bedroom door. She glanced at the clock; it would be another half hour before her alarm went off. Yawning, she propped up on one elbow. "Come on in."

Helen poked her head into the room. "Sorry to wake you," she said. "We were just wondering if we could treat you to breakfast at that little café downtown before we go to the cemetery."

Rebecca smiled. She always enjoyed sharing her home with others, but these ladies were somehow special. They hadn't complained about anything—not once. She was pretty sure they'd noticed the pungent smell in her car, it would have been impossible not to. But they didn't mention the manure, and they voluntarily cleaned up after dinner. Now, they wanted to take her to breakfast. She couldn't remember the last time one of her guests had offered to do something for her. "I'd love that," she said. "Just give me a few minutes."

The Blue Bird Café was a cliché, a cookie-cutter copy of the thousands of small restaurants that dot American's midwestern landscape. It offered booths with cracked red vinyl seats, tables of gray Formica laminate, menus coated with peeling plastic covers, and waitresses with names like Flo and Dottie.

In the front of the café, local weather and the farm report blasted from a grime-covered radio. From the kitchen came the clanging of pots and pans and the staccato sounds of Spanish.

The smell of bacon, strong coffee and grease hung thick in the stuffy room. Like all the other members of the sacred Fraternity of Greasy Spoons, Lynden's Blue Bird Café served up meals specially designed to stick to ribs and clog arteries.

"Edna, split something with me?" Mattie poured over the menu.

"I agree. There's too much food here for one person," Helen said. "Rose, wanna share something with me?"

Rose and Helen shared an order of French toast and ham. Mattie and Edna opted for the Sunny Morning Special and an extra plate. Rebecca and Dolores each ordered the Hungry Man's Breakfast and, despite protests from the others, Dolores asked for three cinnamon rolls to divide among the group.

"We'll burst," Mattie said.

"Don't be silly." Dolores closed her menu and licked her lips. "It's our first morning away from home. We deserve a little treat."

As they waited for their meals to arrive, the ladies told Rebecca about Katie and their travel plans. Rebecca shared stories about some of the other guests she and her husband had welcomed to their home.

While they chatted, Rose excused herself. "I'm going to pop across the street to that grocery store and pick up some flowers to lay on the graves."

"Want me to go with you?" Helen started to stand.

Rose shook her head. "No, stay here. I won't be more than a minute—back before the food comes."

"Feel free to leave the flowers on the car seat," Rebecca said. "It's unlocked and much cooler out there." She fanned herself with a menu.

Helen watched Rose weave through the crowded café. She thought of the story Rose had shared. I need to stay close to her today. *She'll need a friend.*

Rose returned to their table just as Flo delivered the two Hungry Man's Breakfasts and the three saucer-sized cinnamon rolls. Mattie groaned. Dolores grinned.

Helen patted the seat next to her. "Right on time, darlin'." She slid over to give Rose room to sit. Helen noticed a small paper bag poking from the top of Rose's handbag. "Did you find what you wanted?"

Rose nodded. "Yes, and you're right." She looked at Rebecca. "It is too hot in here. I left the flowers in the car."

Rebecca stayed in the Suburban and checked emails while her guests trudged through dew-wet grass to the graves. She glanced up at them and smiled. The ladies walked two and three abreast.

As she watched them move along, slow but steady, arm in arm, Rebecca thought of her mother.

She still lived in her own home, two towns over, but it wouldn't be long now. Rebecca and Todd knew it was only a matter of time until they'd change the guest room around and would welcome her to their home. Rebecca watched the ladies disappear behind a stand of pines and wondered if maybe her mother would like to go on a little trip before all those changes occurred. She wondered if her mother ever thought of doing something out of the ordinary, something risky. Rebecca decided that maybe later, if she got the time, she'd drive over to her mother's house and ask. After all, if these ladies could do it . . .

The morning glistened, fresh and green. A breeze brushed sweet, and clean, and cool enough for a slight shiver. One small sparrow perched on a mulberry branch and sang her song to the day—her steady cheep, cheep, cheep a walking tune for the ladies.

The plots were arranged in alphanumeric order on a tidy grid and were easy to find. While her friends stood by, hands folded, heads lowered, Rose laid the bouquets on her parents' graves. Red roses for her father. Pink for her mother.

"Lovely spot," Edna said.

Mattie nodded. "So peaceful here."

Rose took a minute and surveyed the grounds. As a perpetual care facility, the cemetery featured polished granite memorial plaques sunk level with short Bermuda grass. The names of the deceased were carved on the plaques in curling script. Vases, planters, candles or other offerings were not allowed—too hard for the groundskeeper to mow around. And so people who wished to pay their respects to the dearly departed respectfully left bouquets on the flat stones. On the days he mowed, the groundskeeper collected the flowers. He took the fresh ones home to his wife and dumped the rest in a compost bin.

"This is a good resting spot," Rose said. "I know they'd be pleased."

Dolores asked Rose if she would like them to hold hands and pray. "Or, we might sing a hymn. I know some beautiful hymns. In fact," she warmed to the idea, "I would be happy to sing a solo if you want."

Rose looked at Dolores. "No thanks," she said. "They're at peace."

On the walk back to the car, Mattie mumbled something about Dolores's singing and waking the dead. Helen stifled a grin and punched Mattie on the arm.

Rebecca turned in her seat and faced Rose. "The graveyard where your brother is buried isn't quite as pleasant." She sighed. "Vagrants and probably teenagers. I keep nagging my husband to organize a cleanup committee. The land does belong to the church. I suppose we should, you know, fix the place up a bit. But, what with being so busy . . ."

Rose nodded.

Rebecca continued, "I'll drive you there, but I have a meeting at the church, so when you're done if you can walk back to the house it would be a big help. We're only three blocks away, straight down the hill."

Dolores started to complain about her knees, but Mattie interrupted. "A little exercise would do all of us some good."

Dolores started in again. Edna patted her hand and smiled. Dolores fumed but complied.

"That cleanup committee would have some serious work ahead of them." Mattie reviewed the paper Rebecca gave them. It diagrammed the placement of graves in the long-neglected burial ground. She'd apologized, said the photocopied sheet was probably way out of date. One more thing for the church committee to tackle.

Dolores eyed the uneven ground, piles of trash, and tangled brambles blighting the landscape.

"Rose, dear, would you mind terribly, if I stay and sit here, on this bench? My knees are giving me serious pain right now, and I might trip, maybe fall, in there." She gestured toward the yard.

Rose glanced at her and gave a brief nod. She didn't care if any of them came with her at this point, but she knew the others would.

Dolores lowered herself to the bench with a groan, opened her handbag, pulled out a sack from the café, and unwrapped the last cinnamon bun. A good time for a snack.

"Over there, I think." Mattie pointed toward a far corner. They'd left Dolores a full ten minutes earlier but hadn't made much headway. The cemetery was not large, but the need to edge past blackberry bushes and around piles of litter slowed their progress. They stepped over cigarette packages, fast-food containers complete with burnished chicken bones, and empty bottles: beer, vodka, and Raspberry Ripple. Discarded condoms and a single tennis shoe crowded for space. Faded plastic flowers spilled from toppled and broken vases. Blocks of once spongy floral foam now gripped dried sticks in a crusty hold. A pair of yellow panties dangled from a scrubby plant, the word Wednesday embroidered in blue across the front. Cast concrete headstones lay toppled or smashed. Where there once had been mounds of freshly turned dirt, the earth now sagged. Any semblance of care had long since departed, but the scent of rot and abandonment snarled and stayed.

Helen stopped each time she spotted a toppled American flag lying in the mud. They were small, cheap, faded. The kind of flags people wave during parades then drop to the curb and forget. She didn't say a word but pressed her lips into a tight, hard line. She dug each one out of the dirt, wiped it clean, smoothed the folds, and planted the stick upright next to a headstone.

Despite the mid-morning sun, Edna shivered. "This place is spooky."

Mattie slowed and surveyed the area. "Not so much spooky." She looked down at the diagram, rotated it, and looked up again. "More like sorrowful. All these souls, squandered, forgotten. Such a waste." She made up her mind, turned to the right, and continued.

Rose did not comment. She gripped her handbag with clenched fists and followed Mattie. When they finally located the grave, Edna put one hand over her heart.

"Oh, this is so sad," she said.

A sharp-spiked crabapple bush partially obscured the headstone. Mattie bent over and tugged at the stubborn, thorny plant. She pulled her hand away and shook it. Drops of blood flew from her fingers.

"Don't get hurt," Rose said. "We can't move the bush. It's too prickly."

"Nonsense. Of course, we can." Mattie slid out of her jacket, turned it inside out and draped it over the bush. She pulled the plant away from the headstone before Rose could stop her. "This is your brother's grave. The least we can do is tidy it up."

"She's right," Edna said. She knelt by the headstone and tugged at a clump of weeds. Mattie shook the leaves and thorns from her coat and spread it on the ground. She kneeled next to Edna and went to work scooping up cigarette butts and other bits of trash.

Rose bit her lip. She looked up at Helen, her expression a pain-filled question. Helen looked back at her and held her gaze. Then she lifted her head, jutted her chin out, and squared her shoulders. She didn't say a word, but Rose heard her thoughts, '*You can do this.*'

Rose inhaled, and then she too squared her shoulders. She exhaled, bent down, and plucked a beer can from her brother's grave.

Helen nabbed a plastic bag that tumbled in the breeze. By the time they'd filled the bag, the plot was clear of weeds and garbage. They stood and brushed foliage and dirt from their clothes.

"Now that looks so much better," Edna said. She tied the top of the bag in a knot.

"Yes," Rose said. "It does. Thank you."

Not knowing what to do or say next, the four of them stood quietly and stared down at the grave. Finally, Helen cleared her throat.

"Edna. Mattie. Why don't we find someplace to dump this junk? Give Rose here a little time alone with her brother."

Rose stared at her a moment, her face blank. Then she blinked once and nodded.

Mattie and Edna chatted as they picked their way across the yard toward the bench where Dolores sat snoozing in the sunlight. Helen hung back. She stopped next to a scraggly pine and turned toward Rose.

She stood on her brother's grave with her back to Helen, opened her purse, and pulled a small plastic bottle from the paper bag. Helen remained still and watched. Rose uncapped the bottle, took one step forward and poured its contents over the face of the stone. She tossed the bottle to one side. It landed label up. *Kiwi Liquid Shoe Polish*. A black stain spread over the concrete slab. Helen tilted her head, strained for a better view.

Rose stooped down, removed one shoe, and with fierceness Helen would never have guessed possible, she ground the heel of it into the name of her brother. Then using both hands to hold her shoe, Rose beat the top of the stone. She hit it over, and over, and over again. Helen stifled a gasp, turned and walked with quick steps to join the others.

Mattie and Dolores argued about the correct rules of *Old Maid* as they walked from the cemetery to Rebecca's house. Edna swung her arms back and forth and hummed to herself. 'We're off to see the wizard—the wonderful wizard . . .'

Helen walked next to Rose. Every so often she glanced sideways at her friend. But Rose didn't speak or return Helen's look. She followed quietly along behind the others as if this day were like any other day. When they arrived at the house, Helen retired to the guest room for a nap. Mattie, Dolores, and Edna opted for a rematch of their card game, and Rose joined Rebecca in the kitchen.

In anticipation of her husband's homecoming, Rebecca prepared Todd's favorite meal: bacon-wrapped meatballs slathered in a barbecue glaze, baked beans, creamy coleslaw, and a sweet cherry pie.

"Todd loves this pie," Rebecca said. She handed Rose a flour sifter.

"My mama used to make cherry pie," Rose said. "It's not my favorite, though. My favorite is blueberry." She dusted flour over the cutting board. "Funny, since my favorite color is pink. You'd think cherry, or maybe strawberry would be my favorite."

She continued to chatter on while she rolled pie dough and later as she chopped cabbage. Rose shared how her husband had given her pearls on the day their son was born and how she wore those pearls every day—only removed them to sleep or to shower. She reminisced about her son's childhood, and how she used to love dressing him in little pink suits with vests and bowties. She talked about her room in Florida, how everything, even the toilet tissue, was pink. Rose barely took a breath.

Rebecca listened, curious at what had caused the change in her frail, previously shy and hesitant houseguest. She planned to discuss this with her husband, but she already knew what he would say. *The Lord works in mysterious ways.*

When Reverend Clarenbach arrived, he gathered his wife in a full embrace and kissed her with a loud smack. Then, one by one, he held the ladies' hands between his big paws and squeezed. His face, round and florid, beamed a grin that invited open smiles in return. The ladies liked him immediately.

Over dinner, the reverend entertained them with stories of his young charges, all of them away from home for the first time. He shared how some had played brave, had swaggered, and acted the part of seasoned travelers. And he described how others had clung to the chaperones until they stood in the church parking lot, holding their parents' hands, safe from the world once again.

Mattie watched her friends. She noticed how they played and joked with their hosts. Helen laughed out loud and talked with her hands punctuating her stories with the jingling of her bracelets. Dolores pontificated on every subject while helping herself to seconds and thirds. Edna and even Rose joined in the silliness. Mattie knew they were happy. She felt happy, too. And she knew it wasn't just the reverend's gentle disposition or Rebecca's midwest cooking that filled them, and her, with a sense of peace and well-being. This traveling stuff, she thought, it's not so hard. *We should have done this years ago.*

After their meal, the reverend invited the ladies to join him in his study for a digestif. Rebecca served snifters of warmed brandy, something none of them had ever tasted. Edna had never even heard of warmed brandy.

When Rose reached up to accept the glass, Dolores huffed. "Rose," she gaped at her friend. "You don't drink. You even turn down rum balls at Christmas. Are you all right?"

Rose laced her fingers around the snifter and pulled it close. She felt the heat spread through her hands to her chest. "Why, yes, Dolores," she said. "As a matter of fact, I am all right." She looked across the reverend's study at Helen, who smiled ever so slightly. "I haven't been this all right for a long, *long* time."

Reverend Clarenbach poured another round of brandy; the glasses were small. Rebecca snapped photos of the ladies to post on their Facebook page, and then she brought out a game of Pictionary. Dolores, Edna, and the reverend played against Helen, Mattie, and Rebecca. Rose excused herself and wove off to the guest room.

Helen readied for bed in the dark, quiet and careful not to wake Rose. She slid under the covers and sighed. A long day. In fact, several long days. But they'd started their journey. They were warm and safe and together. She turned her head and looked across the room to the other bed. Rose lay under a quilt beneath the now open window. A sliver of moonlight slipped from behind the guest room curtains and spilled onto her pillow. Her face, peaceful. A soft smile tugged at her lips.

Something woke Helen—a sound or some small movement. The moon had traveled on; it left the room in shadows. She lay still and listened. Only silence now. Strange, she thought. She shrugged, rolled over, and drifted back to sleep.

Chapter Eleven

A Single Strand

The Clarenbachs promised to handle all the arrangements. They would mail her ashes to her son in California along with the sealed envelope she had given Mattie to forward—if anything should happen. Mattie knew the note would say something about how much Rose loved her son and how she wished they had spent more time together; wished they'd watched one of his movies together. Mattie suspected the letter would include a will, and she also suspected that the errant son would stash the ashes in a garage or attic and concentrate on the contents of the will.

The ladies wanted to stay for the service on Sunday when Reverend Clarenbach, Rebecca, and the rest of congregation would pray for their friend. They wanted to remain in Wisconsin a little longer to pay their respects, again, to Rose's parents, and to eat another breakfast at the Blue Bird Café. However, an email from Katie changed their minds.

*Grannies. That old witch, Josephine, told the aunties you flew
the coop. I lied to buy you some time. But you better hustle. Get
on that plane to Europe before they figure out where you are.
Look for some kids at the airport in Dublin. They will help you
get to Cork. Have fun and send pics.*
Ciao, grannies. Katie.

So that her friends might find some peace and closure, Reverend Clarenbach held a private service for Rose in his study. The
ladies took their seats and listened with bowed heads and hands
folded; hankies at the ready. The reverend didn't know anything
about Rose other than what he'd learned in the short time they
shared at dinner and what he'd seen on Facebook: a small woman wearing a pink dress, pearls, and a paper bag over her head.
He did remember, though, that she'd come to Wisconsin to visit
the graves of her family members, and he latched onto that fact as
a focal point for his sermon.

"Family," he said, "was the most important element in our
dear sister's life. Rose was all about family—her devotion to her
son, her love for her parents, and the deep longing to connect,
once again, with her brother."

The reverend went on for several minutes ad-libbing about
Rose's relationship with each of her family members. The other
ladies touched hankies to teary eyes and nodded. But Helen suppressed a croak and covered her mouth. Then she excused herself
and left the room.

"They were close," Rebecca said. She nodded toward

Helen's empty chair. "Traveling companions."

She knew they'd shared the guest room. She did not know about the drawing of straws or Mattie's generosity. Her husband acknowledged the observation with a solemn nod and continued. He added "dear friends" and "traveling companions" to his standard eulogy phrases.

Helen could not stay and listen to the fabricated stories about Rose and her family; stories about her son and her brother. She sat on her side of the guest room and stared at the bed where Rose had rested such a short time ago, safe enough for an open window, at peace enough for a smile in her sleep.

Helen held a single strand of pearls. She couldn't remember Rose without those pearls. They were her signature look, those pearls and all that pink. Where did she get them? A gift from Rose's husband? An heirloom from her mother? Helen shook her head at the thought they'd come from the son. Only cheese came from California. Earlier, Rebecca had offered to send Rose's satchel and clothing to Hollywood, but Mattie had spoken for all of them.

"No," she said. "Give them to someone here, in Wisconsin. Someone who needs them and will appreciate them."

No one mentioned the pearls. Helen made a decision. She would ask Rebecca to post them for her. Katie would cherish them. Pearls and patchouli—a perfect combination. She knew the others would approve, and she was sure Rose would be pleased.

Chapter Twelve

Busted – Tampa, Florida

"You what? You pompous ass. You let them go?" Joan's voice carried from the director's office into the hallway. The janitor and two orderlies froze and listened. This was the most exciting thing that had happened since that old geezer peed on the piano, and then on the Assistant Director.

"Now, now." Roger Simpson's hands shook as he hustled over to the door and closed it. "Let's all be calm about this." He turned and tried to reach the antique coat rack positioned behind his chair. The two hysterical women had breached his sanctuary before he had time to slip into his suit jacket. He tried to focus on the fact that he'd worn his favorite, and most expensive, Hugo Boss shirt, and his new Salvatore Ferragamo tie. These, he believed, gave him the look of a leader. But without the jacket, he felt somehow less in charge, less in control.

"Calm?" Suzanne stepped in front of Simpson. She blocked his way before he could reach his armor or even return to the safety of his desk. The skin on her face pinched Botox-tight.

"Our mother is missing, and you want us to be *calm*?" She shrieked the last word.

Before he could stop himself, Simpson covered his ears. He immediately realized how undiplomatic that appeared, so he thrust his hands into the pockets of his slacks. Then he realized that stance made him look weak, unconfident. He pulled his hands out and held them straight, palms facing the sisters.

"Now, ladies, if we could discuss this . . ."

"If you think for one minute you are going to stay in business after this . . ." Joan moved in. Her upper lip formed a snarl; a blotchy rash crawled up her neck. She pointed a finger at him, her sharp, manicured nail inches from his face. "You'd better go call your lawyer, mister, because you are so sued."

Simpson shook his head. His body quaked. "Now, now." He tried to swallow, to get control. He thought of calling for a nurse; give these harpies something to knock them out. It usually worked with the old poops. "Let's take a look at the documents, shall we?" He stopped short of adding *before we call security.*

"What are you doin'?" Caroline lumbered up to the group gathered in the hall outside Simpson's office. By now, there were four orderlies, two nurses, and a candy striper. They crowded around the janitor who hunched forward, his cupped hand pressed against the door. At the sound of her voice, they straightened. Some stared at their shoes, others at the ceiling.

"All of you scoot. You hear me? If you don't have enough work, then I will be sure you git some more. Now git outta here."

The orderlies sprinted in one direction, the nurses and the candy striper in the other. The janitor grabbed his mop and bucket and limped away as fast as his bowed and aging legs would carry him.

Caroline thought about things for a moment. She could creep on down the hall, follow the janitor and the orderlies. Or, go have coffee at the nurses' station, stay clear of all this mess. That would be the smart thing to do. She shook her head, sighed, and opened the office door. Later, she would tell her cousin that opening that door was one of the stupidest things she ever did.

Chapter Thirteen

Away to Foreign Lands
British Airways

Katie managed to get them on a direct flight from Wisconsin to Dublin; nine hours in the air, a perfect time for long, restful naps. But she was not able to seat them all together.

"I'll give you ten dollars if you let me sit by Helen." Edna searched her friend's face. She and Mattie watched the bags while Helen and Dolores used the ladies' room. "Please."

"No way." Mattie shook her head. "Dolores will babble and eat all the way to Ireland." She remained stationary, moved only her eyes as she scanned the crowded terminal to make sure Dolores and Helen were still out of earshot. "If you remember, I'm the one who wanted to leave her in Florida. I hate all that whining and all her dreary stories about Mr. Will . . ."

Edna interrupted. "I know. I know. But we couldn't leave her. She was part of our lunch group, and she doesn't have anyone else."

"Be honest," Mattie said. "The real reason we brought her along is that she would have spilled the beans. She can't keep a secret, and she would think she was the Belle of the Ball if she had some juicy information on our whereabouts." She frowned and made a quick motion with her head.

Edna glanced over and saw the two returning. She sighed. "All right," she said. "But I don't care who draws the next short straw; this is the last time I have to sit next to her on an airplane. Got it?" Mattie didn't respond.

Helen and Mattie sat toward the back of the plane. They each ordered a miniature bottle of wine with dinner and watched *Forrest Gump* for the third and fourth time respectively. After the movie, they secured their airline-issued eye masks and slipped into sleep.

Dolores and Edna plunked down in the two middle seats in a center row. Once Dolores realized that all she had to do was reach up and hit the call button to receive cartons of milk and small packages of cookies, extra packets of nuts, a second, or even third helping of dessert, she was in heaven.

"I love this international flight." She turned to face Edna. A crumb of Oreo cookie balanced on her lower lip. "Why, these girls are so happy to feed us. They're not at all like those stingy girls on the flight from Florida." The crumb bounced off and landed on her tray table. Edna slumped down in her seat and pulled a blanket over her head.

But Dolores did not take the hint. She chattered until the cabin lights dimmed and the in-flight entertainment began. Dolores ordered one more packet of toasted nuts and finally settled back to watch. Edna sent up a small prayer of thanks.

She pretended to be asleep when the movie ended, and Dolores tapped on her shoulder through the blanket. Undaunted, Dolores struck up a conversation with the woman sitting on the other side of Edna. Actually, it was more monologue than exchange as the other woman was Spanish, and her English was limited. But, as people do—when trapped—the Spanish woman smiled politely and nodded when she thought she should respond. Thrilled with a new listener, Dolores propped herself over the armrest and gouged her elbow into Edna's shoulder. Edna tried to move, but Dolores had her pinned. Rather than let her know she was awake, Edna merely gave in and remained still under the blanket, a captive audience for the umpteenth time to the story of Dolores Ryanna Brackin.

Chapter Fourteen

"All my people were Irish. Through and through. I have a picture of my great-grandfather standing by his barn in Ireland, but I left it in Florida. We are from Florida; me and my friends who are traveling with me.

"Do you know anyone from Florida?" Dolores asked the question but didn't pause—didn't wait for an answer.

"So you see, I know all my people were Irish because my great-grandparents and my grandparents were Irish, and my mother was Irish, and I look Irish. Used to have beautiful auburn hair, you know. Are all your people Spanish?" She fluffed white curls with one hand.

The other woman nodded and started to speak, but Dolores hurried on.

"Yes, that's interesting. So, as I said, all my people were Irish, and that's why my friends are going with me to Ireland. We are going to kiss the Blarney Stone. In Cork County. That's where it is, you know." She opened her mouth wide, tilted her head back, and poured a measure of nuts. She munched on them for a moment, then continued.

"I'd like to see where my people came from. I was too busy as a girl to travel. I had lots of responsibilities and an important position in my town. Joliet, Illinois. I'm sure you've heard of it? Forty miles outside of Chicago. Of course, with my schedule and all, I couldn't get away for travel and other frivolous things."

"You work?" The woman tried one of her recently learned phrases.

"My goodness, not now. But I did. I certainly did. Oh yes, I had such responsibilities." She scooped more nuts from the bag. One fell between her fingers and landed on Edna's blanket. Dolores gazed up at the call button. She considered ordering something else but decided to proceed with her story instead.

"You see, my mother and father did not expect another child. My brother was already eighteen, and newly married, when I was born. I was a big surprise, indeed. Of course, being a miracle baby and all, my parents loved me very much, spoiled me rotten." She laughed and then frowned. "I suppose my life would have been a lot different if it hadn't been for that streetcar."

"Street? Car?" The Spanish woman reached in her bag for her phrase book.

"Yes, it was a streetcar that changed my life." Dolores sighed. "My parents and my brother and his wife and their new baby were all heading to the church—the big one in the city, in Chicago—for the christening. They took my father's Model A. It was his pride and joy, outside of me, of course. I remember that day so clearly, which is strange because it was so long ago. I was five.

"I watched my mother get ready. It was the middle of winter. Sunlight reflected off piles of snow outside the window and lit up my mother's dressing table. She was so beautiful. I remember how she pulled on her best dress. It was navy blue with a white collar and white cuffs. And I remember how she pinned her hat into her hair, the navy blue hat that matched her dress, the hat with the netting, and the row of rhinestones along the rim. My mother touched her finger to her perfume bottle and then touched it behind each ear. *Evening in Paris*, very expensive, you know. They don't make it anymore."

Dolores pantomimed the act while she spoke. The glow from the overhead reading lamp added a third chin to her profile as she touched a finger to her ear. The Spanish woman watched her through the shadows and smiled.

"Mother and father left me with my grandparents. My grandfather couldn't go out because of the wheelchair and his sickness. I don't recall what his sickness was, but he never said anything or even opened his eyes. He just sat in his wheelchair in the corner of the living room. Grandmother took care of him day and night. She pushed spoons of food into his mouth and washed his face and hands with a cloth. She did everything for him: fed him, cleaned him, lifted him in and out of that chair, laid him on the bed. Everything.

"So, of course, she couldn't go to the christening. I don't remember why I couldn't go. But I didn't mind because I loved staying with my grandmother. She made pies. Delicious pies. She let me eat the raw dough and lick the filling off the spatulas— cherry and apple, chocolate pudding, and pumpkin."

At the thought of chocolate pudding, Dolores glanced again at the call button but went on without reaching up.

"I remember when my mother kneeled down and kissed me good-bye. 'Be a good girl,' she said. 'And help your grandmother fix the food for the christening party. We'll be back so soon you won't even remember we left.' "

Dolores closed her eyes and inhaled; the heavy floral scent of perfume and the sweet flavor of cherry pie still so easily recalled. The Spanish woman coughed. Dolores opened her eyes.

"Grandmother cooked all day: chicken soup with dumplings, baked sweet potatoes with brown sugar and raisins, and shepherd's pie. That's ground lamb and beef mixed with mashed potatoes, you know. She cut slices of ham and drenched them with dark beer gravy. And she made shortbread and a ginger cake drizzled with lemon sauce.

"When she got all the cooking done, she put some food in the ice box and the rest on the table with clean dishcloths over the top. She started the logs in the fireplace and lit the candles. 'Won't be long now, little one,' she said.

"But it was a long time. We waited and waited. Finally, a policeman came. He said there was an accident. A streetcar jumped the tracks. All gone. Even the baby. All of them, except my mother. She was in the hospital, and he would take grandmother to her. I wanted to go with them, wanted to be with my beautiful mother. But the policeman said no. It wasn't something a little girl should see. So I stayed with grandfather and waited.

"Grandmother didn't come back that night. The fire went out, and the candles burned down, and they went out too. And it snowed, and the wind blew and something happened to the furnace, and it stopped working, and the house got dark and very, very cold.

"I wrapped a blanket around my grandfather and tucked it in at the edges. He didn't move, didn't notice it was so cold or so dark. He sat there with drool dripping down his shirt, so I put a washrag under his chin. For a while, I stayed in my grandmother's chair wrapped in a quilt, but I didn't like being in that dark room with my grandfather, so I took the quilt and went to the kitchen.

"It was cold in there too, but the snow stopped, and the moon came through the window and lit up the table and all that food covered with dishcloths. I ate a little bit from each dish. And then I went back around and ate more from each one. I did that until my belly hurt. Then I wrapped up in the quilt and slept under the kitchen table.

"Grandmother didn't come home for two days. Outside the snow swirled and the wind howled. It was the worst winter storm ever in the history of Illinois. The house was cold, and it got dark early. Grandfather soiled himself, and he smelled bad. I put more blankets on top of him to cover up the smell, but then I hurried back to the kitchen. I was afraid. Cold and afraid. But at least the kitchen had sun coming in the windows during the day and moonlight at night. And all that food. I ate and ate. It kept me warm and I didn't want it to spoil.

"On the afternoon of the third day, the policeman brought grandmother home. She hugged me and told me mother and father and the others were with God now, and we'd have a proper burial come spring."

The Spanish woman clicked her tongue and made the sign of the cross. Dolores didn't seem to notice. She sighed and plowed onward through her story.

"I stayed with my grandparents. Which was all right, I guess. Grandmother taught me how to sew and clean and do laundry. Mostly, though, we cooked.

While we sliced lamb, and stewed chickens, and kneaded dough for bread, she told me stories about Ireland and how she and grandfather used to dance until midnight at the pub in County Cork. She could sing all the old tunes: "Cockles and Mussels", "Danny Boy", and "Whiskey in the Jar". I didn't need other friends; I was happy with my Irish grandmother. Just the two of us, singing and cooking together in that kitchen."

Dolores paused a moment and savored the memory of chicken, dumplings, and warm white bread cut thick as a doorstop. She shook her head and moved along with the telling.

"At night, after dinner, after we finished all the work for the day, and after grandfather was cleaned up, and tucked into his chair, grandmother brewed a pot of strong Lipton's tea for herself and warmed a glass of milk for me. She squeezed the juice of a lemon into her cup, and then she added a teaspoon of thick honey to her tea. She always let me lick the spoon.

"When the honey melted, she took a square bottle out from behind her pots and pans. 'Not the same as what we had back home,' she said. 'But it will do, little one, it will do.'

"I wanted to taste her tea with the lemon, and honey, and American whiskey, but she said no, it wasn't for young ladies like me.

"So that was my life until I turned nine and my grandmother died. Heart attack. After that, it was only me and grandfather. Like I said, he needed someone for house-cleaning, laundry, cooking. You know. Everything. The state paid for a nurse until I turned eleven, then I took over." Dolores exhaled.

The Spanish woman wanted to use the toilet, but her husband was deep in sleep. He snored and sprawled out in the seat next to the aisle. He would not budge. Resigned, she sighed and tried another one of her phrases. "Do you to school?"

Dolores sniffed. "I didn't finish high school. Actually, I think high school is overrated, don't you?" She glanced at her listener. The other woman shifted in her seat and crossed her legs. Dolores pushed on.

"Like I said, I didn't finish high school, but I did go to secre-tarial school. Much more practical, wouldn't you say, than history and social studies? A girl can make a good living as a secretary. That is if you don't waste your time running around with boys or any of that tomfoolery.

"I worked as the personal secretary for Mr. William T. Broughton. Forty-two years. I was seventeen when I started working for him, and I never missed a day of work. Worked a full nine hours, five days a week, and sometimes I went into the office on the weekends to vacuum and dust.

"The cleaning staff didn't measure up in my opinion. They forgot to dust all the diplomas and photos on the office walls. They even missed the best one, the picture of Mr. William T. Broughton and President Kennedy shaking hands in the White House. I always dusted that one first.

"I went in to work even when Mr. William T. Broughton was on vacation or when he took a few days off. Mr. William T. Broughton was a lawyer, you know. Very important for lawyers to get some time off to rest their brains. I mean, they have to read all those big heavy books and such. Why, I even scheduled grandfather's funeral on a Saturday so I wouldn't miss work."

Dolores paused a moment, took a deep breath, enough time for the Spanish woman to ask a question.

"Married? Me?" Dolores shook her head no. "I'm sure if I wanted to, I could have, you know, had a suitor, but I was too busy at my job. Mr. William T. Broughton, he relied on me. He had so many important papers that needed typing and filing.

"He even sent me to a special course, dictation. We didn't get that at my secretarial school. After I took that course, he talked out what he wanted in those papers and I took notes. That's what dictation is." She focused on her listener for a beat. "Do you have secretaries in Spain?"

The other woman didn't even try to respond.

"I took notes and typed them up. I started over if there was any kind of mistake. But I didn't have to start over much. I am, you see, an excellent typist."

She looked down at her fingers, still proud of them.

Stubby, maybe, and thick. But they certainly weren't all twisted and claw-like the way Mattie's were. Mattie could barely open a jar. But Dolores's fingers—*her fingers*—would still type if she wanted them to.

Unable to hold it any longer, the Spanish woman jabbed her husband in his ribs. He grunted, opened his eyes. She pointed to the aisle. When she returned Dolores picked up right where she'd stopped.

"Now, I know young people today worry about their job security and the like, but I knew that Mr. William T. Broughton would never let me go. He was so appreciative of my work. Why, every year at Christmas he bought me a big box of *Fannie May* chocolates, the special box that only came out once a year. The box with the gold foil. After thirty years, the Fannie May Company stopped making the boxes with gold foil. Too expensive for most people, I suppose. Although I'm sure Mr. William T. Broughton could have afforded them. They started making plain white boxes with red and green satin ribbons. Not gold foil, but still, attractive. Naturally, I ate the chocolates, but I kept those boxes—each and every one—the gold ones and the white ones. Kept them in my closet in my grandfather's house." Again, she stopped long enough for the other woman to insert a question in halting English. Dolores answered immediately.

"Do I still have them?" She sighed, finished off the peanuts, folded the bag, and slid it into the seat pocket.

"I would have. You should always keep a gift, you know. But when I moved to Restful Palms, that's where my friends live with me, I hired a company to move my things. Those foolish young men who moved me? They probably never had a box of good chocolates, so they didn't see the value. They told me they recycled the boxes, put them in the bin. I was devastated. Still am."

The memory of the missing boxes saddened Dolores. She tugged at the wrapper on a muffin she'd rescued from Edna's tray before the flight attendant took it away.

"You boss. He is married?" The woman asked.

"Oh no . . . certainly not."

She broke the muffin over the lump that was Edna. Crumbs tumbled onto the blanket and rolled down the folds. In the dim light of the cabin, the bits of dropped food resembled runty bugs in a scurry to safety. Dolores generously offered half to the other woman. The Spanish woman shook her head no. Dolores took a nibble and nodded in approval. "They have such good food on this plane. I'm going to try to get my friends to take all our trips on this airline," she said. Then she continued with her story.

"As I said, no, Mr. William T. Broughton was too busy being a lawyer to have a wife and children. He worked hard all week, and on the weekends, he went golfing with his best friend from law school, Mr. Daniel W. Witherstop. The two of them, both lawyers, spent all their time outside the office together. It worried me because I knew they worked on legal things, and they never got any time off. But that was how dedicated my boss, Mr. William T. Broughton was. Even when he retired and closed the office, he continued to work." She shook her head in dismay.

"He should have taken time off to rest, but he went on a trip with Mr. Daniel W. Witherstop to some island. I forget where. I know they worked the whole time. They were that kind of men."

The Spanish woman made a face. "You boss. He is alive?"

Dolores's nose turned red, her eyes watery. "No, bless his poor soul. He got some disease and passed away." She sniffed. "I know it was because he worked so hard. No time off for fun.

"I organized the funeral. Mr. Daniel W. Witherstop asked me to do it because he was too broken up to handle the arrangements. That poor Mr. Witherstop, he cried all the way through the service. I guess he thought he'd never find another work partner as dedicated as Mr. William T. Broughton.

"He was so grateful, that is, Mr. Witherstop, was so grateful for my help, that he gave me the picture of Mr. William T. Broughton and President Kennedy. I cherish that picture."

Dolores sniffled, took the last big chunk of muffin, and swallowed. She dusted crumbs from her hands. Like the others, they fell on Edna.

"I'd show you that picture. Naturally, I brought it with me. But it's in my suitcase." She frowned. "I do hope those boys are careful with my luggage." Then she turned toward the Spanish woman and smiled. "Trust me," she nodded with confidence.

"That picture is a treasure. Probably worth a lot of money. Of course, I would never, ever part with it."

Chapter Fifteen

Dublin Airport hummed with the sound of travelers swarming the halls, all on their way to some other place. Young people. People who carried briefcases and lugged bags made especially for computers. People who checked watches, maps, tickets, then nodded and hurried off. People assured of where they were going and what they were doing.

The line for Customs and Immigration snaked along for what felt to Helen like miles. She shifted from one foot to the other, scanned the area. She wanted to, needed to, speed through the line and find the ladies' room. Soon.

Edna stretched and twisted to loosen the knots that kinked her muscles during the long hours she'd spent crunched under the weight of Dolores's elbow. She had hoped to sleep during the story session, but she didn't because, for some reason that she could not conceive, Dolores had shared a different story with the Spanish woman than the one she'd told, so many times, to her friends at Restful Palms. Edna thought that maybe when the time was right, she'd ask Dolores about the new story.

Dolores rummaged through her bag, certain she'd left something on the plane but not entirely sure what.

Mattie bit her lip, anxious about their situation and about how the others didn't seem to notice their predicament. Here they were, in a foreign country, where all the signs were in English, but also in some other strange language that looked something like, but not entirely like, English. What if the signs dropped the English words altogether? And here they were, in a foreign country, each of them with fifty dollars' worth of foreign money. What if they ran out? What if they couldn't find a bank? What if she couldn't remember how to use the phone? What if . . . She read Katie's email for the sixth, or maybe the ninth, time.

Look for some kids at the airport in Dublin. They will help you get to Cork.

She scanned the crowd. Some kids? How would she know these kids? Who were these friends of Katie's? What if they didn't show up? What if . . . What if . . .

She looked at her three friends, so oblivious, so unconcerned. They assumed she had things under control because she worked the phone and because all of this, at least, *most of this*, had been her idea. Mattie gripped the handle of her bag so tight her fingers hurt.

Ruddy-faced Irish Customs agents smiled at each of them, welcomed them to the Emerald Isle, and wished them all a good holiday. Edna, Helen, and Dolores took off in search of a restroom. Mattie waited for a few moments and watched the mass of people. They moved in what looked to her like a type of dance, some sort of choreographed chaos. She swallowed and then followed the others.

Katie had suggested, in fact, she insisted, that they each travel with only a small carry-on and a handbag. They had all agreed. Easier to move around, no need to find the baggage claim in airports. Cheaper, too, as they wouldn't have to pay porters to lift heavy bags. They all stuck with the plan, all except Dolores. At the last minute, she decided that there were things she must not, could not, leave behind. She announced that she was willing to pay the extra fees to have her belongings where she wanted them. So, once again, as they'd done in Wisconsin, they all trudged off to baggage claim.

"Oh, those custom agents were so kind," Edna said. She watched luggage spill from a tube onto the conveyor belt. "Such lovely smiles. And, the language! It almost sounds like a nursery rhyme."

"Yes. Or like music," Helen said. "Even though they're speaking English, I can barely understand what they're saying, but it's so pretty. I have a feeling I'm going to love Ireland." Her eyes twinkled.

Dolores stayed busy commandeering assistance from a security guard. Couldn't he please help an old lady? All her people were Irish, you know. Couldn't he get her bag off that thing?

But Mattie ignored her friends. She felt a tightness in her chest. Breathe, she told herself. *Just breathe.*

"Grannies!" Before she could turn around, two strong arms surrounded her in a hug that lifted her off the floor. She inhaled a sweet musky scent that reminded her of Katie. The girl released her and bounced over to hug Helen with the same enthusiasm and strength.

Mattie turned to the young man who stood smiling and nodding his head. He wore a long sleeved tie-dyed shirt, leather lederhosen, and hiking boots. His blond hair, a thick mat of dreadlocks, was tied together with red string. Feathers, beads, and bells hung from each thread. The bells tinkled as he moved. He stuck his hand out and gave hers a shake.

"Hi, Granny. I'm Peter. This is Eliza." He nodded to the girl next to him. "And that hugger? That's Melissa. We're your Facebook friends. Welcome to Ireland." Peter wore a perpetual grin. He never once stopped smiling.

The ladies stood and gaped, all four speechless. Eliza wore baggy army pants, leather sandals, and a skin-tight T-shirt. Dolores would comment later that it left nothing to the imagination and good thing that girl was flat as a boy. Eliza's hair was boy-like too. No more than an inch all around and dyed a deep, clear violet.

Melissa hugged each of them, Mattie twice, then stood back and beamed. Her walnut hair flowed in waves around her face. She wore a pretty white blouse embroidered with lilac flowers and a floor-length skirt of pale blue satin. A beautiful girl, the ladies would remark later when they were alone. But why on earth would she stick those safety pins through her eyebrows? And that big ring through her nose? And *did you see* her tongue?

Helen finally spoke. "This is great. You found us. But, how did you find us in such a busy place?"

Peter tilted his head to one side. He pointed to Dolores's green felt hat and to Mattie's combat boots. "Lucky guess," he said. Then, he laughed.

Katie's Facebook friends, "The Kids," as the ladies called them, lived and studied in London, but were on holiday, a school break, in Ireland.

"We stopped in Cork for a few days," Eliza said. "Found a room over a pub in the village close to Blarney Castle. For cheap."

Melissa nodded and flashed a brilliant smile. "We follow your Facebook page. And wow." She giggled and gave Edna a quick hug. "We were blown away when we found out you needed help getting to Cork."

"No brainer," Peter added. He grabbed Dolores's suitcase and led the way through the airport.

The ladies and the kids crammed together in a battered truck on loan from the pub owner. Melissa drove too fast for Edna's comfort, and on the wrong side of the road at that, but no one else seemed to notice. It occurred to her that perhaps she should learn to drive. Maybe if she knew how to drive . . . Edna thought about Louis. What would he say if he saw her driving a truck? In Ireland? But Louis isn't around anymore. *Things are different now.* She decided she'd try to remember to ask Melissa for a driving lesson. The idea reassured her, and she turned her attention to the conversations that bounced around in the borrowed truck.

"We wanted to hike the length of the island," Eliza explained. "But our holiday is too short, so we're hitchhiking instead."

"Isn't that dangerous?" Helen asked. Eliza and Peter exchanged a questioning look.

"Maybe in some violent countries," Peter said. "Maybe like in Libya or America. But . . ." he shrugged. "No, don't think so. This is Ireland."

Helen and Mattie exchanged glances. Later they would need to think more about his comment. They would need to discuss dangerous countries.

"Where have you been so far?" Dolores asked.

"Oh, to such beautiful places you wouldn't believe." Eliza waved her arms around. "To Galway, and the Ring of Kerry, and to Kenmare. Ireland is the most beautiful place on earth." She turned to Mattie. "But you, grannies, you are off to some pretty amazing places, too?"

As the truck rattled over rutted and narrow dirt roads and rolled past the ruins of humble stone cottages and once-great castles, the kids told rowdy drinking stories about sharing pints with

Neo-IRA members in Belfast and waxed on about the breathtaking majesty of the Cliffs of Moher.

The ladies shared their dreams of riding camels and petting kangaroos. Mattie described, in grand detail, how their ship would vault over swirling waves on the Mediterranean Sea.

"You guys are so completely cool," Eliza said. "My grandmum and granddad don't do anything except sit and complain."

"Maybe they aren't as young as us, dear," Edna said.

"Hmm, maybe." Eliza thought for a bit. "How old are you guys, anyway?"

"Bloody rude." Peter shot Eliza a look.

Oh, we don't mind." Dolores said. "I'm eighty-one. I am, of course, the youngest."

Mattie rolled her eyes. Helen grinned.

"I'm pretty young," Edna said. "I'm only eighty-three."

"Helen? How old are you? I never can remember." Dolores tapped Helen's shoulder.

"Eighty-eight. I'm eighty-eight years old. Two years older than Mattie. I'm the oldest. But . . . I like to think it's all a matter of how you feel, not how many years you're toting around."

"Geeze," Eliza said. "My grandmum and granddad are way younger than you guys. I think they should get up and do something."

It was difficult to move with all those bodies scrunched together, but Helen managed to pat Eliza's hand. "Don't be too hard on them, dear. We couldn't do this if we didn't have Katie and all her friends, like you, to help us."

"You *do* have a lot of friends," Melissa bobbed her head.

"Over a thousand as of this morning," Peter added.

Edna forgot all about the age discussion when she considered the idea of one thousand friends and how much time it would take to write out and lick stamps for one thousand Christmas cards. She wasn't sure this was such a good idea. Maybe not a good idea at all. She thought about it for a moment and made a mental note to discuss the Christmas card dilemma with Mattie but, distracted by all the laughter and chatter, she lost the note, and later, she lost the thought.

About an hour into their journey, Melissa announced that she had to pee. She pulled the truck to the side of the road, and while Peter tromped off in one direction, the girls headed in the opposite direction toward a clump of bushes in the middle of a meadow. The ladies looked at one another.

"I'm not going to the bathroom outside," Dolores said. "It's, it's . . ."

"It's senseless to sit in this truck and get a bladder infection." Mattie rummaged around in her bag for a tissue, and then she followed the girls to the shrubbery. Helen and Edna exchanged looks.

"Why not?" Helen took Edna's hand, and the two of them traipsed across the field. Dolores stood by herself next to the truck. She straightened her spine and lifted her chin. This was not the sort of thing a secretary to Mr. William T. Broughton did, in Ireland or anywhere else. She could hold it.

"Girls. Over here." Peter waved his arms and jumped up and down to catch their attention. "I found the sacred stones."

Melissa and Eliza squealed and took off in a run toward him. Mattie and Helen looked at each other. "What the . . ." Mattie started.

"Absolutely no idea," Helen shook her head. "But we're here. Let's go see."

By the time the ladies caught up with them, Peter was already lecturing the girls about the history and importance of the twelve boulders that circled a patch of smooth emerald grass. A large black rock flecked with sparks of white quartz held court in the center of the circle.

"It's a druid shrine," he said. "A sacred circle for the early people of Ireland."

"Maybe we shouldn't be here." Edna wrapped her sweater tight even though the morning sun warmed her. She edged closer to Helen.

"Oh, no worries." Eliza skipped to a large stone. "They want us to believe." She pressed both palms against the rock's mossy surface, closed her eyes and hummed a soothing ommm.

Mattie listened for a moment and then twisted toward Peter. "They? Who?"

"The ancient Spirits, of course, Granny," he said. "They are everywhere in Ireland. If you believe in them, and honor them, they will protect you as long as you're on the magical island."

Helen looped her arm around Edna and gave her a quick, re-assuring hug. "Assume, for a minute, we believe in these ancient spirits," she said, "how do we go about honoring them?"

"Look there." Peter pointed to a large tree off to the north side of the circle. Its branches dripped baubles and trinkets and stretched wide like a many-armed Hindu goddess.

"Wow." Mattie stared for a moment and then, without another word, she cut through the circle toward the tree.

Peter grinned. "She feels the Spirits," he said. "Come on, la-dies; you can tie a token to a branch, leave a gift for the Old Ones. Marvelous good luck, you see."

"I'm leaving my other nose ring." Melissa lifted up on her toes and wedged a piece of silver jewelry into the crook of a branch. "It was a gift from my mum so I know the Spirits will be pleased."

"I'm leaving this bell and a feather from my dreads," Peter said. "And Eliza and I are going to make love behind the center stone." He finished a knot, shook the branch and smiled at the tinkle of the small brass bell. He turned and reached for Eliza's hand. "Come on, baby. Let's give the greatest gift of all."

Helen watched as the two young people trooped across the grass to the center stone. She sighed when they laughed and paused for a kiss.

"Pull yourself away from the lovebirds and give me a hand with these bows." Mattie tugged at Helen's sleeve. "Two boot laces, two bows. One from me, down here, where I can reach, and one from you. Up high. You tie it up there." She handed Helen a boot lace and pointed to a branch out of her reach.

"Sure you don't want to keep these?" Helen glanced down at Mattie's combat boots. They flopped loose around her feet.

"Nope. Been carrying 'em in my handbag since we left. Extra weight. Don't need laces." Mattie grunted as she struggled to fasten a loopy bow on a stumpy branch of the sacred tree.

Their boot-lace bows joined coins from around the world, beaded earrings, bits of colored yarn, hair clips, slips of paper folded into swans or small squares, and several baseball caps bragging the names of taverns and sports teams.

"It's like a Christmas tree." Edna's eyes sparkled. "A Christmas tree decorated by total strangers."

"Let's do some oms," Melissa said. She held out her hands to Edna and Helen. Helen reached for Mattie. The four women stood in front of the sacred tree, closed their eyes and ommmed to the ancient Spirits of Ireland.

When they finally returned to the truck, Dolores was beside herself.

"Where *were* you?" she wailed. "I don't think I can wait much longer. What took you so long?" She rocked from one foot to the other. "How much longer before we reach town?"

Helen eyed her friend. "Darlin', I heard how you feel about using the great outdoors as your restroom but maybe, just this once, you might give it a try."

Dolores bit her lip, tried to hold back the tears, and everything else. "Come with me?"

Helen nodded. She sloshed around in her handbag, found a tissue, then took Dolores's elbow and steered her across the meadow to the stand of shrubbery where she and the others had been earlier.

Mattie snorted. "What a piece of work."

Once everyone settled in, Melissa slipped the truck into gear and eased back on the road. Peter and the others told Dolores all about the stones, the sacred tree, and the gifts they'd left.

"Helen and I tied my old boot laces into bows in the branches. Have to admit, they looked pretty good." Mattie grinned.

"Good luck for sure," Helen added. She smiled at Mattie.

Dolores shifted in her seat and adjusted her position. "Those of us who are naturally Irish don't need to be hanging things in trees for good luck. Why I bet . . ."

"I didn't take my handbag with me, so I didn't have anything to leave," Edna interrupted her. "Then I remembered my new socks. Put them on fresh today. Bright green pom poms. Green for Ireland. I left them hanging in that tree." She beamed.

"You left socks to a Holy Spirit?" Dolores stared at her in open disgust. "I can't . . ."

Mattie stopped her with a hard jab to the ribs.

Peter took over. "Eliza and I made love behind the center stone. That's a beautiful gift; don't you think?"

Dolores didn't answer. She was busy rubbing her side.

"I don't agree," Melissa piped up. "You two are like rabbits, and you do it everywhere you can, so I don't see how that was a sacred gift to the Spirits."

"Love is always sacred," Eliza said.

The kids continued to debate the issue for some time, but the ladies dropped from the discussion, content to gaze at the verdant countryside through the truck's smudged windows. They sped over sloping hills, through emerald valleys, past herds of fat, fluffy sheep and thin, slow cows.

When the young people fell silent, exhausted by their debate about spiritual sex and sacred stones, the ladies sang. They warbled the words to *"Chattanooga Choo Choo," "Sentimental Journey," and "Buttons and Bows."* Eliza insisted they repeat the Dinah Shore tune three times so that she could learn the words. When the kids joined in, they harmonized to Beatles songs and to one by a man named Sting.

Edna leaned forward and tapped Peter on the shoulder. "Do you know any songs from that young man? That Elvis Paisley?"

"Elvis Paisley." He and the two girls burst into laughter. "Oh Granny, you are so funny."

But, as it turned out, they did know several Elvis songs: "Blue Suede Shoes," "Jail House Rock," and "Hound Dog." After each song, Peter did his best impression of the King. "Thank you. Thank you very much."

The girls and the ladies collapsed into fits of giggles and pretend swoons. Eventually, they mellowed, and Melissa sang a sad song by a singer named Jannis or Janet or something like that. Her clear, strong voice carried over the rumble of the truck. "Freedom is just another word for nothing left to lose."

Although she didn't know why, the words made Mattie tear up. She turned her head and pressed her face against the window so the others couldn't see.

Chapter Sixteen

They arrived at the village mid-afternoon. The kids dropped the ladies off at The Kissing Fingers Bed and Breakfast and agreed to meet up again that evening at the local pub for a meal of good, old-fashioned Irish comfort food. The ladies promised to treat— the very least they could do for all the help.

The Kissing Fingers, a two-story, whitewashed cottage overgrown with thick green ivy, wore a thatched roof and a bright red door. A moat of pink and lavender dahlias hugged the perimeter. Mrs. Doolin, owner and proprietress of the B&B, arranged for them to share one room on the second floor. "It's a good one," she told them. "The loo is right down the hall. No need to use the stairs."

Peeling yellowed paper dotted with faded violets clung to the walls and sloped ceiling. A porcelain bowl and pitcher of water crowded the top of an oak dresser. In one corner, a wicker rocking chair waited. Three windows, opened for air, offered a view of the flower garden and a neighboring field. Toward the far end of the field a lone donkey, tethered to an apple tree, circled at the end of his line and dug a ring around his captor.

Two double beds, covered with identical lilac-colored spreads, meant that the ladies would be forced to share. This was something none of them wanted to do, but exhaustion won out. Before they could stop her, Edna tore strips of paper from a page in her passport.

"Darlin', I think you just broke a federal law," Helen said.

Edna blinked. "Please don't tell."

They used the passport strips and drew straws for bunk-mates, and within the hour, all four ladies snored softly in the dusty sunlight that filtered through the lace curtains of The Kissing Fingers Bed and Breakfast in County Cork, Ireland.

They woke when a soft gust brushed against the windowsill and pushed past the curtains. Shadows clung to the walls.

After making up the beds, the ladies fiddled with their hair and checked their handbags for critical items: passports, money, hankies. They reached for sweaters. Rested now, hungry, and eager to visit with the kids again, they clamored down the stairs to the front room.

"We'll leave the door open and the light on for ya. We're the third house up, see?" The owner wiped her hands on her apron. "There'll be a full moon tonight, so you'll be findin' your way back, no worries." She pointed down the street. "Pub food is lovely, but remember, we'll be havin' a full Irish breakfast in the mornin'."

"I'm famished." Dolores clomped down the street, several yards in the lead. The others moved at a more leisurely pace. Twilight slipped into the village and a cool evening breeze swept the streets. Warm yellow light spilled from cottage windows. Stars winked on, one by one. In the distance a dog barked; closer, a dove cooed.

Edna threw her head back, wrapped her arms around herself and spun. Dizzy from her spin, she reached for Mattie's arm, tittered, and covered her mouth with her other hand.

"What's so funny?"

"Oh, I thought . . . *can you imagine* what Louis would say if he knew?"

"He'd roll in his grave, for sure." Mattie grinned, stared upward, and pointed. "Look at the sky. I can't believe it. Here we are, in a foreign country, at night, walking to a bar."

"It's not a bar," Dolores called over her shoulder. "It's a pub. Pubs have food. We don't go to bars."

Edna and Mattie ignored her. Together they spun, this time, arms extended wide.

"Oh ladies, I'm so happy." Helen took a deep breath. Jasmine, night phlox, and tuberose scented the evening. She walked a few more feet, stopped, and with her friends, looked to the heavens. For a moment, she smiled. Then her shoulders slumped and shook. She turned away and covered her face with her hands.

Edna stopped, glanced over at Mattie. Without a word, they went to Helen. Dolores ignored them and continued to plod onward toward the pub. Edna put her arms around Helen and held on. Helen pressed against her and let tears drop. Mattie patted her on the back. "What is it?"

Helen took a breath, straightened, touched Edna's hand, and then pulled from the hold. She dragged a hankie from her pocket and swiped at her eyes. "Oh, I'm a foolish old woman." She blew her nose, shook her head, and stuffed the hankie back in place. "This is so lovely. I just wish my Roy was here. He, he . . ." She hiccupped once. "He would have loved this place." She sniffled again and then gulped air. "My boys, they would love it too." Then Helen smiled, sad and wistful.

"Who is Roy?" Edna slapped her hand over her mouth the second she said it. Maybe she'd drifted off when this story was told, or maybe she'd heard this name a hundred times but forgot. She thought that . . . maybe . . . she forgot a lot of things these days. And forgetting frightened her.

"Oh," Helen said, "I don't talk about him much. Clarence was such a good man, kind and gentle. But Roy, he was my first love. My true love."

Edna exhaled. She hadn't forgotten. This was new information. Good.

"Roy and I had the boys together. Twins. Jesse and James. That was Roy's idea. He had such a sense of humor, that man. My man." She took another gulp of air. She didn't want any more tears.

"Do you want to talk about him? Mattie tilted her head to one side. Helen shook her head.

"No, I'm all right." She reached over and gave Mattie's wrist a quick squeeze. They walked on in silence until they reached the corner of the pub. All three stopped at once.

"It's like something you'd find in a magazine," Edna said.

"Or like something you'd see in a movie," Mattie added.

Logs and planks framed the structure. River stones of green and gray, cemented together in splendid disarray, formed the chimney that covered two-thirds of one wall.

"It's classic," Helen said.

A brass lion with his mouth frozen in a roar served as knob and knocker. An iron grill guarded a small opening in the center of the dark green door. Stained glass windows, three feet tall and two feet wide, bracketed the portal, and rippled with amber light from the fireplace inside. Flowers clustered in boxes below each window and spilled their fragrance into the night: carnations, asters, jasmine, and tendrils of honeysuckle. A narrow bench painted green to match the door, propped against the pub's outer wall.

"You know, Helen," Edna said, "I don't know much about Roy or your twins. But the evening is so warm, and it's so peaceful here, I'd like to sit for a spell. Sit on this bench and hear your story." She lowered herself and settled with her back against the wall. The wood still held the warmth of the late afternoon sun. She looked up at Helen but saw only shadows. "That is if you feel like talking."

Helen cleared her throat. "Aren't you ladies hungry? Don't you want to go in?"

Mattie took a seat beside Edna and patted the spot next to her. "Come sit with us for a while," she said. "Sit here, in this lovely place, and tell us about your Roy."

Chapter Seventeen

We met when I was in college—Martha Washington Academy for Young Women. Not many black girls attended college or even finished high school back in those days. My folks had to scrimp and save every penny to send me there. I worked real hard, too. Got all the best marks, volunteered for all the school events, did whatever it took to get good enough evaluations. And I made it in.

My folks were so proud. They figured I'd meet a nice rich boy from the men's college on the other side of town. A light-skinned black boy with a college degree. We would go far. I'd have the life they wanted for me. And things were going according to plans. Then I met Roy.

Roy was everything my folks didn't want for me. His skin was ebony, and he worked as a gardener on campus. Roy didn't have two dimes to rub together, but he had a smile that . . . let's just say his smile sent a heat wave over me. He was so smooth. There was me, in my plaid skirt, white blouse, and a maroon sweater, my hair tied back with a matching ribbon. I clutched my books, walked fast and with purpose, head down on my way to class. And there was Roy, dirty work overalls covered with grass stains, sweat making his face all shiny and slick.

He flirted with me and charmed me, and Lord as my witness, I could barely think about European history or the use of proper nouns after a few minutes talking to Roy. At first, I tried to take a different route to class, but no matter where I walked, he was there. He'd stand with a rake like it was a rifle and he was at attention, or he'd push a wheelbarrow right across where I was about to step. There he was with that smile of his.

One day, he asked me out. Go to a movie and get an ice cream after and maybe take a stroll by the river. All so sweet. But I knew my folks would have a fit if they knew.

He came for that date dressed in pressed white linen slacks, a red-and-yellow-checkered shirt, and a yellow sweater vest. He looked just like . . . he looked more handsome than any of the rich boys who went to the young men's college. Years later I found out that he saved for two months to pay for that date and those clothes. Roy, he had his eye on me, and when Roy wanted something, he found a way to get it.

When we learned I was pregnant, I had to drop out of school, and I had to tell my folks. They were heartbroken. For a while there, I feared they would never talk to me again. But Roy charmed them almost as much as he charmed me. We got married in their backyard and when the twins were born my folks let us live in a room over top of their garage.

Roy started a landscaping business, and I enrolled in nursing school. My mother watched the twins. We did okay. And love. . . *my Lord* . . . my life was so full of love sometimes I thought I couldn't stand it. Sometimes I thought my heart would burst right out of my chest and scare the babies.

We went to dances when we could afford it. Sometimes we went to the roller rink on Saturdays. When summer rolled around, we took our little ones to a park and ate picnic lunches on the grass. Roy and I would stretch out on a blanket in the sun with our babies snuggled between us. Love.

Roy used to come home with two baseball bats, or two footballs, or two tennis rackets. Always two. He couldn't wait for our twins to be big enough to play with him.

Then, in the fall, Roy was called to join the Army. I remember the day he left. We posed for a picture together in front of the train station, and then he posed with the babies. He looked so sharp, so handsome, in that uniform. My heart swelled up with pride like a birthday party balloon. Then fear pricked it down. Roy laughed at my fear. He grabbed me up and spun me 'round.

"When we win this war," he told me. "I'm coming back, and we're going to make another set of twins. Girls this time!"

But we didn't make another set of twins. When Roy came back, he was stretched out in a casket with an American flag draped over the top. A lot of the girls and women from town came to the funeral to comfort me, but most of the boys were still overseas—fighting.

I worked at the hospital until the twins turned six. Then I met Clarence.

Clarence was fifteen years older than me. He sold insurance, owned his house, and everybody in town, including my parents, said how stable he was. He didn't dance or do sports. The twins went next door to play ball with the neighbor boys and their father. Clarence didn't like to spend money, but he paid for the food and clothes, and he was quiet and clean and not too demanding.

When Jesse and James turned eighteen, they went off to join the Army. They enlisted together, which scared me so much. If something bad happened, I might lose them both. But those boys, they looked so much like their father. Shiny jet hair, snapping eyes, smiles so bright and open you couldn't refuse them anything.

The Army sent them to Australia to train the Australian troops who would go to Vietnam to train the Vietnamese troops. They wrote to me regular. Told me all about Australia and how beautiful it was. They sent me postcards with pictures of the beaches and the natural wonders like Ayers Rock. And they sent me a card with an architect's drawing of what the Sydney Opera House would look like once the construction was done. It looked like a big old ship with sails puffed out like it was riding a summer storm. Jesse was so inspired by the beauty of that building that he decided to go to college for architecture when he got out of the military.

I cherished those words from my boys and I loved learning about that enormous and mysterious country. I especially liked the cards that showed pictures of strange animals like the wombats. Oh my, they are something. They look like fat, pudgy bears without tails, or maybe like flat-nosed pigs in brown fur coats. Cute, in their own sort of way. Also, there were tiny blue penguins and platypus. Lordy! Those are the strangest animals you ever would want to see. And kangaroos. Huge rabbit-like animals hopping over the fields at sunset. "Animals with attitude," my boys called them.

"Oh Ma, you got to come to Australia and see the kangaroos!" That was James. He loved animals. "They are the craziest critters the Lord ever put on this good earth." He wrote that to me. It was the animals of Australia that made James decide he would go to vet school when he got out of the Army.

The Army decided they could come home for a short while before they went on over to Vietnam. As you can guess, I was beside myself with excitement. I couldn't wait to see my boys again. Couldn't wait to look into those eyes, couldn't wait to hug my grown-up babies.

Like their father, my boys didn't follow through on their post-war plans. But unlike him, they didn't return laid out in a casket draped with an American flag.

It happened the day they were supposed to leave Australia. They were on their way from the base to Sydney when the helicopter crashed. That young recruit who came to our door, he had his hat in his hand, his uniform pressed so tight it cut. All he gave me was one dog tag. That was all that was left. All they could find.

Clarence was kind and gentle, and he went to the cemetery with me. The Veterans of Foreign Wars put on a ceremony complete with a bagpiper and a soldier who played taps. Everyone in town said how moving it was. The Army gave me two American flags, each folded in a triangle. I took them and said 'Thank you.' I didn't tear up, not once, at that ceremony. When Clarence and I got home, I put those flags under my sweaters in the bottom drawer of my dresser and left them there for all those years until Clarence died and I moved to Restful Palms.

Helen closed her eyes, breathed low and slow. Her spine pressed against the pub's outer wall. Her friends sat still and quiet. Muted sounds slipped from under the door; the tinkle of glassware, a fiddle's refrain, a laugh. Outside the pub, a band of crickets tuned for their evening song. Finally, Mattie looped one arm around her friend.

"I'd like to see that building," she said. "The one that looks like a ship."

"Me too." Edna reached across Mattie and squeezed Helen's hand. "I can't wait to see those kangaroos, either. And, while we're there, I think we should look for a wombat."

Chapter Eighteen

Dancing the Granny D

Mattie slapped her thigh with a hoot. "Would ya look at our girl Dolores." She held the door open for Helen and Edna.

They expected to find Dolores hunkered over a mountain of gravy-smothered mashed potatoes. They thought she would scoop spoons of lamb and onion stew from a wooden bowl. They assumed she would shovel Irish comfort food as fast as a rat terrier digs dirt. But she did not scoop. She did not shovel. In fact, she did not even eat. Dolores danced.

To be truthful, her motions smacked more of gambols and hops than the steps of a dance, but still, her flesh jiggled and slapped and shook in time to the music. When she spun, her skirt lifted enough to show the rolls of flesh that spilled over the top of her knee-high nylon stockings. Circles, the color of salmonberries, blotted her cheeks, and a smile curved across her face like a slice of summer melon.

Her partner, only an inch or two taller, leaped to his toes to twirl her around. His brown work pants, frayed and stained with the blood of fish, touched the tops of leather clogs and when he landed on his heels, their wooden soles beat time on the hardwood floor. A knitted vest stretched over his barrel chest. His face flushed pink and slick with sweat, although unlike hers, his color would stay. Years of wind over salt water and thousands of pints of Guinness gave him a permanent glow.

"Oh, my Heavens." Edna stared through the smoke-blue air that circled the room. She pointed to the end of the bar where Peter balanced on a stool. He aimed his cell phone toward the dance floor. Eliza and Melissa stood on either side of him and held onto his legs. "I think Peter is taking a picture of Dolores."

Mattie nudged her. "Look." She jerked her head toward the back of the pub. Three rugged and hardy-looking men, all at least in their seventies; practically youngsters, Edna would say later, sat at a round wooden table. They hoisted glasses, laughed, and called out encouragement to the man who spun Dolores round and round to the lively tune.

The man held Dolores's hand high, and he stomped as she twirled. He grabbed both of her hands, and the two of them whirled in a wide circle. They had the floor to themselves as the other dancers cleared the way for them. When the last strains of music died, the audience clapped and cheered, and the man pulled Dolores in for a tight hug then released her with a broad grin.

Dolores followed him back to the table; her chest heaved as she gulped for air. Curls lay plastered against her forehead. She glanced toward the door and waved to her friends who stood like stage-shy students—their mouths open in shock, gobsmacked. She beckoned them to join the group. The men, too, waved to the ladies and splashed beer as they hoisted froth-topped pints in welcome.

While the ladies settled in, Dolores's dance partner spoke with the waitress. The beer arrived followed by a jumbo platter of spicy chips smothered with cheese sauce. Edna made a mental note. He already knows the way to Dolores's heart. *Best to keep an eye on this fellow.*

Done with the order, he turned to Dolores and dropped his arm over her shoulders. It barely reached around. "My girl, you can dance." He gave her a squeeze. "I'll be takin' you to the county fair in the spring, I will. We'll enter a contest and win a blue ribbon for sure."

He picked up her leprechaun hat, now soaked with spilled beer, and gave it a shake. Droplets of dye landed on the table. He arranged the hat on her head and pulled it to one side at a raffish angle. Wet green felt pressed against her damp white curls. Dolores giggled and blushed a shade deeper than her already flushed face.

Helen and Mattie looked from the man to Dolores, to each other, and then to Edna. Edna straightened and took stock of the fellow. Yes, best to keep an eye on this one, and on his beer-swilling buddies too.

"Grannies!" Melissa swooped in and hugged each of the ladies almost knocking the air out of them. Then, much to their surprise and delight, she hugged each of the men.

After catching her breath, Helen gestured to Peter and

Eliza. "These are our friends," she said and nodded toward Edna. "Her granddaughter's friends. They picked us up at the airport." She turned to Eliza. "Let's find some more chairs."

"No. So sorry, grannies," Peter said. "We have to go tonight. We found a ride with a guy delivering a load of chickens to a market up north. He's going to drive all night, and he said we can tag along. Have to go."

"Oh, shoot. We wanted to buy you dinner." Helen pouted.

"That's cool." Melissa bounced over and hugged her a second time. "Life is beautiful. Love abounds. And we will never forget you, grannies."

"Impossible to forget you," Peter grinned. He waved his cell phone in the air. "Now that Granny D is dancing on YouTube!"

His comment went over the heads of the ladies; however, an American tourist sitting at the next table heard Peter's announcement and told his wife to remind him to look up that video when they got home. For years after, the couple would tell the tale over and over again, and the video of the elderly American woman dancing in an Irish pub would become the focal point of their vacation story.

After another round of hugs, the kids gathered their backpacks from behind the bar and left the pub to search the village for a truck stacked with chickens.

"So, Luv." The man across from Dolores smiled wide. His red beard brushed the table and swept through a puddle of beer.

"Will ya be introducin' us to these fair colleens you've brought with ya?"

In a practiced move—one that Helen and Mattie would later discuss in some detail—the men had managed to sit the ladies between them—girl boy—girl boy. Dolores made the introductions around the table clockwise. Mattie, then Jamison O'Hennessy. Edna and Patrick Tomelson. Helen next to Roger Sommerfield and she, Dolores, snuggled against Mr. Charles Michael O'Reilly. Dolores insisted on saying his full name, every time. But the others called him Chuck.

"Dolores," Helen said, "I didn't know you danced."

"Dancing . . . isn't that in the blood of all Irish folk?" Dolores made a face and fluttered her hand in the air as if Helen's comment was absurd.

Caught up in the moment, Mattie winked at Jamison O'Hennessy. Jamison tipped his beer to her and winked back. Mattie blushed and turned toward Dolores. "How *di*d you meet these charming fellows?" she said.

Dolores sniffed, eyed the plate in the center of the table. "You ladies were taking your time, and I was looking for a spot with room enough for all of us." She turned and smiled at Chuck. "Mr. Charles Michael O'Reilly here came right over to assist me." She reached out and lifted a wedge of fried potato from the plate. She pushed the chip into her mouth. A dribble of cheese dropped on her chin. Chuck scooped it off, then licked his finger, sighed, and smacked his lips. Dolores giggled and squirmed under his arm.

"Wow." Mattie raised her eyebrows.

Jamison, Patrick, and Roger ordered more beer, more appetizers and several shots of whiskey. They regaled the ladies with tales of country life and of the eccentric tourists who traveled through their village on the way to Blarney Castle.

Helen, Edna, and Mattie laughed at their stories, nibbled on the bar food and shared anecdotes about their lives back in America. But Chuck and Dolores decided to move away from the group to a smaller table—better for close conversation.

"I've never met such a fine-lookin' woman," Chuck said as he helped Dolores up from her chair. "My girl. She is a magnificent beauty." Dolores fluttered her eyelashes and blushed.

"Wow," Mattie repeated.

Despite jet lag and a long exciting day, the ladies managed to stay at the pub until just past ten. It was a chore to pull Dolores away from Chuck, but they reminded her that they were going to the castle early the next morning and that they all needed some rest.

"At least, let me walk you ladies to your accommodations," Chuck said. Mattie rolled her eyes and started to say that they were only a couple houses up the street but the look on Dolores's face—pure enchantment—stopped her.

Edna, Helen, and Mattie hurried on ahead barely able to control themselves. They couldn't wait to get to the room where they could sort all this out. When they reached The Kissing Fingers they let themselves in and left Dolores alone with her suitor.

"Five minutes, tops." Edna checked her watch. "Then we go rescue her."

"No way, darlin'," Helen poo-pooed the idea. "She's havin' fun. First time ever is my guess." She shook her head and smiled. "Let her be."

Dolores and Chuck did not hurry. They blushed and stuttered and sighed. And they strolled, hand in hand, through the village, under the big, full, Irish moon.

Dolores wanted to talk. The others wanted to sleep. Mattie said goodnight, rolled over and buried her face in the crook of her arm. Within minutes, her soft snores rocked a low, steady rhythm in the room. Edna turned and pulled a quilt over her head. She wondered if she would spend most of her trip hiding under blankets while Dolores babbled. Helen propped up on one elbow and tried to listen for a while.

"Um . . ." she said. And, "Uh huh . . ." and, "My goodness. Isn't that just lovely." But finally, she yawned, rested her head on the pillow, closed her eyes, and slipped into sleep. Dolores didn't seem to notice. She kept going. On and on. Charles Michael O'Reilly this, and Charles Michael O'Reilly that. At last, even she wound down. She pulled the chain on the lamp next to the bed and within moments, snored her way to dreams of fiddle tunes and wedges of cheesy potatoes. For the first time since Mr. William T. Broughton passed away, Dolores forgot to place his photo—the one with President Kennedy—on her nightstand.

Chapter Nineteen

The Slippery Gift of Gab

Morning fog rolled over the village and blanketed The Kissing Fingers Bed and Breakfast. Mrs. Doolin cleared the last of the dishes from the dining table. The ladies, minus one, sat in the parlor and sipped tea while they waited for the weather to clear and for Dolores to select "the perfect outfit."

She'd caused them alarm earlier when she had disappeared from the cottage before dawn without so much as a word to anyone. She didn't leave a note and, of greatest concern, she had not been the first at the table when breakfast was served.

Mattie and Helen wanted to organize a search party. Edna said they should call the police as she was sure Dolores had been kidnapped. Maybe by those IRA people the kids told them about. But Mrs. Doolin convinced them to wait awhile before they jumped.

"From the looks o' yer friend, she won't be missin' our breakfast."

Mrs. Doolin was right. The moment she sat a platter on the table, a platter piled high with buttered potatoes and steaming pork sausages, Dolores burst through the door, her face flushed from exertion and the chilled morning air.

"Look." She plopped herself on a chair and held out a white cardboard box tied with green and gold ribbons.

Mattie eyed Dolores, looked her up and down and noticed a swatch of green curls tangled among her patch of white. "Where have *you* been?"

"Bakery." Dolores beamed. She either ignored or missed Mattie's tone. "I've got cookies."

"Cookies?" Edna's brow furrowed. She held two fingers to her lips. She wondered how, or when, Dolores found a bakery. And cookies? Were they supposed to buy cookies?

"Dolores, darlin', you about scared the daylights out of us." Helen shook her head. "You have got to get a grip on your eating."

Dolores pouted for an instant. Then she brightened. "They're not for me. Not only for me. Mr. Charles Michael O'Reilly is *very* fond of shortbread cookies. He told me so. He said, next to me . . ." She halted briefly, blushed. "He said next to me, shortbread was his favorite sweet. She tapped the top of the box. "I went to the bakery, that one at the end of the road. I was there when they first opened. Wanted to get the freshest shortbread cookies. For tonight. For dessert."

"Tonight?" Now Edna panicked. What about tonight? Did she remember? No, no not at all. Would the others be ready for tonight? Would she miss it?

"Yes." Dolores bobbed her head up and down. "Mr. Charles Michael O'Reilly is going to pick me up tonight and we are going to the pub in the next village over." She reached across the table and speared a sausage with her fork. "I told you that last night. Don't you remember?"

Edna started to confess, but Helen jumped in.

"Dolores, darlin', you sure must have told us but we were all so excited . . ."

"And exhausted." Mattie snorted, disgusted. She broke a scone in two.

"We are going out to dinner. We are going on a date. A real date." Dolores sighed.

"Are you supposed to take cookies on a date? To a restaurant?" Mattie spread marmalade over the pastry.

"I'm sure I don't know." Dolores scooped scrambled eggs onto her plate. "But he likes shortbread, and I think anything goes when you're . . . you know, on a real date."

"Dolores." Mattie leaned forward, the half scone still in her hand. "Did I get this right? This is your first date?"

Dolores flushed. "Some of us had to work, you know. Some of us didn't have time . . ."

"Here we are, ladies." Mrs. Doolin entered the dining room with a massive bowl of steaming breakfast pudding. A thick cream and whiskey sauce dripped over the mound of dense brown cake. All thoughts of Dolores and her first date were usurped by the scent of cinnamon, and nutmeg, and plump, warm raisins.

After three complete outfit changes, Dolores selected her best, a pale peach suit with a cream-colored blouse. She wore peach earrings that matched the buttons on her jacket. After much debate with herself, she decided to wear a single strand of sparkly peach beads. She surveyed the results in the mirror and congratulated herself for insisting that she bring a big suitcase. After all, how else could she have been ready for this date with Mr. Charles Michael O'Reilly?

"Don't you think that's a little dressy for dinner at a bar?" Mattie asked when Dolores stepped into the parlor.

"We're not going to a bar. We're going to a pub." Dolores snapped at Mattie. "And besides . . ."

"You look stunning," Helen said. She brushed a crumb from Dolores's sleeve. "That man of yours is going to be the talk of the town. Why just think, he's found a lovely American woman to hold on his arm."

Mattie glanced at Edna and rolled her eyes. Edna looked away and picked a piece of lint from her sweater.

Mrs. Doolin poked her head into the room. "Ladies, your ride is here. Enjoy the castle. We'll be havin' dinner at seven." Then she glanced at Dolores and smiled. "For those of you who don't have a date, that is."

"The guidebook says the grounds around the castle are absolutely beautiful and from what we saw on the way in, I'm guessing the book is right." Helen pushed her reading glasses up her nose and skimmed the glossy pages. She nodded, removed her glasses, and rested against the stone wall. Seconds later, she stood straight up. "Oh, darn."

Mattie stopped mid-step and turned back toward Helen. "What's the matter?"

"The wall. The wall is covered with some sort of green stuff. Wet moss or something." She twisted to one side. "Is it all over my clothes? Think it will stain?"

Mattie brushed Helen's jacket with the heel of her hand. "It might. But show it to Mrs. Doolin. Maybe she has some kind of stain remover."

"Shoot." Helen held her jacket out and scrutinized the soiled spot. "I really like this outfit." She sighed, draped the fabric over her arm, looked down on a stretch of foliage surrounding the castle, and changed the subject.

"You know, Mattie, after we kiss the stone, we should take a stroll around, check out the grounds. I'd love to spend some time in those gardens."

Mattie followed Helen's gaze. She frowned but nodded yes. She wanted to appear positive, but she wasn't sure the group could do much more than hobble back to the taxi once they'd completed the climb. Over breakfast, she'd volunteered to lead them up the stairs to the stone. Now, in retrospect, she wished she hadn't.

Mrs. Doolin had warned them about the long, tedious hike to the top of the castle. "There's a hundred twenty-seven steps, and ever' one of em slick as a young eel," she said. She shook her head. "I don't know why so many want to go up there; it's not that grand. Gardens are better. And for sure you'll be stuck behind a carload o' tourists."

Their hostess had been right about the steep, slippery climb. However, as luck would have it, an art festival in a neighboring village drew most of the tourists away from the castle that morning, leaving the stairway, for the most part, open and clear. Dolores took credit for the luck, her people being Irish and all, but it really didn't make much of a difference, because with or without the luck of the Irish, and tourists or not, the ladies moved up the steps at a slow, plodding pace.

Despite their ages, Mattie and Helen were comfortable. They could talk, check the guidebook, and even snap photos without running out of breath. But Dolores struggled and Edna appeared distracted.

"I'm glad we don't have to be in a big crowd." Dolores stopped to catch her breath. She gripped the railing with one hand and the bakery box with the other. Rings of perspiration stained the fabric under the arms of her suit jacket. She brushed against the wall but didn't notice the wet growth on the stones. A slide of sweat caused her blouse to cling to her skin. She looked over the edge of the railing and down three stories to the grass below. She opened and closed her mouth and gulped for oxygen.

"Dolores, we'll never make it to the top if you stop all the time." Edna had insisted that she be the last one in their line. She demanded that she take the role of protector so she would be the one to keep them all together.

But with each of Dolores's many stops, Edna wished she'd been second, after Mattie, who made steady headway up the narrow passage. In fact, she and Dolores were so far behind that a couple of Canadian tourists politely asked if they could go around. This, Edna found embarrassing.

Mattie and Helen stopped at the final landing and lingered a full fifteen minutes. They smiled and nodded when the Canadians passed them. While they waited for Dolores and Edna to catch up, Helen read the history of the famous castle out loud, and Mattie visualized herself as a knight, perhaps a Joan of Arc sort of knight. A brave knight who poured hot oil down the parapet onto marauding enemies. She figured she already had the gift of gab—certainly didn't need that from the stone. But the history, the romance . . . it was all quite thrilling.

By the time Dolores and Edna reached them, Helen and Mattie were rested and ready to go again. But Dolores was exhausted.

"Those steps are too dangerous." She fanned herself with her hand. She'd taken her suit jacket off about halfway up and thrust it at Edna. Edna folded the jacket and carried it inside out so Dolores wouldn't notice the streak of green slime that stained the back.

"You went too fast." Dolores pointed her finger at Mattie. "You should have been more careful. Someone could get hurt on those stairs."

Mattie glanced at Helen. Helen shrugged and turned toward the last short set of stairs. Ignoring Dolores's protests, the ladies crossed the top floor of the castle together. When they finally reached the cavity over the famous stone, Mattie volunteered to go first. She settled onto the mat next to the hole and flashed a smile at the man who wrapped his arms around her waist. She did her best to uncurl her fingers, grasped the iron handrail, leaned back and wriggled downward. Mattie smacked the worn spot that a billion lips had kissed; it was smooth and cool. The man pulled her up and grinned. Mattie stood and thrust both arms in the air. "Yes!"

"Next! Next!" Edna hopped up and down and clapped her hands like a little girl. "Please let me go next." The man tilted his head, amused, and waved her over. Edna repeated Mattie's performance, and when she came up, there were tears in her eyes.

"Ya all right, girl?" the man asked. He kept his hands on her waist.

She nodded. "Yes. Yes. So excited."

He helped her stand, and in a move he couldn't explain later when his co-workers teased him, he gave Edna a heartfelt hug. Embarrassed, he turned toward Helen. "Set to go?"

"Oh how fun." Helen beamed when she stood. "I'm so glad you wanted to do this. I would never have thought of it." She faced Dolores. "Come on now, your turn. I'll hold the box."

Dolores shook her head no. "I'm not going to do it."

"What?" Mattie said.

"I'm not going to do it," Dolores repeated. She scowled at Mattie.

"I just can't believe you. We came all the way to Ireland so *you* could kiss the Blarney Stone. What do you mean you're not going to do it?" Mattie stood with her feet wide, her arms akimbo.

"I'm not. I don't have to, and I'm not going to." Dolores stomped her foot on the stone walk.

"Excuse me." A woman behind Dolores tapped her on the back. "Could we go around you?" Dolores stepped aside and let the woman and her three companions by.

Mattie, Helen, and Edna formed a circle around their friend. "Now, now. Don't be scared." Helen patted Dolores's shoulder. "We're all right here. We won't let you fall."

Edna nodded in agreement, smiled big and held out her hand.

Dolores slapped Edna's hand away. "I'm not afraid." She smoothed her skirt, lifted her chin. "I'm not going to lie down on the ground and get my best outfit dirty to kiss that disgusting stone."

"But this is your . . ." Edna wondered if she was getting all this right. It certainly didn't seem right.

"Dolores, darlin', there's a mat on the ground." Helen pointed toward the man who lowered another tourist down the hole.

Dolores shook her head again, this time with more force. "No. That mat is small. My skirt will be on the ground. I've got a date with Mr. Charles Michael O'Reilly, and I'm not going to go with filth on the back of my skirt." She grasped the box to her chest and glared at the others.

Mattie sighed. She looked at Edna and Helen. Edna's lower lip trembled; she patted her mouth with her hankie. Helen shook her head and made a "What can you do?" gesture with her hands.

"It's settled," Mattie said. "Let's get going. If everyone has enough energy we can walk around the gardens and maybe have lunch at that little café next to the gift shop." She turned toward the passage that wound down the castle, but Dolores reached out and grabbed the back of her sweater.

"I'm going first this time," she said. "Down is a lot easier than up. I want to lead."

Mattie shrugged. "Suit yourself." She stepped back and let Dolores pass.

"I'll take that now." Dolores grabbed her suit jacket away from Edna, and without another word, she stomped to the stairs and disappeared around the curved wall. Edna stood still, her mouth formed a small "O." She turned to Helen and blinked.

"Never you mind her." Helen looped an arm over Edna's shoulders. "She's grouchy on account of she wore that suit, and she knows it was a ridiculous thing to do. She should have worn something more practical for today and changed back in the room before her date. Don't you worry." She gave Edna a quick squeeze.

"Come on." Mattie nodded toward the stairs. "We had better get going. No telling where she'll go or what she'll do if she gets to the bottom much before us."

Dolores took off down the stairs at a fast clip. It occurred to her that she would have to change her clothes at the B&B before dinner because her suit jacket looked terrible, and even though she'd been careful, her skirt was wrinkled. If she could convince the others to skip the garden tour she'd have time to switch out-fits. She thought about her strategy to get them to change their minds. She could offer to buy them lunch. Maybe not lunch, but, at least, dessert. Surely they would go along with her plan. After all, *it's just another garden.* "We have gardens in Florida, for heaven's sake," she grumbled.

The steps that led down the castle were as narrow, worn, steep, and slick as the ones that led up, but Dolores did not pay attention to them, and she did not hold onto the railing. She was too busy thinking through what she would wear for her big date with the ruggedly handsome Mr. Charles Michael O'Reilly. Ob-viously, it would have to be one of her denim skirts and a smart top.

"The red one with the daisies looks good on me," she mut-tered out loud to herself. "But maybe something green—that green one with the rhinestone Siamese. That one is stunning. Very slimming."

Most tourists would have called the smell in the narrow passageway musty or moldy, but it reminded her, in some vague way, of the man she would dine with that evening. Maybe even kiss, that evening. The idea of that potential kiss—her first kiss— sent her heart racing. They'd fall in love, of course. He was probably already in love. The other ladies would be bridesmaids, maybe. At least, Helen, she was graceful and dignified enough to be a bridesmaid. Dolores Ryanna Brackin O'Reilly. Has a very nice ring to it.

Oh! A ring. They'd have to go shopping for a ring. Something with an emerald, most likely. Of course, they'd live in Ireland because of her family background and because he probably already had a house. But then, maybe they'd buy a different house, one that was new to the two of them, and naturally, she'd decorate it, and they would have parties, and he would adore her and—

She missed a step. Her heel touched the edge of the next tread and slid off. Dolores swung her arm out and tried to catch the rail, but failed. She dropped her jacket but continued to clutch the box of cookies. She slid down a third step. Her knees buckled under her. She fumbled and tumbled, head first, down the flight. She flipped over in a slow somersault. Skidded. Her face bruised against the stones.

If there had been other tourists close by, they might have broken her fall, might have stopped her plunge. But the way was clear. Nothing, no one, to prevent Dolores Ryanna Brackin from catapulting down, down, over, around, over again, and down the spiraled stairs of Blarney Castle. She didn't call out. The only sound a thud, thud, thud.

When the others rounded the last curve, they saw her sprawled face down, one shoe missing, her peach skirt crumpled high on fleshy thighs, one hand stuck straight out, over her head. Blood seeped through her green and white curls. A corner of the bakery box, now crushed flat, poked from beneath her belly.

Mattie screamed. She leaped down the last four steps and flung herself on her friend.

They waited outside the surgery for three hours. A nurse called Mrs. Doolin to let her know what had happened. Mrs. Doolin rang Chuck. "They're at hospital," she said.

Mr. Charles Michael O'Reilly solemnly joined the ladies in their waiting.

Chapter Twenty

A R a i n b o w f o r D o l o r e s

Each morning, for the next three days, they gathered around Mrs. Doolin as she phoned the hospital for news of Dolores. Each morning, the news was the same. Dolores lay in a coma, wrapped in bandages and a hospital gown. Despite visiting hour rules, Chuck never left her side.

As if in mourning, the sky wept. Soft, but steady rain turned the village streets to swirling, chocolate milk streams. Somber clouds blocked the sun. Except for meals, Helen and Mattie stayed in their room. They read, chatted about childhood, old age, and life in general. And they slept. Other than sharing the news in a brief email to Katie, they did not mention Blarney Castle.

The village priest stopped by the bed and breakfast every afternoon to console the ladies, but only Edna and Mrs. Doolin met with him. Although Edna wasn't Catholic and wasn't sure that she followed their conversations, she enjoyed the time spent in the parlor with the hostess and the holy man. She delighted in the lyrical sound of their voices and in the snacks her landlady set out on a silver tray.

Mrs. Doolin served brownies and lemon bars and mugs of hot coffee flavored with good Irish whiskey and dollops of heavy cream. She and the priest gossiped about the neighbors, grumbled about the new government, and commiserated about the rising cost of groceries. Once in a while, they would ask Edna about America, or Florida, but most of the time the three of them were the happiest munching on sweets, sipping strong coffee and chatting about life in the village.

On the morning of the fourth day, Mrs. Doolin held her breath as she pressed the phone to her ear and listened carefully. Her eyes widened and then she let out a whoop and slammed the handpiece into the phone's receiver.

"Come on, ladies," she shouted. "We're heading to hospital. Your friend is awake and chatting up a storm!"

Mattie held her breath as she pushed her way through the crowd in Dolores's room. All the fellows they'd met at the pub were there, along with the bartender and two barmaids. Mrs. Doolin's neighbors jostled for a view of the now, somewhat famous, American granny. The priest and three members of the church choir stood together, holding sheets of music, ready to sing at a moment's notice. Chuck sat tight on the narrow bed, his left hand clasping Dolores's right. Mason jars filled with garden bouquets covered every flat surface in the small space—their scent mixed with the smell of wet wool and hospital food. Dolores sat up, propped against a mountain of pillows. Her leprechaun hat balanced like a crown on the white gauze circling her head. She beamed and motioned for Mattie and the others to enter her world.

Before leaving the hospital, Mrs. Doolin chatted with the doctor who told her there was nothing to worry about now and that Dolores was out of danger. Other than broken ribs, a nasty bruise on her head, and a twisted ankle, the American woman was fit as a fiddle. They'd like to keep her for a few more days however—just to be sure—but after that, with several weeks rest, she should be able to join Chuck for another twirl around the dance floor.

Mrs. Doolin passed the information along to the other ladies and insisted that Dolores and they continue to stay with her, at the cottage, while the recovery took place. She'd offer them a special discount.

"Don't you worry," she told them over a dinner of pigs in a blanket and buttered greens. "We'll put her in the downstairs room; soon she'll be up, rested, and ready to continue her travels in no time. It's the perfect plan."

But Helen, Mattie, and Edna were not convinced. An email from Katie the day before had them worried. Once again, Edna's daughters were on their trail. If they stayed, it would be just a matter of time until Joan and Suzanne found them and would make them return home. Besides that, even with Mrs. Doolin's generous discount, they hadn't budgeted such a lengthy stay in Ireland. Finally, there was the matter of Chuck and Dolores. The two of them were fast becoming more than just dance partners—that was evident to everyone.

After dinner, the three friends donned sweaters and plastic rain caps and went for a stroll through the village. The rain had slowed to a mist, the streets were only slightly muddy, and the crickets were back to practicing their evening songs. The three friends stopped to rest on the bench outside the pub.

"We need to get going," Mattie insisted. "We can't afford to stay here, and besides . . ."

"I agree, darlin'." Helen nodded. "But we can't just leave her here, and she can't travel for several more weeks."

"We have to give up. We have to go home with my daughters." Edna hung her head. "I'm so sorry . . ."

Helen cut her off with a snap of her fingers. "I know! We'll send Katie an email—she will use that computer of hers—she will figure out what to do."

Brightening at the thought, Edna fished through her handbag for her pencil, and Mattie dug the phone from her sweater pocket. The two went to work with Mattie's words and Edna's eraser. When they finished, Mattie slipped the phone into her pocket and sat back.

"Now all we have to do is wait," she said.

Two hours later, as the ladies prepared for bed, the sharp notes of a calliope called from Mattie's pocket. A phone call from Katie! They leaned in close to hear her voice.

"Grannies," she shouted, "I have been thinking about your problem, and I have an idea!"

Katie suggested that she reschedule their flights and rearrange their accommodations. Dolores could stay in Ireland until she felt well enough to travel and then, Chuck would take her to the airport. Katie would pick her up when she arrived in Tampa, and the others could continue on with their quests for sailing ships, camels, and kangaroos.

Mattie and Helen worried that Dolores would be offended about being left behind. Edna fretted about their friend getting enough to eat if they weren't around. But Mrs. Doolin was delighted with Katie's proposal and Chuck and Dolores were over-the-moon.

"Don't you worry none, ladies." Chuck beamed and tightened his hold on Dolores's hand. "I'll be taking care of my girl here. Best care she's ever known."

Dolores's eyes sparkled, and her smile lit the room. "Mr. Charles Michael O'Reilly and I have so much to catch up on. Really, I couldn't have left now even if I didn't take that fall." She blushed and flicked her free hand at Helen. "You make sure these girls stay in line," she nodded toward Mattie and Edna. "You and I always were the responsible ones. I'm sorry, but you'll just have to go on without me." She turned her head and gazed up at Chuck. "I'm needed here now."

Chuck offered to drive them to Dublin and so, on the morning of their last day in Ireland, Helen, Edna, and Mattie stood by the front door of The Kissing Fingers Bed and Breakfast with their satchels packed and ready. They'd said their goodbyes to Dolores during visiting hours the day before. Now, as they waited, they chatted with Mrs. Doolin and took one last look around the charming little cottage.

"Um . . ." Edna pointed to a large framed photo mounted on the front room wall. "Isn't that Dolores's photo of Mr. William T. Broughton and President Kennedy?"

"Right you are." Mrs. Doolin beamed. "I asked your friend if I could hang it in the cottage—just temporary—while she was recovering. We get quite a few Americans you know, and they'd be pleased to see a photo of the greatest American president here in Ireland." Mrs. Doolin paused and smiled wide. "And you know what she said?"

Edna shook her head no.

"She said I could hang it there forever. Something about her not wanting to dust it anymore."

Chuck wore his fishing clothes and an old wool cap. "Yer chariot awaits, ladies." He gestured toward the door. "The rain's stopped, and there's a bow as wide as Heaven. Come see."

The four women followed him outside, crossed the street, and then turned back toward the cottage.

"Oh my," Edna gasped.

A shining rainbow stretched from one end of the village to the other—all seven colors clean, clear, and iridescent with light.

"It's magical," Helen whispered.

"It's so beautiful," Mattie said.

"Almost as beautiful as my girl," Chuck added. He removed his cap and pressed it to his heart.

Chapter Twenty-one

Dublin Airport's Terminal One was long, and the hike between gates a challenge. They walked at a steady pace for twenty minutes and availed themselves of the moving sidewalks whenever possible, but still, it was slow going. Not so much from the actual distance, or the weight in their satchels, but more from the heaviness in their hearts. They'd started with five; now there were three.

The tram driver spotted them and glanced back at his riders. They had all paid the fare. Certainly, there was room in his electric cart for three tired old women. Probably on fixed incomes, couldn't afford the tram fee. Give them a rest; he would. Besides, the tall one, the dark one, the one in the maroon suit, now *she* was a looker. "Girls, can I take ya to yer gate?" Ignoring the grumbles of the other riders, he motioned for them to make room for the ladies.

Mattie and Edna squeezed into the middle row next to a businessman. He kept his head buried in *The Irish Daily Times* until they reached his stop. Even then, he quietly folded his paper, picked up his briefcase, and stepped off the tram without a sound or a flicker of eye contact.

"Bet he's fun at a party." Mattie nudged Edna. "Move."

Edna scrunched over. "Poor guy." She grabbed the front seat as the tram lurched into motion. She watched the man meld into a surge of business travelers. "Bet he's never even been to a party."

Helen accepted the driver's invitation to sit on the front seat with him. She nodded, and smiled, and offered phrases like, "Oh my," and "That *is* impressive," and "I wouldn't have guessed that." The driver carried the rest of the conversation. He sat taller and straighter as he told her how, for fifty-six years, he'd driven the people of Dublin wherever they needed to go.

"Sixteen when I started, I was. First, it were streetcars, then a taxi, double-deckers and now, this tram." He slowed the vehicle, stopped, and waited while two passengers stepped from the back seat and collected their luggage. "Takes a lot of patience." He eased the tram forward. "And ya have ta be alert all the time." He leaned over Helen. "ON YER RIGHT!"

Helen jumped.

"Bloody tourists." He shook his head. "Son wants me to retire. Go live with him and his missus. But I'm nowhere near that. Nowhere near."

The driver nattered on, and Helen did her best to appear interested. Behind her, Mattie and Edna sat back and watched as the tram rolled past other travelers, tourists, and day-trippers. Some pulled wheeled bags behind them, others pushed carts piled high with luggage, several bent under the weight of backpacks. There's something to be said for looking like a feeble old crone, Mattie thought. She adjusted the bag at her feet and propped against the back of the leather seat.

In a sudden move, Edna grabbed Mattie's arm and dug her fingers in with such a fierce grip that Mattie yelped. Edna slapped her hand over Mattie's mouth and with eyes wide and alarmed, she pointed toward two women who walked abreast of the tram.

They moved with determined strides, lips turned down in severe, angry expressions, eyes narrowed in concentration. They wore tailored wool pants, trench coats, and sensible shoes. They did not speak to each other. Edna turned her head and ducked down as if she were tying her laces. The tram rolled past the women.

"What?" Mattie said.

Edna remained hunched over. She crowded toward Mattie and whispered. "My daughters. We just passed my daughters. Joan and Suzanne."

"*Are you sure?*" Now Mattie whispered, too. Edna's head bobbed up and down. Her lower lip trembled, and her left eye twitched.

Mattie checked her watch and peered at the crowd behind them. Somewhere, in the river of walkers . . . Edna's daughters. If the girls found the three of them, they'd be whisked back to Restful Palms and locked in their rooms until they died—because it would be *for their own good*, and because of Edna's money. Mattie set her jaw and narrowed her gaze. She drew in a breath, then released it slowly. "We have quite a bit of time before we board," she said. "I think we should hide."

They offered the driver a tip, but he shook his head no and brushed the air, dismissive.

"Ladies' loo is right there." The driver pointed across the hall. He brought the tram to a stop, engaged the parking break, stepped down, and offered his hand to Helen. "Now remember, Miss. If yer ever in Ireland again, you be sure ta look me up. You do. I'll show you 'round Dublin. Private tour." He held onto her hand an extra tick, took one last breath of her soft lilac scent. "I know all the streets."

Helen thanked him and flashed her best Lena Horne smile. It was a smile that he would remember during many, many journeys up and down the length of Terminal One.

As they do in public restrooms the world over, a dozen or so women resigned themselves to a scraggly line that snaked the length of twelve stalls and wound past six sinks. Trapped and exposed, the ladies panicked. What if Edna's daughters found them? How did they find out about Ireland? Where were they headed?

"Come on." Helen put her arm around Mattie's shoulders. She spoke in a loud voice as if she were trying to reach someone with poor hearing. "Come on, dear; we'll help you. Don't worry that you soiled yourself." She raised her voice higher. The women in line turned to watch. "We have a change for you. No need to be embarrassed. Happens to everybody at some time." She pulled Mattie toward the stall reserved for disabled travelers.

Mattie twisted one way, then the next. "Let go of me." She tried to wriggle out of Helen's grasp, but Helen held a firm grip. "What the . . ."

"Shhh . . ." Helen squeezed her and pushed her forward. She turned to the line. "My auntie here is . . ." She paused, sighed. "It's hard when they get this old."

Several women nodded, sympathetic. Two of them entered into a conversation about aging relatives.

"Thank you, thank you." Helen nodded and smiled as the women parted the line and let them through. Edna wasn't sure what was happening, but she followed along.

The three friends wedged into the cramped space. Once inside, with the door secured, Mattie punched Helen's arm and glared at her. Helen shrugged. They rustled around, flushed the toilet, and made noises they hoped sounded like changing a "soiled auntie." They stayed in the stall for about ten minutes.

"Think they've passed the bathrooms yet?" Without waiting for an answer Mattie turned the lock, held her breath and pushed the stall door open a slit. She peered out. At first glance, nothing more than a typical line in a ladies' restroom. Women waited their turn, checked watches, calmed fidgety children, applied lipstick, and eyed themselves in compact mirrors. Mattie jolted back and pulled the door tight. She locked it and spun around. "They're here." She held one finger to her lips and jerked her head toward the door. "In line."

Edna made a fist, pushed it against her mouth, and squeezed her eyes shut. She started to crumble. Helen wrapped her arms around her friend and drew her in close. They stood frozen and silent, and they listened.

"This is absurd. The whole thing is ridiculous." The voice was hard. Cold. "When we get back, she goes into a locked facility. End of story. I'm done with this nonsense."

Edna opened her eyes, dropped her hand and mouthed her daughter's name—Suzanne.

"God, I'm exhausted. I love her, of course, but we've been taking care of her all our lives. It's like we've been the adults, and she's been the child. She's always been frail and weak. Now, I think she's losing her mind, and she's missing, and I feel like such a failure. What would Dad say?"

"Joan?" Mattie mouthed. Edna nodded. Her shoulders hunched forward, her skin paled. Helen tightened her hold.

"He'd say we should have made her sign those papers the last time we saw her. He'd say we should have kept a tighter watch over her. We should have taken better care of her. We *have* failed."

"I say, no matter what, when this is over we get a full-time nurse to watch her and then we are so suing. That Restful Palms place can kiss their operating license goodbye this instant."

"Got that right."

A toilet flushed.

"And Katie, she better learn how to wait tables because she isn't getting one more penny for school or anything else. I knew she was trouble from the day we took her in."

The ladies strained to hear, but an electric hand dryer roared over Suzanne's next words. The dryer stopped.

"I agree," Joan said. "Can you believe she helped them escape? I heard she dressed them in costumes. Put one in a leprechaun hat. And you know that really old woman? Katie made her wear Army boots. I wouldn't be a bit surprised if she convinced them to get tattoos."

Helen's eyes widened. She stared down at Mattie's combat boots, pointed to them, and then toward the stall door. Then she gestured toward the stool. Mattie pursed her lips and handed her bag to Edna. She placed one hand on the wall and one on Helen's shoulder and climbed onto the toilet seat. She balanced one boot on either side of the open ring and stooped down so that her head wouldn't protrude over the top of the stall. Her boots slipped a bit on the rounded surface.

Helen released Edna and gripped Mattie's legs to steady her. Edna pressed against the door and peeped through the crack. She watched her daughters, both grim-faced and stern. Later, when she thought about them, she'd be sad. But now, they frightened her.

The ladies held their breath when Suzanne leaned against the door of the stall where they were hiding. "I'm so tired," she said. She dug through her purse for their tickets. "I miss him, but I'm sort of glad Dad isn't around to know we lost her. He'd be furious."

The loudspeaker crackled. *"Flight 11 for Cork now boarding gate 24G."*

"That's us," Joan said. "Let's go."

The ladies remained still for ten more minutes before Mattie climbed off the toilet seat. They stayed huddled in place for another half hour. Helen crunched seat protectors and flushed periodically for effect. Edna pressed against the wall and stared at the floor, her face without expression until Mattie nudged her and handed her a pencil. She whispered the directions in Edna's ear. When they found Katie's email, Mattie held the phone out so Helen could read it.

Grannies: OMG Soooooo sorry to hear about Granny D. I hope that Mr. Charlie guy takes good care of her. You should know this—the aunties are in Ireland. They figured stuff out. They talked to Josephine and that weird Director-guy, Roger Simpson.

He blamed it all on Caroline. She got fired. RUN. Send more pics. The whole world loves you.
Me most. XXX Katie.

Edna's eyes welled up when she read the message, but she did not let the tears fall. Helen came up with a plan and made a mental note of it. She didn't know how she'd do it, but she vowed to herself that when they returned to Florida, she would help Caroline get her job back.

Mattie's lips pressed together. She shot a quick look at her dress held so perfectly in place by hidden Velcro. It was Caroline who'd given her the freedom, the dignity, to dress herself. And Caroline who'd kept her secret.

Mattie didn't have the time or emotional energy right then to allow feelings of guilt to surface, but she knew they would. Although she and Helen did not share their thoughts out loud, they did share the same plan.

Even though they realized the flight to Cork had departed, the ladies scurried to their gate, crouched in their seats, and kept their faces buried in newspapers left behind by other travelers.

When an airline agent offered to board them early, they jumped at the chance to hide in the safety of the cabin, but they didn't let their guard down until the plane reached cruising altitude and the captain turned off the seatbelt sign.

"Dolores would have loved this airline." Edna held the glass of Australian shiraz to the window and watched as sunlight, high above the clouds over Europe, shot through the liquid and splashed color on seat backs and tray tables. "All this lovely wine and food and the stewardesses are so sweet."

"Flight attendants," Mattie said. "They're flight attendants." She struggled to open her wine bottle.

"Here, let me help you with that." A steward took the bottle, gave the top a quick twist and poured half the liquid into her glass. He sat the wine and cap on her tray. "Can I bring you anything else?"

Mattie shook her head no. She should have thanked him and was a bit ashamed that she hadn't, but she looked down at her hands and gritted her teeth. She stared at her fingers; at her curled, knotted crab-like fingers. They made her angry and afraid. These hands, *her hands*, they could do so many things. *Did* so many things. Now they couldn't even twist the top off a miniature wine bottle or push a button through a hole.

"I agree," Helen said. She leaned over Mattie and spoke to Edna. "She would have felt like a queen."

"Maybe . . ." Edna took a tentative sip of her wine. "Maybe we should go back. Go home. Maybe my daughters are right, and maybe Josephine was right, too."

"Now Edna darlin', whatever are you talkin' about?" Helen moved even closer. Mattie grimaced and pushed further back against her seat.

"First it was Rose. Now poor Dolores stuck in that foreign hospital. Maybe this is too much for old . . . for us." Edna's nose reddened. "Maybe we're not outrageous women. Maybe we're just tired, old fools."

"Oh now, shush. Don't be thinkin' that way. Rose was happy. Probably for the first time in her life. At least since. . ." Helen hesitated, thought for a second, and then continued. "Never mind. She was happy. And she would have had that heart attack if she'd been in Wisconsin or in that tiny room of hers in Restful Palms. And Dolores . . ."

Edna's eyes brimmed. "If we hadn't climbed up to that stupid old stone, she'd still be walking around."

"Now, now." Helen reached all the way across Mattie and stroked Edna's arm. "She wanted to visit that castle. And, she was, she is, in love. She was probably thinking about that fellow when she fell. Probably feelin' sorta, sexy and alive. You know, I bet it was the first time she ever felt that way in her whole life. And now, who knows what magical things may happen with her and Chuck. Why, I wouldn't be at all surprised if there's a wedding in their future." Helen closed her eyes a moment, hummed a few notes to an old love song—one that made her both happy and melancholy at the same time. She opened her eyes. "I think we should make a toast to her, to Dolores, because she deserves to have attention from a man." Helen lifted her glass and nudged Mattie. "Come on, let's toast to Dolores," she said.

Edna held up her glass. "Still, I miss her and wish she didn't take that fall. She was such a dear, dear friend. I wish she was still traveling with us."

"Wait a minute." Mattie pushed Helen back into her seat. "I hate to speak poorly of anyone who's in the hospital. But, let's be real, here. Dolores is a pain in the butt, and you both know it."

"Mattie," Edna said. She lowered her glass and stared.

Helen huffed. "You can't be serious. She is our friend."

"*You* can't be serious." Mattie gulped her drink, swallowed. "She is whiny and self-absorbed, and she caused us all a lot of extra work. Let's not forget that damn big suitcase of hers. And do you know how many times I found bits of food stuck to my bag or crumbs on my dress? How did she manage to get *her crumbs* on *my dresses*?" She took another gulp. "I'm not saying I'm happy she fell, of course not. All I'm sayin is it's going to be easier to move around without her extra weight."

Edna cringed as if she'd been slapped. She turned toward the window and slumped in her seat.

"Oh my." Helen could think of nothing more to say. She retreated and turned her attention to the flight attendant who walked down the aisle collecting dinner orders; Beef Wellington or roast turkey with dressing.

Mattie slurped more wine, poured the rest of the bottle into her glass. She wasn't proud of herself at the moment, but still . . .

Chapter Twenty-two

Take Your Bundle and Go, Caroline
Tampa, Florida

Caroline stood in the lobby of the Restful Palms Retirement Home. She held the cardboard box the janitor had helped her to pack.

"Leave all that shit there," her cousin had said. But Caroline couldn't leave without her uniforms or the withered cactus from the break room—the one that didn't want to live but refused to die. She couldn't leave without the cards that grateful families had given her when they came to pay the final bill and clear things out. Six cards—fourteen years.

Most folks rushed past her, past the nurses and the orderlies who'd cared for their mothers and fathers, and in a few sad cases, their severely wounded children. Caroline liked to think that more relatives recognized the value of the work she and the other staff members did for their loved ones, but that they didn't say much or show their appreciation because even an extra couple of minutes in the retirement home—with all those memories—would have been too painful for them.

Caroline liked to think that.

And what about her jewelry? She had an extensive collection of macaroni necklaces. She could never figure out why activities directors, usually young girls straight out of college, thought people in their eighties would enjoy projects they'd done as children. She reckoned the residents went along with these idiotic assignments out of sheer boredom and to be polite to the young people.

She debated. Bring the strings of pasta home? Or just dump them in the trash and be done with it. Finally, she decided that a resident might discover them in the garbage, and she didn't want to hurt anyone's feelings. She figured she'd toss them out at home. Although, many years later, she still strung them on her tree at Christmas.

Caroline wasn't angry with the ladies even though they had, more or less, tricked her into signing that form, which ultimately cost her job. How could she be mad at those women who finally took things into their bony, arthritic hands and broke free? She chuckled and shook her head as she thought of them—wondered what those old gals were up to. Last she heard from one of the young orderlies, they were dancing in some bar in England or Ireland or maybe Scotland. The orderly couldn't remember which, but he remembered he didn't like the music much.

No, she couldn't be angry at them. But she was disappointed in Josephine. *Shouldn't ever tattle on your friends,* she thought.

"Girl, they did you a favor, kickin your black ass outta that place." Her cousin did not like the retirement home. "Those people never did appreciate you. You go on unemployment now, see? And have yourself some rest time. You deserve it," her cousin said.

"Mr. Johansen," Caroline called out to the man speeding by on his motorized wheelchair. Three small American flags, duct-taped to the seat, flapped in his wake. He leaned forward, face grim, determined—didn't stop or even nod. She stifled a laugh. "Never mind, sugar. I can see you got places to go. Things to do."

She shook her head and drew in a long breath. The smell of urine and *Lysol* and the cloying scent of *Youth Dew* perfume competed. She listened. Canned laughter spilled from a television. *The Price is Right* would be on about now. Someone practiced chopsticks on the piano in the recreation room. Caroline grimaced and remembered how difficult it had been to clean between the keys.

She would miss this place.

Chapter Twenty-three

The Best Medicine – Qantas Airlines

They didn't speak much for the rest of the evening. After dinner and the first movie, they tucked under the wool blankets offered by the flight attendant. Lulled by the steady purr of the jet and rocked by exhaustion and their emotions, they slept. If they'd remembered their dreams, they would have been alarmed: stairwells that wound endlessly into darkness, blood on pink roses, yawning hallways, and trench coats cinched tight. But they didn't remember these dreams.

Breakfast came drenched in brilliant sunlight reflecting off mounds of clouds, streaming through Plexiglas windows. The tension of the day before melted. Helen tapped Mattie's arm before she left for the bathroom. The two friends exchanged smiles. The rest had done them good.

Mattie wrestled with a small container of cream. Her fingers continued to cramp and curl, but they gripped a little better this morning, behaved a little more as she wished.

"Do you want some help with that?" Edna said.

Mattie shook her head no. She managed to catch the tag on the top of the container. She took a deep breath and gave a tug. The top ripped off. Cream splashed into her scrambled eggs and sprayed Edna's blouse.

"Oh!" Mattie stiffened. She gaped at the spots as they spread, dark and wet, into pale blue cotton. Edna held for an instant and stared at her shirt. Then, she laughed. A full on, hand-to-the-heart, head back laugh.

Mattie glanced down at her eggs; they swam in hazelnut-flavored creamer. And she too laughed. Heads turned, necks craned. Fellow passengers smiled. Old women laughing. Yes, the rest had done them good.

"So, darlin', now that we don't have to go to baggage claim, how will we find Katie's Australian friends?" Helen secured her tray table and then reached for Mattie's.

Mattie chewed her lower lip and furrowed her brow. "I'm not sure. But that's where we met the others, so I guess that's our best option." She nodded toward the table. "Thanks."

"No problem." Helen smiled. "Who are we looking for this time?"

"Some college students on break. Surfers. She said it will be easy to find them."

Edna sighed. "What would we do without Katie?"

"I don't even like to think about that." Helen shuddered.

"I don't," Mattie said.

Chapter Twenty-four

Steak and Kidney Pie
Melbourne, Australia

Melbourne International Airport bristled with travelers, many of them young, fit, and tanned. Khaki shorts bagged to knees; T-shirts advertised board wax and rock bands. Sandals slapped the cement floor. Surfboards and scuba gear rode round and round on conveyor belts until collected. Phrases like "G'day, mate," and, "Ow ya goin?" buzzed through the building. Excitement effervesced. The ladies circled, backs to each other, mouths open in awe.

This time, Helen spotted them. "Look." She pointed across the room.

Two girls, two boys. The girls stood arm in arm and surveyed the crowd. One, tall with long blonde hair and blue eyes; the other, short, Asian in appearance, hair straight—obsidian. Almond eyes blinked behind black-rimmed glasses. A sling, tied at her neck, cradled her right arm in a heavy plaster cast. Both wore capris, tank tops, and combat boots without laces. Boots exactly like Mattie's. The boys wore flower-print shorts that brushed their knees, T-shirts, flip-flops and green felt leprechaun hats. All four sported tattoos.

"Oh my," Edna stared. "Are they making fun of us?"

"Grannies!" The blonde spotted them and raced over, her smile wide with perfect teeth. The ladies found themselves swept up in hugs and laughter. Names flew—Minh, Sarah, Ben, and Trevor. More hugs.

Before the ladies could catch their breath, their new friends hustled them out of the airport and across the parking lot to the side of a rusting, oversized station wagon. Ben piled their bags in the back compartment while Sarah and Helen climbed in the front. Edna slid into the back with Trevor.

Mattie stood next to the old car and stared at it in wonder. She couldn't decide on its color: something between sand and tan, or faded beige. The front panel on the passenger's side came from another, probably newer, vehicle. It was a shiny metallic blue and didn't quite fit. Wraps of bailing wire secured its place. A spider web of bungee cords held three surfboards balanced on the roof. Stickers from beaches and parks across Australia plastered the rear bumper.

The tires looked dangerously bald, especially for the load of three old women, four muscled young people, piles of luggage, and camping gear. Still, something about the ancient vehicle charmed Mattie.

"Sweeeeet," she said.

Ben laughed. "She is a sweet old gal." He slapped the side of the car. "This is Myrtle—1968 Holden. She's been hauling surfers around since she rolled off the line. My dad bought her new. He gave her to my big brother and then my brother passed her down to me." Ben grinned and slid in next to Trevor. "I um . . . had a little issue with the local coppers, so Minh is in charge of driving until I get my license back." He patted his thigh. "Come on, now. It's a tight fit, but you can sit on my lap, Granny. Let's roll."

Mattie perched on the lap of the grinning surfer boy; Minh drove with her left hand, and Sarah babbled on and on about how excited they were to meet the Outrageous Grannies.

"Women." Mattie reached forward and tapped Sarah on the shoulder. "We are outrageous *women*." This spun the surfers into waves of laughter.

"Are you . . . are you making fun of us?" Edna said.

Myrtle hit a bump. Edna seized the back of the front seat. They all popped upward then landed, hard, in their seats. Except for Mattie, who landed back on Ben's lap.

"Sorry about that." Minh glanced up at the rearview mirror.

"Wha ya mean, makin fun a ya?" Trevor's thick Australian accent all but obscured his question.

"The hats." Edna pointed to the crumbled green felt clutched in his hand.

"And you girls, wearing those boots." Helen pointed at Sarah's feet.

"Oh, no." Sarah wriggled around enough to put her arm around Helen. "You are our heroes! That video of Granny D dancing? Viral. You should see the clubs. Everyone is doing the *Granny D*."

"Totally viral." Minh bobbed her head and started to turn around.

"Road!" Ben and Trevor yelled in unison.

Minh laughed but refocused on her driving.

"Chickies—lots of chickies—wear granny boots now," Sarah said.

"And lots of blokes and sheilas wear leprechaun hats, too." Ben pitched in. "It's a crazy-cool thing."

Helen looked over her shoulder, caught Mattie's eye. Mattie shook her head and glanced at Edna. Edna's mouth formed its little "O." Viral? Clubs? Granny boots?

Eager to learn more about this viral thing, their new friends, and what Katie had scheduled for their trip Down Under, Helen tried to chat with Sarah, but Myrtle was shy two windows, so the roar of the wind and the road made conversation all but impossible, plus Minh's driving was less than steady. Finally, Helen gave up, and like the others, she hunkered down and hung on.

Forty-five minutes later Minh pulled into a truck stop for fuel and meat pies. While the ladies used the restroom, she and the boys ordered lunch. Sarah found a picnic table away from the rows of gigantic tour buses with their big engines left running. Edna was the first to join her.

She scooted into place, then contemplated the view beyond the truck stop: wide open stretches of short grass punctuated with stands of wattle and scraggly pine trees. Upwind from the diesel fumes the air smelled of sweet sage. A light breeze fluttered the edge of a plastic cloth stapled to the table. "This is a pretty country," she said.

Sarah followed her gaze. "Yeah, it is. But it's much prettier up north, where I come from."

"Where is home, dear?" Edna turned to face her young friend.

"Katoomba. In the Blue Mountains." Sarah paused for a moment and closed her eyes. "It's the prettiest place in Australia. The mountains look blue, and the air is crystal clear." She opened her eyes and continued. "My parents run an art gallery downtown. I'm going to run it when I get out of school." She smiled at Edna. "You grannies should come up to Katoomba and take a tour. You'll love it!"

Edna thought about blue mountains. *Very strange.* She'd never heard of such a thing, but before she could ask Sarah how the mountains turned blue, her thoughts were interrupted by laughter. Helen and Mattie joked and poked at each other as they rounded the corner of the building and made their way to the picnic table.

"Surf is great now," Trevor said. "Wait 'til you see the waves. We'll git you grannies out there on a board for sure." He plopped down cardboard trays of food holding what looked like a chicken pot pie and a paper boat filled with fried potatoes.

"We're on holiday from uni, out for ten days," Sarah said. She helped pass the food around.

"Here. Gimme that, Black Granny." Trevor took a squirt bottle from Helen and jammed the pointed nozzle into the center of one of the pot pies. "Ya push it in the pie. See? And squeeze. Tomato sauce goes in the pie. See?"

Helen grimaced. A little ketchup would be tasty. But she guessed there was now more ketchup—tomato sauce—in her pie than meat.

Mattie reached for the bottle, pushed the nozzle through the thick crust on her steak and kidney pie and squeezed hard. Ketchup squirted from the top of the crust and splatted on her shirt. Big red blobs. She swore softly and glanced at the others, but they'd missed it as all eyes focused on Minh while she adjusted her sling.

"What happened to your arm, dear?" Edna touched the cast. Sarah reached over and helped Minh with the knot.

"Fell off my board into a gnarly wave." Minh shrugged as if careening off a short board into house-sized surf happened on a regular basis. Probably did. "My board went flying. When it came down, it smashed my arm."

"Oh dear . . ." Edna's hand flew to cover her mouth, but she stopped herself, pretended to cough instead.

"No worries, Little Granny," Minh said. "It's all good." She gave Edna a gentle pat on the back. "The doc said I'll be stuck in this bloody cast for a few weeks. That's the bad news. But good news? I get to take you ladies on a mini-tour of Australia. Your granddaughter, you know, Katie? She and I Skyped and set it all up. First stop, tomorrow morning, the Wild Animal Park to feed the roos." She smiled at Helen. Helen slid her plate to one side and turned to face Minh.

"Skyped?" Edna said. "What is . . ."

Helen pressed her hand on Edna's arm and interrupted. "We can feed them?" She stared at Minh.

Minh laughed. "You can hug 'em if you want."

Helen sat back and placed her hands flat on the table. "Lordy," she said.

"But wait," Trevor said. "There's more. See?"

Minh bobbed her head so fast her glasses slid down her nose. She pushed them up with one finger and continued. "He's right. Katie told me to take you ladies to Tassie. On the Spirit."

"Tassie?" Mattie wiped at a blob of ketchup on her shirt.

"Tasmania. *Spirit of Tasmania*. It's a ferry boat. We can take Myrtle on board and sleep overnight in cabins. And we can go to Penguin. You'll love Penguin. It's a village and the penguins, the little blue ones, they come in from the sea in groups. And, oh yeah . . ." She reached across the table, pulled a handful of napkins from a holder, and handed them to Mattie without missing a beat. "If you want to learn to surf, we have an extra board for you."

Edna and Mattie stared at Minh.

"Lordy," Helen repeated.

Following a lively discussion, the surfers decided they would have enough time to catch a few waves before dark. And so, instead of stopping at a hotel first, they drove directly to the beach.

Even though Ben generously offered to teach them how to catch and ride a perfect wave, the ladies politely declined surfing lessons. Helen noted that she'd never learned to swim. Edna mentioned that she didn't like cold water, and although Mattie showed some initial interest in the sport, she finally gave it up when she realized it might be hard to grip the slippery board with her curled and arthritic toes.

The three friends did, however, sit with Minh on top of a cement break wall to watch Ben, Trevor, Sarah, and, at least, twenty other surfers ride the waves—waves as clear as glass, the color of slivered kiwi in the curls, frothy as whipped wax at the crests.

"I feel like a teenager on summer vacation," Helen said.

"I wish I was a teenager." Mattie kicked her heels against the wall. She watched a bronzed boy with straw yellow hair sprint toward the water. "Can you think of all the fun we could have if we were young again?"

Edna pressed against Mattie and rested her head on her friend's shoulder. "I'm having fun right now, Mattie," she said.

Mattie wrapped her arm around Edna and gave a squeeze. She continued to watch the boy as he leaped into the waves. "Me too," she whispered.

Hesitating a few final minutes before plunging into the sea, the Aussie sun colored their skin with warm, ginger light.

After the surfers rinsed under beach showers and slipped into dry clothes, they joined the ladies for a stroll. The little town of Cohen survived on money from tourists who came to watch buff young people tackle giant and not-so-friendly waves. Minh explained that each season, a few of the braver gawkers signed up for beginning surf lessons, which frequently resulted in extra income for the part-time medics who administered first aid from a 1969 VW Westfalia van.

Helen counted three restaurants, four bars, six souvenir shops, and one nail salon. Nobody wanted to go for American-style fast food, so, after some debate, they all agreed that the Mama Mia Señorita Bar and Grill sounded like a winner; close to the beach and packed with cost-conscious surfers and unsuspecting tourists.

The ladies bought dinner for the group. Everyone ordered the special of the day: pasta, beans, and some kind of meat all tucked into pita bread smothered in green chili sauce and goat cheese. It might not have been the best choice.

After dinner, the ladies checked into a small, shabby hotel that squatted two streets back from the beach where their new friends and about a hundred other surfers camped.

Helen wrinkled her nose when they first stepped into their room. The smell of disinfectant, tangy salt air, and laundry detergent almost overpowered her. Mattie thought the smell made her ill, upset her stomach. But Edna was sure it was the food, not the cleaning products, that attacked their bellies and made them run for the toilet.

"Who ever heard of Italian-Mexican?" she said. "And what do you think we ate? I bet it wasn't beef." She belched without covering her mouth. She knew it was rude and was something she'd never considered when Louis was alive. But now, for no particular reason that she could think of, the very act of belching gave her a little thrill.

Edna sat on the edge of the double bed that she and Helen would share. Mattie had drawn the long straw this time; a strip from the restaurant's takeaway menu. "Can you believe it? All those young people wearing leprechaun hats?" She shook her head. "I don't understand what this video stuff is all about but they seem to enjoy it." She wiped the bottoms of her feet with a damp washrag. "And can you believe we are in Australia? Why, before we started all of this, I never even thought about Australia." Edna laid the cloth on the floor next to the bed, pulled her legs up and slid under the sheet. She propped herself against the headboard.

An ancient window box air conditioner wheezed, rattled, and generated enough tepid air to flap dirty cobweb fringe in a half-hearted wave.

"Darlin', I can't hardly believe it myself. I'm all excited and confused both at the same time." Helen eased down to the bed and sat next to Edna. Every movement hurt these days—her joints so stiff now and her muscles so sore. But she didn't wince or complain. Best, she thought, to keep this to herself lest Edna and Mattie felt obligated to slow down for her. She would not let that happen. She stretched her legs and stared absently at them.

She'd always been proud of her legs. Long, *like the legs of a stallion*, Roy used to say. Now, blue veins mapped the years. Even so, her legs were still good, and strong. She looked at Edna.

"But you know, here we are. And tomorrow, I'm going to see those animals, the ones my boys wrote home about so long, long ago." Helen brushed her hand through her hair. "It makes my heart throb to know I'm in the place where my sons were so happy." She closed her eyes, took a deep breath, and exhaled slowly.

Edna placed her hand on Helen's. "It touches my heart, too," she said.

They sat still and quiet. From the bathroom, the rush of the shower competed with Mattie who belted out the words to a song she sang a lot lately—something about freedom.

Chapter Twenty-five

Kangaroos and Kookaburras

Minh arrived at dawn and kicked the door. "Sorry about the noise. Couldn't knock. No hands." She balanced a cardboard container of cups in her left hand. Steam rose from hot coffee. A paper bag of jelly donuts nestled in the crook of her cast.

Mattie slurped coffee. Edna wiped a glob of jelly she'd dribbled onto her blouse. Helen, way too excited for donuts, plied Minh with questions about the Wild Animal Park.

"It's super fun." Minh bobbed her head up and down, then jabbed at her glasses. "You buy little bags of food at the gift shop. Make sure to hold your hands flat when you're feeding the animals, or they might go for your fingers."

"They bite?" Edna stopped her mop-up efforts and stared at Minh. "Bite hard?"

"Not if you keep your hands flat and hold the food out. You'll get the hang of it. No worries." Minh pulled a donut from the bag, tapped excess powdered sugar onto a napkin. "You know, you could follow a park ranger on a guided excursion." She took a bite. Swallowed. "But the tours are pretty lame. So you should think about going off on your own. You can figure things out, and you won't be stuck with a bunch of helpless Americans." She stopped and considered what she'd said. "I don't mean all Americans . . . I mean, you know, no offense."

Mattie reached over and patted Minh's hand. "No offense taken, dear."

Because she'd already visited the animals, three times so far, and because today was her turn to buy groceries for the surfers' communal kitchen, Minh left them at the gate to the park with a promise to return later that afternoon.

Once inside the gift shop, Mattie took charge of purchasing day passes and packets of pellets while Helen and Edna perused the souvenirs. Edna played with snow globes and squeezed the paws of talking koalas. She gave a little squeal and tittered each time a stuffed animal squeaked out "G'day mate" and "Ow's ya goin?"

Helen selected a canvas hat with a stiff, wide brim. Wine corks hung from strings of fishing line tied around its edge. The corks swung like soundless wind chimes each time she moved her head. "The movement keeps the flies away," she said. She stood in front of the display mirror and rotated first one way and then the next to check her profile.

Edna nodded her approval and went back to shaking the globes. She watched, enthralled, as flurries of plastic snow covered the Sydney skyline and Uluru.

When Mattie joined them, she tilted her head and eyed the swinging corks. She thought the hat made Helen look ridiculous. "It's um," she floundered for words. "It's not exactly your style, is it?"

Helen glared at Mattie through narrowed eyes. She lifted her chin, straightened her shoulders and marched to the checkout stand without another word. The corks danced merrily around her head.

With tickets in hand, they joined a group of tourists clustered around an elderly fellow dressed in movie-set safari clothing complete with multi-pocketed jacket, Crocodile Dundee hat, khaki shorts, snakeskin belt, and hiking boots over thick, olive-colored socks. "Now ladies and gentlemen." He motioned for the group to crowd close. "The park spreads over 60 acres. Approximately one hundred different species live here, including insects and other creepy crawlies. I say approximately because we expect more sneak into the park and take up residence on a fairly regular basis. Good place to live, this is. Plenty of food and natural predators are housed in cordoned-off areas." He paused, took a reading of his group. So far . . . so good. Attentive, interested tourists meant better tips. He glanced at Mattie, sized her up. "Nice boots, miss." He nodded toward her.

"Nice socks," she countered.

"Hmm," he cleared his throat. "As I were sayin', the animals are in native settings. Enclosures designed like natural rock formations keep 'em from eatin' each other or from scamperin' all over the whole of Australia. Feel free to feed and pet most of 'em." He monitored the crowd—still following his words—a good sign. "Except the Tasmanian Devils. Leave them buggers alone as they will rip yer face right off, they will."

A woman in the front gasped and snatched at her husband's arm. The guide changed tack. "Not to worry. Those of you who are with me are perfectly safe as I know the territory." He patted the Bowie knock-off strapped to his hip. *Realistic reproduction*, he always thought. "Yer are all welcome to follow along, or you can goes off on yer owns. Willy-nilly like."

The ladies glanced at each other and made a silent, joint decision. They'd follow Minh's advice and take the willy-nilly route.

Although disappointed that the group of attractive, mature women (American types for sure), had decided to go off alone rather than follow him for an experience they'd never forget, the ranger shrugged. No matter, the show must go on. He turned his attention to the rest of the tourists, thrust his arm straight up and drew a circle overhead. "This way folks. To the wild animals of the deep, dark land Down Under."

Mattie gave the fellow with his hat and knife some thought. Might be fun—a little flirting, maybe lunch . . . But this day was all about Helen. Helen and the kangaroos that bounced, somewhere, on the sixty acres of park land. Old men in snakeskin belts would have to wait for another day.

The first animals to greet them were six friendly and perpetually hungry wallabies.

"Are they baby kangaroos?" Edna bent down and offered a handful of pellets to the eager animals.

"No." Mattie paraphrased the description in the pamphlet that came with the price of admission. "Same family, marsupials. They carry their babies in purses. But these guys are a lot smaller, and they don't jump about as much as kangaroos."

The wallabies clustered around Helen and Edna. They pushed at each other and pulled on open palms with nimble paws. Mattie snapped photos, and after playfully admonishing her friends for not doing a better job of rationing treats, she went back inside and picked up five more bags of animal food. She grinned and hummed the entire time.

As she waited in line to pay for the pellets, Mattie thought about her friends and how great she felt just watching Helen be so . . . so happy. They were all happy. *Weren't they?*

Yes. And this was better—so much better than what she'd considered that afternoon in the private dining room at the Restful Palms Retirement Home. True, things hadn't worked out exactly as planned. Who plans to fall down the stairs of a castle in Ireland? But still. Yes, this was better than what she'd ever dreamed. And soon, Helen would pet her kangaroo, Edna would ride her camel, and she, Mattie Snorgenson, would sail on her ship. She smiled at the clerk, paid for her purchases, and stashed a couple of the small bags in her pocket.

So happy in the moment, Mattie skittered up to her friends and startled the wallabies. "Got 'em!" She beamed and divided the rest of the bags between Helen and Edna. Then, like the park ranger, she thrust her hand straight up and lassoed the sky. "Come on, ladies," she said. "Let's go hug a kangaroo!"

Kookaburras laughed and sang, and Edna insisted they lived in old gum trees. She didn't know how or why she knew this, but she knew this for certain.

Enthralled with the echidna, Mattie snapped so many photos that Helen reached over and gently took the cell phone from her. "Come on, Mattie-Girl," she said. "Katie might send an email. We don't want to run the battery down."

"Yes, but look at this thing." Mattie pointed to the spiny creature. It resembled a cross between a hedgehog and an anteater. "Its feet are on backward." She stared as the strange, awkward animal dug into the soft wood of a rotten log and explored the terrain with its elongated finger-shaped nose. Helen coaxed and pleaded, and even threatened before she managed to tear Mattie away from this new wonder.

The main trail stretched in an oval that originated and ended at the gift shop. Narrow pathways crisscrossed the route, which allowed visitors to view and interact with the animals in natural-appearing but protected enclosures. The three friends took their time as they wandered along the paths.

Now and again they stopped to pet and feed animals they'd never seen or even heard of. Occasionally they caught a glimpse of the tour guide and the tourists who followed along behind him. Once, a short way past the parrots, the ranger noticed the ladies watching him, and he waved for them to join his tour. But they only smiled, waved back, and continued on their way.

The wombat, a sturdy fellow who looked more like a fur-covered ottoman than an animal, stood on stumpy hind legs and pressed fat front paws on the wooden bridge suspended over his enclosure.

"I could snuggle with him," Edna said. "He's so cuddly."

Helen knelt down and poured out a handful of treats. She stroked his thick, coarse fur as he snorted through the pellets. Despite her concern about saving the cell phone's battery, she and the others each posed for a photo with the wombat. After every shot, Mattie and Edna dutifully worked together to send the small image to Katie. They still weren't quite sure what she did with the pictures, but, as with everything else, they trusted her.

The three friends ambled along the park's main trail and ventured down smaller dirt paths. They chatted, and laughed, and pointed to strange snouts and bright flecks of color on feathers overhead. They pulled back—fast—from the sharp beak of an emu and stood still, with respect, as a stately peacock swept by with his jeweled fan of sapphire, emerald, and gold. After an hour or so they passed a large open area where lean yellow dogs roamed and lounged in the sunlight.

"Those dingoes remind me of our dog," Helen said. "Except that they don't bark. We used to have a golden retriever, got him before the babies were born. Now that dog barked. Oh boy, could he bark."

She watched two pups play together and thought about Roy and how he used to roll around on the grass with that big yellow dog. "We called him Max," she said. "I sure missed that dog when we moved. My parents took Max. They loved him, too. But Clarence, he wasn't much of a dog guy. Not much of an animal guy at all."

Mattie placed her hand on Helen's shoulder. Helen shifted her gaze to Mattie. The two friends exchanged a gentle, understanding smile.

Toward the end of the loop, they found the enclosure that served as home to a family of Tasmanian Devils. Edna stretched over the high rock wall that separated tourists from the legendary creatures. She gazed down into the shady enclosure.

"They don't look so fierce, do they? They look like cats or maybe . . ." She thought hard—worked hard—for the words. Concentrated. *Black and white . . . black and white.* "Skunks!" She beamed. Triumphant.

"They may look all furry and cute, but remember what that ranger man said." Helen sat her bag on the ground and sloughed out of her cardigan. The sun hung directly overhead now. Mattie stood next to her. She thought about the ranger, his swagger, his big Bowie. Then she too removed her sweater.

The ladies clung to each other behind the thick glass window that separated tourists from the venomous coastal taipan, a snake with a deadly bite for which, according to the placard, there are no antidotes. *All Bites Are Fatal*, the sign said. *Please Inform A Park Ranger If You Are Bitten.*

Normally, Mattie would have had something to say about a sign like that, would have questioned the logic. But here, in this place, where animals wore their feet backward, where birds laughed, and dogs refused to bark . . . Here, in this place where real life bordered on magical, who could argue?

Helen scrutinized the map on the back of their pamphlet. "It looks like we have two choices." She traced the lines with one finger. "We can go have lunch at the café in the gift shop or," she looked up at Mattie and Edna, "we could veer off here and go to the field where the kangaroos are." She waited for a beat and then added, "If you two are hungry, I can wait to see the kangaroos until after lunch." She held her breath.

Mattie stomped one foot. Dust swirled up and settled back down on her boot. "Are you kidding? Eat? We don't need to eat. We need to go see those animals." She turned to Edna. "Right?"

Edna nodded emphatically.

Helen exhaled.

"But I think we can try something that isn't on the map," Mattie said. She stood close to Helen and looked at the page. "I saw a gate back there. I don't think it's part of the park, but it looks like it might . . ." She leaned in closer to the paper. "Yep, I think there's a forest that connects the park to the open field. Let's go through that. Let's explore on our own."

"Can we?" Edna tilted her head and scrunched her face in worry. "I mean, wouldn't it be dangerous? You know, to go off the path?" Her eyes darted from Mattie to Helen and back to Mattie. "Would we be safe?"

Across the way, the ranger called out to his group. "And now we will view the vicious, the frightening, Tasmanian Devils. Stick close to me. It's safer that way."

For a moment, the three women stood as motionless as photos on a postcard. Around them, the sounds of the park continued— grunts and snorts, the flap of feathers, the thump, thump, thump of wallabies hopping on the hard-packed path. A gentle breeze ruffled their curls, brushed across Mattie's housedress, and pushed the corks on Helen's hat into a slow swirl.

Helen spoke. Her voice now almost a whisper. "You know, we were safe at Restful Palms. But we went there to wait. We were waiting to die. Now, here we are, and we're not safe. This is dangerous. But dangerous or not, we came here to live, at least for a little while. Dangerous doesn't worry me. Dying doesn't worry me. I'll see my boys and my Roy when that time comes. What worries me now is *not livin'*. Followin' a bunch of scared people. Walkin' along a regular path, or sittin' around in that old folks' home, waitin' to die . . ." She reached over, touched Edna's hair and smiled. "Darlin', that's safe. But that's not livin'."

Edna's worry lines softened. She looked up at Helen and smiled back at her. For a moment, Helen did not see a muddled, confused old woman in Edna; she saw a loving, trusting friend.

Mattie tented her eyes with one hand. She looked up at the sun and then at the gate. "Come on," she said. She turned away from the ranger and stepped off the path. "This way."

Their shoes turned wet and muddy when they wandered into a marshy swamp, but they finally found the trail that led into the forest. The sun, now slightly skewed to the west, filtered through thick foliage.

Mattie was amazed that she could still remember the names of so many different plants. Still have my green thumb, she thought. Puffing her chest with confidence she identified gum trees and whistling thorns, iron-buds, and bloodwoods, turpentines, and cypress pines. Shadows played between leaves dusted in silvery grays and muted pewter.

"I know this one," Helen said. She reached out and touched a branch. She rubbed her thumb and fingers over the surface of a leaf and breathed deep the healing scent of eucalyptus.

The day was flawless. One of those rare days when the temperature was so perfect that Helen couldn't tell where her skin ended and the world began. She daydreamed. Her thoughts traveled with particles of dust. They rode on motes that floated on rays of sunlight and settled on the petals of small blue flowers. She might have stayed right there, in that spot forever, if Mattie hadn't yelled.

"Holy mackerel. It's coming right at us!"

Jarred, Helen looked up in time to see a huge, chestnut-colored kangaroo bounding down the dirt path, aimed directly at them. Edna gave a little squeak and covered her head with her arms. Mattie kicked her foot up, poised as if to stop the creature with a boot, but Helen opened her arms wide and called out one word. "Yes."

The animal took a final leap and stopped abruptly. It stood eye to eye with her, so close she could feel its moist breath on her face. It must have weighed at least two hundred pounds. It stretched its paw toward her and lightly scratched at her sweater.

"Oh! Treats! You want treats." Helen struggled to pull the paper bag from her pocket. The kangaroo continued to paw at her until she managed to tear the bag open and pour food into her flattened palm. The creature lowered his head and with a certain delicacy and grace, nibbled at the pellets. Mattie had enough time to snap a couple of shots before she and Edna were confronted with beggars of their own.

Some of them bounced down the trail like the first one. Others crept from the dense brush on either side of the forest path. None of them shy, all with agendas. Animals with attitudes.

One smaller roo, lighter in color than the rest, bore a joey in her pouch. The infant poked its head out from time to time, took a sniff of the air, and then slid back into the furry warmth of its mother. The animals were gentle but insistent. They knew about people and about the food they carried.

"We should save some for the kangaroos in the field," Helen said. She realized that her bags were close to empty. "Those are the big ones, the reds and the greys. We should have something to give them."

Shooing the creatures away wasn't easy, but eventually, when the animals realized these people were not going to play anymore, they hopped back into the speckled shadows. The three friends continued their walk along the forest path until it opened onto acres of grasslands that stretched over round hills and flat fields.

Except for the gum trees, the emus, and the kangaroos, the land reminded Mattie of the farms that bordered her childhood town in eastern Washington. There, a frisky river tumbled over sand and rocks. Brown-and-white cows stood in groups of threes and fours placidly chewing their cud. Clean, cotton clouds floated across the vast blue sky. She rarely thought of that town or those farms anymore. But here, in this sunny field with both strange and familiar animals all around, and with dear friends close by, she decided that someday, maybe soon, she would spend a little time remembering. She'd know when the time to remember was right.

"Mattie." Edna waved. "Come here. Let's get a picture of us next to one of these big birds. Katie won't believe it."

While Edna and Mattie chatted and posed for selfies with gangly flightless birds in the background, Helen wandered the land. She stopped several times and extended her open, pellet-covered palm to the lazy young reds that languished in the weeds. She walked right up to them, felt their pelts, their fur toasty with afternoon sun.

Helen adored the kangaroos, all of them, but the greys were the most interesting. Large, lumbering creatures with expressions like wizened, Tibetan monks. One particular grey, a senior animal resting in a nest of grass, captured her heart.

As with so many old men and elderly dogs, the animal wore his beard scraggly, untrimmed. His whiskers, the color of dry concrete, bristled at his lips. He moved with awkward jerks and drags and slowed to catch his breath with each feeble bounce. Helen guessed arthritis, a pain she shared.

He continued toward her as if he knew her. As if they were friends. She offered him food. The aged roo sniffed the pellets, but gently nudged her hand away with a nose, once moist and cold, now parched and cracked. He rocked back on his haunches and his sad old tail, and he stared up at her. Golden eyes searched hers. Helen dropped the pellets into her pocket. She reached out and touched his face. "Did you know my boys?" She brushed his cheek with the tips of her fingers. "Did you make them laugh? Did you make them happy?"

The grey turned his face and nuzzled his nose in her palm.

"I miss them, you know," she said.

The animal sighed, his breath warm and wet.

"Maybe you miss them too and . . ." Helen could not finish her thought, but the roo nodded, ever so slightly, without moving his muzzle from her hand. A soft, warm breeze ruffled her hair, his fur. They stood together for a moment or more until an emu stiff-walked toward them, a bead on Helen's pocket. The kangaroo pulled back, looked into her eyes one more time and blinked. Then, halting and slow, he turned and crossed the field to his nest in the dry grass.

When all the pellets were gone, and the breeze glossed their arms with gooseflesh, the three friends crossed the field and found a gate that bypassed the forest and opened directly into the parking lot next to the gift shop. Minh sat cross-legged on the hood of the station wagon. She waved her left hand and called to them.

"Grannies!" She scrambled down and jerked the back door open. "If we hurry we can make the last ferry tonight and be in Tassie in the morning." She helped Edna climb into the backseat. "Let's go grab your stuff and beat feet to Melbs."

Chapter Twenty-six

No Help. No Help at All
County Cork, Ireland

Most of the people in the small village, the one in County Cork, the one close to Blarney Castle, were not helpful. Not even when Edna's daughters offered them cash, American dollars, for information.

Joan and Suzanne asked at the bakery; they went to the church; they stopped at the local bed and breakfast. "Four old women traveling? One of them quite large? One the size of a bird? Someone must have seen them."

"Maybe." Mrs. Doolin scrunched her face in thought. "But, I mean . . . we *do* get so many tourists through here; don't you know?" She didn't invite them in, but she smiled and held a silver tray toward Joan. "Lemon bar, dear?"

The village priest couldn't recall anything with absolute certainty. "Americans, they do all look alike, you know." However, he offered to pray for the safety of their dear old white-haired mother, wherever she might be. Joan and Suzanne considered the activity a waste of their precious time and declined.

Exasperated, Edna's daughters finally tried the pub. Two elderly fishermen sat outside on a dark green bench under a flower box. Unlike the other residents of the village, they chatted free and friendly-like with the two rather angry women from the States.

"Older ladies, you say?"

"Went up to Belfast, didn't they?"

"I seem to recall that's about the long and short of it. Went to that hotel that was bombed, but fixed up; didn't they?"

"Could be that."

"That it could be. Right. But I'm old. Might have made it up."

Suzanne squinted at the roadmap. "It looks like Belfast is about four hours away," she said. "Let's go."

Joan pulled a bill from her purse and handed it to one of the men.

"Why, thank you, miss. Very generous of you," he said. But she had already turned away.

When the taillights of the rental car were no longer visible, Jamison O'Hennessy and Roger Sommerfield took a short walk through the village. Jamison dropped Joan's five-dollar bill into the poor box outside the church, and then he and Roger shuffled back down the road to the pub, to a pint, and to a hearty laugh with Patrick Tomelson and Charles Michael O'Reilly.

After their expensive, frustrating, and fruitless trip to Ireland—including a wild goose chase from Cork to Belfast—Edna's daughters turned to Uncle Sam for assistance.

"What do you mean there isn't anything you can do? You're the United States *government*, and our mother is a *citizen.*" Joan held the phone out far enough for Suzanne to hear.

The representative from the State Department explained, for the third time, that their mother had completed all the necessary and legal paperwork required in Florida and that she carried a valid passport along with the appropriate visas needed for travel abroad. Since she had not committed a crime, had not been diagnosed with Alzheimer's or dementia, and was not suspected of any breach of national security, well, she—their mother—was in fact, free to move about the world as she wished.

"You people . . . you people are horrible." Suzanne snatched the phone away from her sister. "And incompetent. Just see if you ever get any more campaign financing money from *this* family." She slammed the receiver down.

"Damn government," Joan said. "No help at all. And that Director, that ass . . . Stimpson or whatever his name is . . . no help either." She wrung her hands. "So now what?"

Suzanne set her jaw, crossed her arms. "Now," she said, "it's time to turn the screws on that stupid girl."

Chapter Twenty-seven

The Spirit of Tasmania
Bass Strait, Australia

The setting sun splashed a blast of copper light against the hull of the *Spirit of Tasmania* as the stately ferry pulled from its berth and pointed south for a journey across Bass Strait.

Due, in part, to the fact that the ladies habitually left their bags packed and ready to go before leaving their rooms, and to the fact that Minh kept the gas pedal flat on the floor all the way to Melbourne, they managed to slide into line at the ferry terminal with a good seven minutes to spare. Minh locked the car and then she and the ladies set out to find their cabins and to freshen up before dinner aboard.

The roll of the boat required a sort of crab-like, sideways two-step to negotiate the long passageways. Helen stretched both arms toward the walls to steady herself. Her satchel hung from one arm, her heavy handbag from the other. She still wore her hat with its bobbing corks.

"You look like you're drunk," Mattie said.

"Look at yourself. Weaving down these halls in your dress and combat boots. If anyone ever looked like a drunken sailor woman, Mattie-Girl, it's you."

They kept up the banter until they found their cabin, a few doors down from Minh's. Helen turned to the girl. "Give us

about three-quarters of an hour," she said. "We'll meet you upstairs in the cafeteria. Don't bring your pocketbook. Dinner is on
us."

Their cabin housed two twin bunk beds and a built-in table
with one straight chair. A bathroom cramped the shower, sink,
and commode together in an area the size of a standard toilet stall
at the Restful Palms.

"It's like a dollhouse," Edna said. "All miniature."

Mattie bit her lower lip and eyed the top bunks. "We're gonna
have to draw straws."

"Oh, no need." Helen reached up and tossed her satchel on
one of the top bunks. "I'm tallest. 'Sides, I did like climbin'
when I was a girl. Used to climb a willow in our front yard. Sit
there for hours reading books. Did most of my studying up in that
old tree." She glanced at the narrow berths. "We should be happy
we're not sharin' one of these doll beds tonight." She grinned
and poked her elbow into Mattie's side. "If we did, we would be
drawin' straws, for sure."

After a quick peek at the cafeteria, they all agreed on the formal dining salon. Expensive, true, but worth it—dark mahogany
walls, red velvet chairs, white linen, and bone china. Rather than
bright lights and pop music, globes of frosted pink lit the salon,
and nondescript jazz soothed jangled nerves.

Helen splurged and bought a carafe of red wine for the table. Mattie and Edna sprang for a tray of mixed appetizers. Minh offered to buy dessert for everyone, but the ladies waved her off.

"You're doing all the driving." Helen patted Minh's cast. "Least we can do is treat you to a fancy dinner."

While they waited for the wine, they told Minh all about the Wild Animal Park and showed her the photos they'd taken. She squinted at the phone. "You grannies are so cool," she said. "All my friends at uni are jealous 'cause I get to hang with you. Everybody is following your Facebook page." She pushed the handle of a fork under her cast and scratched. "Oh yeah, that reminds me. My father saw the picture of us with all our stuff packed into Myrtle. He wants to know how you guys can travel so light. Mum has a ton of luggage and expects him to carry it." She made a face. "Sometimes he even pays porters to lug Mum's things around. You guys only carry your purses and those little bags."

The three friends looked at each other. Helen and Mattie smirked. Edna stifled a giggle and blushed.

Minh tilted her head in question.

"Simple," Mattie said. "We share."

Minh still looked confused.

"It really is simple," Helen said. "We divide up all the things we use every day: toothpaste, shampoo, face cream, you know, the basics. Everyone carries one or two things, and we share."

"You share *everything*?"

"Except we have our separate toothbrushes and deodorant," Edna said.

"And lipstick," Helen added. "Some things you have to carry on your own."

"But what about your clothes? Your bags are so small."

"I can answer that," Edna waggled one finger in the air. "Shampoo." She sat back, clearly pleased with herself.

"But . . ."

"It works like this," Mattie said. "We each wear one set of clothes and carry a second set. If we can't use the soap in the hotel, we use shampoo to wash our clothes. When one outfit is dirty, we wash it out in the hotel sink and wear the other one. We can go for weeks like this." She picked a large pink shrimp from the appetizer tray, bit it in two, and swallowed the first half.

"You mean only two pairs of underpants? And shoes?"

Helen nodded. "One to wear, one to wash. One pair of shoes." She smiled at her young friend. "When you get older, things don't matter so much. And bags feel heavy no matter what you put in them. The less we carry, the farther we can go." She looked at Mattie in her housedress—the fabric worn so thin it threatened to tear. "And the more adventures we can have."

"That's so freakin' rad," Minh said.

The waiter arrived with the wine, poured, took their orders, and with a quick bow, disappeared. Helen held her glass high. "This is a celebration day." Her hand trembled, and her eyes misted over. "After all these long years, why, I've finally seen those kangaroos. Even felt their fur." She touched her finger to the corner of one eye. "Today I visited the most wonderful place on this good earth."

"Yes, indeed." Mattie held her glass up. "This was a great day." She smiled at Minh. "A toast to you, dear, for helping us."

Minh blushed and reached for her cell phone. She snapped a shot of Helen, glass held high—face aglow.

"To Minh and the kangaroos and all those other animals, too," Edna said.

Minh sat the phone down and lifted her wine. "To the outrageous *women*." She emphasized the last word and nodded to Helen.

"About time," Mattie muttered.

Glasses clinked.

Over dinner, the ladies shared stories about Florida and their lives in America. Minh told them about her classes at the university and about her crush on Trevor. They agreed with her; he was the more charming of the two. Although, to be fair, Ben did have his high points.

Comfortable with their company and warm with wine, Minh asked the ladies questions—questions her friends didn't have enough life experience to answer, and questions she could never ask her mother. She asked about marriage and childbirth, and how it felt when children grew up and left home. Minh even asked the question all the girls at school wondered—can women still have sex when they . . . um, you know, get old? The ladies answered every inquiry, though their take on several questions varied, which led to lively debates and a good deal of laughter.

It must be true; joy is contagious. The other diners in the formal salon lingered longer than planned, ordered more wine, and they too, laughed. The waiter brought a half carafe to the table and refilled their glasses. "Compliments of the house," he said.

The mood was upbeat and light until Minh asked Mattie about her family. "Were you married? Kids?"

A small, dark cloud drifted over them as Mattie shared that she'd lost her daughter, her young son, and her husband, all during the same year. She didn't say how—just that they'd all gone within three months of each other. Mattie closed her eyes for a moment. "That was a rough one," she said. Then she opened her eyes, cleared her throat, and waved her hand in the air, motioning for the waiter and brushing the cloud away. "Let's order something really, really fattening," she said.

The moment of gloom faded, and the laughter resumed as they divided dessert four ways: a triple-decker Death by Chocolate affair complete with two large scoops of French vanilla ice cream, chocolate sprinkles, and four maraschino cherries.

After their meal, they decided to help their digestion by taking a stroll around the boat. But after ten minutes of crashing into walls and banging against railings, they elected to plant themselves in one place. Minh, who had much stronger sea legs, trounced up to her cabin to get her computer while the ladies settled into stable, overstuffed chairs in the lounge on the third deck.

"Grannies, check it out." Minh placed her laptop on a table where they could all see the screen. "We have free Wi-Fi on this boat. I get to show you guys your Facebook page and the video of Granny D in Ireland." She hit a few keys. "Now watch." She pushed one more button, and then sat back, far enough to give them a good view, but close enough to grab her computer if the boat made a sudden lunge. She crossed her arms and smiled. The ladies scooched in closer to the screen.

The faint but unmistakable strains of "Whiskey in the Jar" piped from the computer's tiny speakers. There, on the screen, big as . . . big as eleven inches on the diagonal, was Dolores. Dancing. She held the fabric of her skirt in one hand and swished it from side to side as she hopped and twirled. Her other hand gripped the fingers of Charles Michael O'Reilly, who stood on his toes and whirled her around.

"Oh, my." Edna slapped her hand to her mouth.

"Lordy." Helen shook her head.

"Wow." Mattie grinned and tapped her boot in time to the music.

They stared at the screen, mesmerized. The video ran a full three minutes. By the time they watched it through twice, a throng of fellow passengers had crowded around the computer with them. Minh couldn't stop smiling. After watching Dolores dance for the third time, she clicked on related YouTube videos. Videos of young people in Canada, Scotland, and New York City, all dancing the *Granny D*.

A video from Japan showed an animated Hello Kitty figure dressed in boots and a green hat jumping about. One short clip featured street kids skateboarding to a hip-hop rendition of the traditional Irish tune.

As the videos played, two couples spontaneously twirled into an onboard version of the *Granny D*. They lurched and stumbled with the jerking motion of the boat. The other passengers whistled and cheered. Edna continued to stare, her mouth now covered with both hands.

Helen kept repeating, "Lordy, Lordy."

Before the start of one video, a promo urged viewers to tune in next Wednesday when Dr. Phil would discuss the psychology of seniors who break out and take chances. *Senior Adventures: Daring or Dementia?* Four p.m. Eastern Central Time. In the background, two young girls held a sign:

Go, Grannies, Go!

Mattie wasn't sure if she should feel proud or sneak back to the cabin and hide.

When the other passengers finally drifted away, Minh clicked on more keys and found their Facebook page. The ladies sat in wonder as she scrolled through photo after photo of all the places they'd been, doing all the things they'd done. Some of the pictures were the ones they'd sent to Katie, but many more were new to them, taken by total strangers, shared with the whole world.

"Oh look." Mattie pointed to the picture Rebecca snapped in Wisconsin. It was the photo of Rose and Reverend Clarenbach toasting with snifters of brandy. "She was happy then."

Helen swallowed hard and looked down. She pretended to search for something in her handbag.

"That's where we live." Edna pointed to a shot of Roger Simpson attempting to hide his face behind his briefcase as he scrambled toward the door of the Restful Palms Retirement Home. A gaggle of cell phone photo snapping people crowded the front lawn. One man held a large video camera and filmed as a young woman chased Simpson with a microphone. In the background, the building looked flat, industrial, and lonely.

"Hard to believe that's home," Mattie said. She chewed on her lower lip.

"Katie!" Edna waved to the screen. They huddled together to take a closer look at the photo of Katie and three other girls—all with dreadlocks, piercings, and million dollar smiles. They held a poster board painted in bright colors, decorated with glitter and bits of string.

WE LOVE YOU, GRANNIES!

"Katie's cool." Minh nodded and clicked through more photos. "Here's a fun one." She nudged Edna.

"Oh no." Edna blushed. Someone, some total stranger, posted a shot of the man on top of Blarney Castle, giving her a hug. "Who can see these pictures?" She turned to Minh.

"That's the great thing," Minh said. "Everyone. Anyone. The whole planet can travel along with you guys." She tapped the down arrow. "And see, all these people who like you, and all these people who put comments under your pictures." She focused on the screen. "Looks like you have over . . . oh my God!"

Minh took her glasses off, huffed on the lenses and wiped them on her T-shirt. She put them back on and leaned in toward the screen. "Yep, that's right. Over 650,000 friends—worldwide." She shook her head. "This is so sweeeet!"

Before leaving the lounge for their cabins, the four women spent another forty minutes scrolling through digital photos. Minh read the posted comments out loud. Over and over again, they wondered at the pictures of total strangers wearing leprechaun hats and combat boots; pictures of strangers smiling and holding signs offering words of encouragement to the "grannies." The ladies did not completely understand all of it, didn't get how this Facebook stuff worked, but they agreed that there was something magical about the whole thing. Yes, something magical, and later Mattie would confide to Helen, maybe something sinister, as well.

Chapter Twenty-eight

It took several minutes for Josephine to answer the knock. Her left knee bothered her a great deal these days—so much so that the physical therapist had replaced her cane with a walker. The walker took some getting used to.

"Mrs. Tarpin?" The orderly craned his neck and tried to see past her. Josephine followed his gaze. Wearing only boxer shorts and a necktie, Tobias struck a Napoleonic pose on top of their dining table.

"Tobias. How in the world did you . . . Get down! Right now!" She turned to the teenager. "Help me. *Please.*"

The orderly bolted into the room, dropped his laptop on the sofa, and scrambled onto the table. Together, he and Josephine managed to coax Tobias down from the table and maneuver him into his wheelchair. The teen fastened a restraining strap around the old man's waist and then stood back, arms at his side. Josephine exhaled.

"Thank you." She leaned on the walker, wheezed as she caught her breath. She thought for a moment and then asked, "What was it that you wanted?"

"I, ah . . ." He scratched at what was perhaps the start of his first beard. "I found that YouTube video you wanted to see. Do you still want me to set it up?"

The young man moved the wheelchair closer to the sofa so that both Josephine and Tobias could see the screen. He balanced his computer on the edge of a cushion, pressed play, and waited while the couple watched the video. At Josephine's request, he pressed play a second time, stood back and waited again. Then he asked if they'd like to see it a third time.

Josephine said, "No."

She grasped the handles of her walker, pulled herself up, made her way to the table, fished a dollar bill from her handbag, gave it to the teenager, and asked him to leave. Josephine closed the door and clumped her walker back to the sofa. She lowered herself to the cushion where the boy's computer had been, the space still warm from the machine. She released a long sigh, closed her eyes, and slumped against the rear of the sofa.

"Do you wish you'd gone with them?"

Josephine jolted upright. Had she heard correctly? She stared at her husband. Tobias rarely had moments of lucidity anymore. She swallowed, leaned toward him, and placed her hand on his arm. She searched his face. His eyes met hers, his gaze soft, tender. After a moment, she shook her head no. "I would never want to be without you," she said.

Tobias slapped his left hand on his thigh. His lips stretched into a crooked grin. "Hot diggity, Eleanor," he said. "Happy days *are* here again."

She sighed and pushed herself from the sofa, her smile both gentle and wan. "Do you want me to get Mr. Churchill on the line, dear?"

Chapter Twenty-nine

A Town Called Penguin
The State of Tasmania

She planned to get up in the night, to walk the decks, to feel the chill wind on her skin, to breathe the sea air. But Mattie slept deep and dreamless all through the night. She didn't stir until the cabin lights came on and the announcement sounded:

Disembarkment in thirty minutes.

They skipped coffee and met Minh on the car deck where she wiped salt spray from the car's windshield. The big boat bumped against a piling as another announcement blared:

Welcome to Tasmania. You may now start your engines.

"I know this place is part of Australia, but it sure feels like a different country." Edna looked up from the souvenir map she'd found on the ferry. "Greener. Prettier somehow." They buzzed along the Bass Highway toward Ulverstone. An early morning mist played hide and seek with sloping hills and stands of stringy-bark gum trees, silver wattle, and pencil pines. Sheep rubbed against wooden fences while lambs, new and wobbly, learned to prance.

Minh turned off the highway and slowed as they entered the city. "We could have breakfast here," she said. "There are lots of restaurants. Chains mostly. Maybe . . . probably . . . a Macca's."

"Macca's?" Edna said.

"Oh, you know, McDonald's, The Golden Arches. But it's not much farther to Penguin." She breathed out and then added, "That is if you grannies can wait."

Mattie reached forward and tapped Minh on the shoulder. "Keep your foot on the gas, girlie. Cause that's the way we roll."

Helen tried to stifle her laugh as she swiveled around to wink at Mattie. "Margaret Lynn Snorgenson, where on earth did you learn to talk like that?" The two women high-fived over the back seat. Minh chuckled, shook her head, and turned at the next intersection.

After a quick check of Edna's map, they drove west on a two-lane road that bordered the sea. The sun, now bright, chased the mist away and threw diamonds on waves that crashed against sharp black rocks snugged along the shore. Helen rolled her window down; Mattie did the same. With all the windows open, crisp, clean air rushed through the car and teased the corks on Helen's hat into a swirling frenzy.

Twenty minutes later, Minh pulled into a spot across from the Penguin Café. "Look at this place," Mattie said. She stood by the car and looked around the town. "Everything is named Penguin." She pointed toward the Penguin Butcher, the Penguin Dry Goods Store, and the Penguin Bicycle Shop. All of the store windows displayed painted penguins. Street signs, even the Please Pick Up After Your Dog signs, featured smiling penguins. The trash cans, shaped like birds with open beaks, stood ready to receive rubbish.

"Fun, huh?" Minh bobbed her head and smiled wide. "It's my favorite place in all of Australia. Except, of course, for the surf beaches. Come on, let's get breakfast."

Their meal included pancakes in the shape of penguins, a blend of "penguin juice" (orange and cranberry), and poached penguin eggs. This last item caused concern until the waitress assured them the eggs came from local chickens. "Happy, free-range chickens," she added.

After breakfast, they walked the length of the main street— Penguin Boulevard, explored shops, and spent a great deal of time in the Penguin Tourist Information Bureau where they met the docent and learned about the tiny blue birds that afforded the village its identity.

Her name badge read Penny. A black skirt, white shirt, and black sweater stretched to cover her ample figure. She looked to Mattie as if she might have penguins for parents, or at least for distant cousins.

Penny smiled at the ladies and handed each of them a complimentary postcard as she presented her often-rehearsed lesson. "In the season, our fairy penguins come in at night, right after sunset. They wait in the water until it's dark so predators don't see them shuffle across the sand." She went on to list the names of seventeen different species and to relate dozens of facts about penguin life. And she even described, in somewhat embarrassing detail, their dating and mating habits.

"Will they come out tonight?" Helen said. She examined a display of penguin stickpins and wondered if one might look good on her hatband.

"Oh yes." Penny stretched her arms wide as if to encompass the whole penguin universe. "They'll be out in full force to-night." She stalled for dramatic effect, a technique she'd learned in the Adult Education course titled Volunteers as Teachers. Guessing the drama at its height, she continued. "They come in groups called rafts. You only have to sit still and wait. You won't be disappointed."

"Why do they come out of the water?" Edna asked. Despite all the photos, paintings, and plastic reproductions of small blue birds, she could not shake the thought of man-sized, tuxedo-wearing creatures waddling in military formation up from the beach to the café. This image disturbed her.

"They're heading home, of course, to their burrows in the sand dunes." Penny beamed, pleased to have all the answers. "Of course, some of them, you see, don't have their own burrows. They live in the boxes the Wildlife Service constructed for them."

"Government housing," Mattie said. She edged toward the door. She'd reached the end of her interest in the life and times of fairy penguins, or any other penguins, or in all honesty, any other birds.

Penny winced, but continued to describe penguin burrow construction. When she finished, she stepped back and waited for any additional questions her audience might have. Mattie decided that there could not be a single fact about these birds that Penny did not know, or share. To her great relief, the others didn't have any further questions and so, with words of thanks and a promise to watch the fairies dance in from the sea, the ladies stepped from the classroom of the Penguin Tourist Information Bureau into the relative quiet of the boulevard.

"Maybe a little too much information," Mattie said when they were finally free.

Helen nodded. "Much too much." She shielded her eyes from the sun and pointed across the street to a poured-cement penguin two stories high.

"Let's go take a picture in front of that statue. Katie will get a kick out of that one for sure."

A local woman out for a walk with her fat, elderly corgi, stopped and snapped photos with their phone as Edna, Helen, Mattie, and Minh posed together in front of the giant bird. The corgi, most likely happy for the pause, lowered to the walkway and promptly fell asleep.

As she framed the pictures, the woman offered all sorts of suggestions on things to do along the coastal highway, places to go, museums to visit, restaurants to try. "If you have some extra time, you should stop at Buttons Beach." She handed the phone to Mattie and smiled. "It's a lovely stretch of sand, and the weather is perfect today, you'll have a special time."

Chapter Thirty

Every Little Ting – Tampa, Florida

"Let's put this one in." Katie flipped her phone around so her friends, Tanya, Abbey and Liz, could see. "I think it's super cute."

"Oh yeah, that's darling." Tanya clicked keys and transferred the photo to the web page. "Help me think of a caption."

The four girls leaned toward the screen and studied the photo of Minh and the ladies standing in front of a giant painted penguin. Minh sat at the statue's feet. Mattie and Helen each held a flipper. Edna blew the bird a kiss.

"I just love my grannies." Katie sighed. "All of them." She touched her finger to the computer. The image expanded, filled the screen with the smiles of Mattie, Helen, and Edna.

Liz hit a key and a shot of Dolores, dressed in a peach suit, holding a white bakery box appeared. In the photo, Dolores glowed. "It's like they're free," Abbey said. "They're finally doing what they want. They're finally doing what makes them happy, even though they are . . . like . . . you know, ancient. Most people never do that. Even college kids don't do that. Know what I mean?"

Katie nodded. "My dads . . . they did what they wanted. They loved each other, and they loved me, and they didn't care what anyone thought. They especially didn't care what their relatives thought. My granny was always on their side, and I think that pissed everybody off." She swallowed, looked past the computer screen and stared, unfocused, at a concert poster on the far wall.

Tanya and Abbey wrapped their arms around her; Liz clicked to another shot of the grannies. They posed together next to a bird-shaped trash bin, in front of the Penguin Bakery. In the photo, their arms were linked, and the ladies were laughing.

Katie leaned into Abbey. "Maybe we should go on an adventure," she said. "The four of us, best friends. You know . . ."

They continued to click through photos and to muse about adventures, and freedom, and friendship. The room smelled of sweet smoke and musky perfume. A bottle of red wine sat almost empty on the countertop. The lilting strains of Bob Marley softened all sharp edges. *'No worry . . . 'cause every little ting, gonna be all right.'* Outside, a gentle Florida rain washed the streets and polished broad-leafed palms to shiny perfection. A sleepy Sunday afternoon with close friends and a labor of love. Until the knocking, the pounding, on the door.

"Katie. Open this door. Right now. This instant." Suzanne hunched under a newspaper she'd grabbed from the car. Joan pulled her coat up around her neck.

"Oh shit. It's them." Katie shut her laptop down. The other girls grabbed and stashed contraband, then slipped out the back door. Katie opened a window and turned a fan on high. Suzanne continued to pound on the front door until Katie, reluctantly, invited her aunts in from the rain.

"So here's the deal." Joan laid down the terms while Suzanne sniffed the air and eyed the rainbow-colored sheet dividing the studio apartment into two rooms. "We know that you helped our mother get out of that place. And we know, *that you know*, how to find her."

Katie held her hands out, palms up. "Hey, I didn't . . ."

"Don't you lie to us missy." Suzanne jabbed her finger at Katie. Katie took two steps back. "We want to know where she is and we want to know right now."

Katie smirked and swayed from side to side. "Or else?"

Joan raised her eyebrows. "You want to know what else? I'll tell you, you little freeloading freak . . ."

Suzanne interrupted. "Simple. You are completely cut off from all of your college money. No more trust fund. Nada. And you are on your own. We have had enough of you."

"You can't do that," Katie said, still rocking from one foot to the other. "My dads put that money aside for me so I could go to art school. It's my money."

Joan crossed her arms and gloated. "Sorry, missy. But you are wrong. Your 'dads,' as you call them, gave us control over that money until you're twenty-five."

"That's right," Suzanne said. She, too, crossed her arms. "We can do whatever we think is in your best interest until then. And we think having your grandmother here, in a retirement home, where you can visit her on Sunday afternoons, is best for you. Better for you than," she sniffed the air again, "whatever it is you typically do on Sunday afternoons. So . . ."

Joan took a step forward. "So. If you don't help us get her back here, we are going to hire someone who will. And guess where we're going to get the money?" The two sisters glared at Katie. Triumphant.

Katie stopped moving. She stared at them, slack-jawed. Finally, she found her voice. "But she's happy. How could you want her to go back to that place? *She's having fun.* She's . . ."

Joan cut her off. "Look, she's our mother, and whether you believe us or not, we love her and want her to be safe. We do want the best for her. But she's a doddering old fool. Probably has dementia or worse. Our mother is senile and has no idea if she's happy or miserable."

Suzanne nodded in agreement. "It's our job to take care of her, and she's probably in danger, wherever she is." The three women stood silent for a few moments. Joan and Suzanne dripped rainwater on the carpet. Katie gathered her focus, her center.

"Aunties," she said, "my granny is fine. She is happy. I'm not going to do anything, ever, to hurt her." She reached up, took the end of a dreadlock and twirled it around one finger. "If you hunt her down and lock her up, that will be the end of her."

Joan started to speak, but Katie stopped her.

"You want to steal the money my dads entrusted you with? Your Karma is what it is. But I'm not part of your Karma." Then, with a beatific smile, she pressed her palms together and bowed deep. "Namaste, Aunties."

Chapter Thirty-one

The small troupe of friends journeyed slowly along the highway taking their time. They pointed out particularly pretty stretches of scenery, laughed at the antics of crows squabbling in blue gums and Blackwood trees, and when something struck their fancy, they stopped. A short visit to a craft gallery to look at student artwork, a brief bathroom break at the High Tides Bar where Minh discussed surfing with a fellow twice her age. The man smelled of beer and cigarettes. He stepped close to her as they spoke and touched her arm or brushed his fingers across her shoulder to make his points. The ladies watched for a couple of minutes and then intervened. Politely citing the need to continue with their tour of Tasmania, they pulled Minh away from the man.

Still full of penguin pancakes, they decided to skip lunch and head straight for the beach. A sign at the entrance of the parking lot indicated that Buttons Beach was both people and dog-friendly. No doubt the old corgi had napped here.

Minh led the way along the narrow footpath to the beach. Shells and chunks of driftwood littered the trail. Tufts of sharp-bladed beach grass marked the edge of the route. Bundles of tall grasses and scrawny brush obscured the view of the water until the path ended and the beach stretched like pulled taffy in both directions. Directly in front, Bass Strait glistened.

"Oh my," Edna whispered.

Long, lazy waves the color of pale green jade rolled to shore. Overhead, cirrus clouds traveled fast on the high, cooler breeze. A luminous halo ringed the sun with the shimmer of fish scales.

"I'm takin' my shoes off and wadin' in that ocean," Helen said. She sat on a log and removed a shoe, tucked her sock into its toe, rolled her pant leg up past her knee, and adjusted her hat. Despite the ache in her joints, this was a moment she didn't want to miss.

"Grand idea." Mattie joined her. She kicked off her boots and rolled her housedress under her belt to shorten the length. "You coming, Edna? Minh?"

Edna protected her eyes from the glare. "I don't think so. No cold water wading for me. I want to walk along the beach and look for shells."

Minh shook her head no. "I'm going back to Myrtle to find something to sit on. Be back in a flash."

Mattie and Helen stepped around mounds of kelp and carefully picked their way over piles of jagged rocks. Once at the water's edge, they spontaneously reached for each other's hand, then stepped into the froth and squealed. Holding tight, they moved slowly until they stood in calf-deep water. From a distance, the high waves were as translucent as glass. But here, in the shallows, the water swirled in murky, opaque olive tones. The first wave rumbled over a layer of loose pebbles. It gurgled and pushed forward a thick line of mustard-colored foam that clung to their legs.

"This is so beautiful." Helen let go of Mattie's hand and held her arms out wide. She threw her head back, her face to the sky. "Lordy! Lordy! I am full of your praise today."

Mattie took a step backward as the sea retreated. She didn't like the pull of the water on her legs, and the fact that she couldn't see below the surface frightened her.

"This is great," she said. She feigned indifference. "But I don't like the cold. It's too cold for me." Helen didn't seem to notice when her friend turned and hobbled back to shore.

Mattie wandered down the beach, dipped her toes in the cool, clear water of tide pools and teased tiny crabs into their shells. She found a stone the shape of a heart—burgundy with a line of white quartz—wiped it clean from sand, and dropped it into her pocket. All the while, she fussed at herself.

"You've lived eighty-six years, Margaret Snorgenson, without so much as a broken bone. What made you so fearful of a silly little wave? They wouldn't be following you all over the planet if

they knew you were afraid of water that comes up to your knees."
She tossed a shell into a pool and watched the ripples expand.

"This would be a super place for a picnic." Edna plodded
through the dry sand at the edge of the beach grass. "I wish we'd
thought to pick up something along the way." She turned toward
the water and watched Helen kick her foot in the surf. With each
thrust of Helen's long leg, a puff of foam flew into the wind.
Edna smiled and then searched the beach until she saw Mattie
poking at something with a stick. "I bet they're hungry, too. But
they probably aren't ready to go yet."

"No worries, Little Granny," Minh said. "We passed a grocery not too far back. I'll go get sandwiches or takeaway noodles,
or whatever, and we can have a picnic." She started toward the
trail and then turned back. "Oh. Here. Trev left his towel in the
car. We can all sit on it. It's huge."

Mattie leaned down for a closer look at the dead gull. It lay
belly up with its head corked down, beak forced into the sand.
Feathers fluttered, one wing stretched full, the other tucked in
close.

"What happened to you, buddy?" She poked at the bird with
her stick. A flurry of shiny black bugs skittered from under the
body. Mattie stepped back. "I guess it's freedom time for you,
fellow. Nothing left to lose." She tossed the stick to one side and
trudged up the beach toward the grass.

Edna patted the towel. "Minh found this in the back of the car. Sit."

Mattie groaned as she eased down. "Where is she?"

"She's gone to get us a picnic." Edna picked a string of seaweed from Mattie's leg. "This is the best day ever. Here, in the sun, at the beach." She closed her eyes, tilted her face upward, and let the sun warm her skin.

"You know, Louis would never let us go to the beach. He thought there were too many dangers like sand fleas, rogue waves, and gypsies."

"Gypsies?" Mattie turned to face her. "In Michigan?"

Edna's eyes snapped open. She pursed her lips. Maybe it wasn't gypsies. Maybe it was seagulls that Louis was afraid of, or maybe . . . She couldn't remember. Gypsies just popped out.

Mattie watched her friend. "How are you feeling?" She kept her voice calm.

Edna's lip quivered. "I'm . . . I'm . . ."

Mattie reached over and touched Edna's arm. "You're fine. You're absolutely fine. Everything is perfect, and so are you." She smiled. *Here we go*, she thought. But out loud she said, "Right?"

Edna nodded. She shifted her weight, bent her knees, drew her legs to her chest, and wrapped her arms around them. "Right," she said. "I guess I'm just hungry."

Mattie cleared her throat. She sat up straight and changed the subject. "Helen should get out of that water soon, or she'll catch a cold." She looked toward the shore. "Oh God. No." She pointed to the water, then pushed herself up using Edna's shoulder to get to a standing position.

Helen was on her hands and knees in the shallow surf. Her head hung down. Her body swayed as a wave drenched her, retreated, and slid over her again. Mattie grabbed Edna's hand, helped her stand. They hurried, moved as fast as possible toward the water.

Mattie waded out and circled Helen's waist with her arms. "Please, Helen. Stand." Helen tried to move, but her limbs trembled. She looked up at Mattie, her eyes glazed with pain. She lowered her head and vomited into the froth swirling around her arms.

Mattie panicked. "Edna, get in here. Help me get her out."

Edna searched for a place to sit to untie her shoes.

"Forget your shoes. Help me!" Mattie tugged at Helen. Helen crumpled, her face inches from the water.

"Grannies!" Minh dropped the grocery bag and her backpack and dashed across the sand to the shore. She splashed into the water.

It took all three of them to drag Helen far enough up the beach to be safe from the incoming tide. They propped her in a sitting position. Helen's body quaked. She gulped for air. Her mouth opened and closed like a fish pulled from the sea. Mattie tried to get her to talk, but Helen was not able to speak.

"Look." Edna pointed to Helen's leg where three long welts wrapped around her calf.

"Jellyfish," Minh said. "Shit." She glanced around. "Here, you two hold onto her. I'm going to call for help." She stood. "Don't worry, Black Granny. Help is on the way." She turned and ran up the beach to her backpack.

Helen clutched at her heart. Her eyes rolled back, and her body jerked.

"Helen! Helen!" Mattie shook her.

She was already gone when they strapped the oxygen mask to her face. Still, Australians don't give up easily. They tried. Gave it their best. Edna and Mattie stood off to one side. Salt-soaked cotton clung to bone-thin frames, teeth chattered, and tears rolled down hollowed cheeks. Minh draped the beach towel over their shoulders and stayed close, her left arm around them both. No one noticed the canvas hat drifting away in the slow current. Its corks floated and stretched strings of fishing line, transparent as tentacles.

Chapter Thirty-two

Little Blue Birds

She stayed as long as she could, but eventually Minh needed to return to Melbourne for the start of the school term. Mattie couldn't, or wouldn't, discuss anything, so Edna and Minh made plans without her. Minh promised to pick them up at the ferry dock when they were done in Tasmania. She would drive them to their hotel and later, to the airport and she would help them with reservations or whatever else they needed. Minh programmed her number into their cell phone. Finally, she helped Edna compose and send the sorrow-filled email to Katie.

Edna and Minh stood beside the old station wagon and held each other for a long time before finally pulling apart. They didn't speak, and they didn't wipe their faces—both now slick with tears.

Penny insisted that Mattie and Edna take the spare room above the Penguin Tourist Information Bureau. They would be dry and safe in the state-owned apartment. "Stay as long as you need. No. Don't even think about money. We are all family, helping family."

Edna accepted the situation. She spent her days visiting with the residents of Penguin. Everyone, from the youngest school child to the folks at the Senior Center, knew the story of the grannies, and everyone wanted to both comfort them and to become a part of what looked like a wondrous adventure. Edna loved the visits, and she cherished the people of Penguin, especially the children. But Mattie refused to come out of the apartment. She barely ate, and although her eyes never misted, a dark cloud hung over her like a threatening storm.

"She says her entire body aches. She says she hurts all over." The lines on Edna's face furrowed deep with concern. "Maybe she's got the flu. Maybe we should call a doctor."

"It's not illness," Penny said. "It's grief."

She and Edna shared a table by the window in the Penguin Café. As it had done in Ireland, the sky opened and poured its sorrow. But unlike the gentle drops of the Emerald Isle, the Australian rain pounded down, splat hard against plate glass windows, and hammered onto the sidewalk like a thunderous waterfall hitting rocks. Three days of heavy rain. Three days of waiting. It would be another two, five total, until Helen's ashes would arrive from Hobart.

"I've seen the same thing with the birds," Penny said. "If one of them gets smashed by a car or dragged off by some feral cat, the rest of them go around so sad-faced it breaks my heart." She drizzled a teaspoon of honey into her cup and watched it melt in the steaming tea. She blew across the top, inhaled the warmth.

Edna dipped her spoon into the jar, pulled it out, and slid it into her mouth. She closed her eyes and felt the thick sweet amber melt over her tongue; she tasted sunshine and the hum of bees. "Mmm."

Penny smiled. "It's Tasmanian Leatherwood. Best in the world."

Edna placed her spoon on the saucer and looked across the table at the other woman. "You know, we've gone through this before—lots of times back at Restful Palms. But Mattie's never acted this way. Even when poor Rose passed. Why, we hardly had time to say good-bye to Rose because we had to leave Wisconsin so fast. I knew Mattie was sad then, of course. We all were sad. And I'm sad now. But Mattie . . ."

She watched a young mother hurry across the street, head down, her child's hand gripped tightly. The little girl wore green rubber boots molded into frog faces. She pulled her mother's hand as she tried to stomp in each and every puddle.

Edna smiled. She thought of Joan and Suzanne. Her smile faded. What happened to those little girls? Had she been a burden to them? Were they *really* the adults and was she *really* the child? Should she have been stronger? Stood up to Louis more? The clink of Penny's spoon against her teacup startled Edna from her thoughts. She refocused on her companion.

Penny sighed and took a sip of tea. "I don't know for sure. But I relate life to the penguins. How they view the world—it's so . . . so honest, so natural. They go to work, fish in the deep sea. They play in the surf. They protect each other when they run across the beach. They stick together. They live in their little burrows; some cleaner than others, some more elaborate than others. They make love, have babies, get in arguments, split up, and love again. They grieve when their friends die.

"I don't think they blame themselves or each other. I think they are just little blue penguins, living life the best they can. So . . ." She took a deep breath and exhaled. "So, I don't know what I'm saying. Maybe, you know, give her some time." She reached across the table and took Edna's hand in hers. "The penguins keep going. Your friend will too."

Penny had placed a chair by the front window that overlooked Penguin Boulevard, but Mattie couldn't watch all the smiles, the waves, the neighborly nods. She pushed the chair around to face the back window, the window with a view of the alley.

There were no cars parked in the alley. The hard-packed dirt strip provided just enough room for one vehicle to pass and for a single row of trash cans to line a faded gray fence. On the boulevard, hanging baskets and window boxes exploded in riots of color from marigolds, begonias, petunias, and zinnias. In the alley, everything was gray, including two scrapping cats.

With the floral print of her dress such a close match to the chintz fabric, Mattie all but disappeared as she wrapped her sweater tight, folded her legs beneath her, and sank into the chair's overstuffed cushions. She knew her behavior must seem rude or, at best, peculiar.

Even so, the people of Penguin were kind and caring. Twice a day the cook in the café brought hot meals wrapped in foil. Each morning, the girl at the bakery delivered raisin scones or cinnamon buns to go with the pot of strong coffee Penny brewed before dawn. No one asked for payment.

These people, total strangers, offered to embrace the ladies, to give them solace. These people, whose existence revolved around awkward, twelve-inch-tall birds, had taken her and Edna under their human wings to protect and comfort them in their time of grief. Edna accepted and returned their embrace, but Mattie could not. Instead, she spent her days fading into the chair, watching the rain wash down the alley, and waiting for Helen's ashes.

On the morning of the fifth day, the local doctor hand delivered the urn. Mattie thanked him but did not ask him in for tea. She closed the door behind him, locked it, and then opened the vessel. She removed the plastic bag, tucked it in her satchel, and hid the urn in the back of the cupboard behind the pots and pans. Then, for the first time since that day on Buttons Beach, she left the apartment and went for a stroll around Penguin.

Edna and Penny spotted her and quickly crossed the boulevard to stand with Mattie.

"Oh, do come tonight," Penny said. She searched Mattie's face. "You'll be leaving early tomorrow, so this will be your last chance to see our beautiful birds." Edna, too, looked hopeful. She touched Mattie's shoulder.

Mattie gazed past the two women, past the giant bird statue and past the break wall to the sunlit waters of Bass Strait. She hesitated a moment and then turned to Edna. "I guess we should watch the penguins return from the sea," she said.

Chapter Thirty-three

The Contract – Miami, Florida

"That's pretty pricey, don't you think?'' Suzanne stiffened, narrowed her eyes and glared at the man across the desk. He certainly looked impressive: three-piece suit, expensive tie. His partner stood to the left of his chair. In her black silk shift, she too was dressed to impress. She smelled of Chanel.

Joan sat rigid in the chair next to Suzanne's. This was their sixth attempt to find a private investigator who would travel halfway around the world to find and return their aging—and in their opinion, addled—mother. Citing the legality of the form signed at Restful Palms and all the reasons given by State Department, the other investigators had refused the job. This man and his attractive female partner were the only ones who appeared unperturbed or dissuaded by legal details. But their fees were more than double, almost triple, what the others would have charged if they'd accepted the task.

"It is high." The woman purred her words; calm assured. "But you have to consider our costs: flights, hotels, any equipment we might need for the job."

"Exactly," the man said. "From your experience of searching in Ireland, you know how expensive foreign travel can get. And you knew who you were looking for. We'll be going by photographs." He waited a beat, then added. "From what I understand, we may be your last hope?"

Suzanne bit the inside of her cheek. He had a point. On the other hand, while it was a lot of cash, there was a lot more money at stake.

"Why so much up front?" Joan looked from one to the other. "Why not half now and half . . ."

"Look," he steepled his fingers and leaned back. "That's our policy. Seventy-five percent up front. The rest when you get our text. If we are unsuccessful, you will get a full refund. Minus expenses, of course." He nodded toward the papers in Suzanne's hand. "It's all in the contract."

Chapter Thirty-four

Our Helen – Penguin, Tasmania

The rain had stopped, and the bright Tasmanian sun steamed and then dried the grass in the park adjacent to the beach. Families gathered on blankets spread with picnic food and bottles of good, local wine from Launceston and the Tamar Valley. Children chased each other in games of tag. Young people held hands. Old friends sat on park benches. The temperature remained warm enough to be pleasant, yet cool enough for the comfort of a sweater or the arm of a loved one.

Penny folded a quilt and laid it on the top of the break wall, making a cushion for the ladies. After ensuring their comfort, she crossed the park, eager to share curried egg sandwiches, veggies, hummus, and tumblers of lemonade with her son and his family.

Edna and Mattie split a turkey sandwich and a bottle of carrot juice. As the sun shot its last spike of light across the water, a church bell chimed three times, and the crowd hushed.

One by one, the stars twinkled, and as if by divine direction (maybe it *was* by divine direction), the first raft of fairy penguins emerged from the sea. They grouped together—six or seven of them—shook salt water from their feathers, cocked their heads one way, then another, scanned the beach for predators, and then with calls that sounded like a cross between a wheeze and a coo, made their mad-dash waddle up the beach to the dunes and to the safety of their burrows. The people of Penguin sighed, and smiled, and remained respectfully silent.

The path to the dunes coursed under the wall no more than four feet below where the two friends sat. Raft after raft of the little birds gathered along the water's edge, waited for all the members of their group to assemble, and then made their run for home.

Mattie watched, mesmerized. It seemed that every bird had an individual look, expression, or mannerism. And it occurred to her that if a person spent enough time around these small creatures, it might be possible to identify each one by its personality. She wondered if a person, a mature, observant person, could get a job identifying little blue birds. Might be a fair way to spend one's time. Something to think about. Something to consider.

Edna laid one hand on Mattie's arm and pointed toward the middle of the beach. She leaned in close and whispered. "Look at that one."

Mattie strained to see through the deepening shadows. In the center of a raft, a single penguin stood several inches taller than the others. It waddled along with them, but it moved with a slightly more graceful gait.

"Look at that one," Edna repeated. "That's our Helen. She's come to say goodbye."

Chapter Thirty-five

Ashes to Dust

They called her from the ferry. As promised, Minh was there for them when it docked. Instead of going straight to their hotel, they asked her to take them to the Wild Animal Park for one more short visit. So, once again, Minh sat cross-legged on Myrtle's hood in the parking lot and waited. And once again, a gentle morning breeze blew soft and skin-warm.

Edna followed Mattie along the trail where Helen had seen her first kangaroo. In the distance, a sad-faced old grey rose up and watched them. Mattie clutched the single bag of treats she'd purchased on the way into the park. At a bend in the trail, she turned and handed it to Edna.

"Here," she said. "You stay and feed the little guys. I'll be back real soon."

"Promise?" Edna opened the bag of pellets.

"Promise."

While wallabies and kangaroos gathered around Edna and her bag of food, Mattie wandered along the trail until she found the perfect spot. She paused, breathed in the beauty and peace of the place, and then pulled the plastic bag from her satchel.

Helen fluttered through the gum trees and the iron-buds, through the turpentines and cypress pines. She floated on rays of sunlight, settled on blue flowers, and dusted silver eucalyptus leaves.

Chapter Thirty-six

Time to Go Home – Melbourne,
Australia

Minh drove them to Melbourne and helped them check into a rundown hotel near the airport. Her glasses fogged, but she didn't even try to stop the tears as she hugged them goodbye. Edna wept too, but Mattie remained stoic and dry-eyed. She hugged Minh and thanked her for all the driving and for being such an excellent tour guide. "Helen thought the world of you," she said. "She would have wanted you to have these." She pressed a couple of Helen's jangly bracelets into Minh's palm. This brought on another rush of tears.

Across the street from the hotel, in the window of a small restaurant, a neon sign flickered Open. Though hungry, neither Mattie nor Edna were in the mood to venture out. They took showers and padded around in their nightgowns. They organized and repacked their bags, tossed old brochures, tickets, and receipts, and by seven, turned out the lights.

Edna lay in the dark and entertained herself with a mind game she played a lot these days. It was an activity that gave her comfort although she wouldn't consider sharing it with Mattie or anyone else. She toyed with random images, let them drift into her thoughts, watched them curl and twist as if they were ribbons of film unwinding from a movie reel. Then she watched them dissolve.

Once in a while, she would reach out and grab a stray word, or the colors of a place, or the picture of a face. She would try, as best as she could, to hold onto that word, or place, or face until she could recall what it meant, where it was, or who owned that smile. She would give herself points for what she hoped were correct guesses although she could never quite remember the point count.

Mattie stretched out on her back and tried to rest, but her eyes would not close, and sleep would not come. She stared at the shadows cast by the hotel furniture—a cheap blond-wood dresser and a single straight-backed chair. She exhaled in a huff and rolled to her side, stayed only a moment, then flopped back and faced the ceiling again.

The hotel was not well-insulated. Subdued sounds of a TV program, an argument, laughter, and lovemaking pulsed through the walls. She huffed again.

"Edna?" She cleared her throat. "You awake?"

Edna, stumped by a face intimately familiar yet worn by a complete stranger, was relieved for the distraction. "Yes. Do you need something? Can I get you water or another blanket? They have more blankets in the closet, you know."

"No. No more blankets. I've made a decision, and I wanted you to know."

"Oh?"

"Tomorrow, when we get to the airport, I'm going to cancel our tickets to Egypt. Book us flights to Florida. We're going back to the Restful Palms where we belong."

"Oh."

"Look, I know you wanted to ride a camel. I wanted to sail a ship, but I was wrong to encourage you. All of you: Rose, Dolores, Helen. We were safe and secure. We were old women having lunch and tea and organized trips to the movies and the shopping mall. Our lives were normal. Now, it's just you and me in a shitty little hotel room in Australia. And this is my fault. All of it. We're going home." She curled into a fetal position and pulled the blanket over her head.

Edna remained still for a moment. Then she spoke. "You really shouldn't swear, Mattie."

The wake-up call came at six. Mattie groaned and snapped on a light. At first, she thought she must be dreaming. She blinked, rubbed her eyes. But no, it was not a dream. It was Edna, in the flesh. She sat in the straight chair next to the door fully dressed with her satchel packed and ready at her feet. Mattie propped up on her elbows. "Edna?"

Edna nodded. Her handbag lay on her lap. She gripped the strap with both hands.

"What are you doing?"

Edna's voice wavered, but she held her back straight, her head high, and stuck her chin out. "I am going to Egypt," she said.

Mattie sat up. She clutched a pillow to her chest. "Now, Edna. We discussed this last night. We're going to change the flight this morning. No Egypt. Back to Restful Palms. Remember? You probably don't remember."

Edna stood up, slowly, with great care. She twisted around, placed her purse on the chair, and turned back to Mattie. She put her hands on her hips, swayed a bit, then reached out and grasped the edge of the television for support.

"You, Mattie Snorgenson, might be going back to Restful Palms. But I am going to Egypt." She pointed her finger at Mattie. "You don't have the right to take this away from me." She took a step forward. "All my life people have been telling me what to do. My parents, Louis, my girls—they all told me what to do. Took my dreams away from me. It was my fault. I let them do it. But, no more. Not you, or my daughters, or anyone else is going to take this away from me. I am going to Egypt, to ride my camel." She stomped her foot. It made a muffled thump on the carpet. She turned, picked up her purse, turned again, and sat down.

Mattie stared at her friend. "Wow," she said.

Chapter Thirty-seven

Under the Veil – Emirates Airline

"Excuse me, ladies." A dark-skinned man dressed in a black uniform leaned over Edna. She stopped her inspection of the safety information card and looked up at him.

"Ladies, I need you to gather your belongings and come with me. Please." He neither smiled nor frowned. His face an unreadable mask. Handsome, but without expression.

"Why?" Mattie said. "Here are our boarding passes." She held the papers out to him. "I'm pretty sure we're in the right seats."

"I need you to come with me. Now."

Edna reached for her seatbelt.

"Our bags are in the compartments." Mattie pushed her elbow down on Edna's arm. Edna froze. "And we're all settled. I'd like to know what this is about."

The man's mouth barely moved, but Mattie thought she caught a slight, swift smile. "I shall collect your bags, madam."

"It's Suzanne and Joan," Edna said. "They found us. We're done for now." Her hands trembled as she bent to pull her purse from under the seat in front of her.

"Don't say anything, Edna." Mattie moved closer to her and whispered. "Let me do the talking." Edna looked back at Mattie and started to respond, but stopped herself. What could she say? The adventure was over. Her daughters had won.

The man followed them up the long, narrow aisle. He carried their satchels, one under each arm.

Ladies and Gentlemen, may I have your attention. We have a few more things to prepare in the main cabin and then the Captain will give the all clear. Please power down your electronics . . .

The announcement droned on and on, but the other passengers on Emirates Flight 405 did not listen. Instead, they gaped as the serious-faced steward escorted two elderly women from their seats; something you don't see every day. They whispered and speculated.

"Spies?" one asked.

"Smugglers," someone said.

"Probably drugs," said another.

Mattie felt their eyes bore into her back, row after row.

Once they'd passed the flight attendants' station and stepped into the first-class cabin, the man stopped and pulled a thick black curtain behind him separating those with money from those with lots and lots of money. He moved past the first couple of seats and then stopped. Edna and Mattie continued to slog up the aisle.

"Excuse me, ladies," the man said.

Mattie turned.

"These are your seats." He nodded toward two spacious chairs—the ones that recline all the way down and have linen and real pillows. He stretched up, opened the overhead compartment, and carefully placed their satchels inside.

"Edna. Stop."

Edna was so busy preparing what she would say to her daughters, so busy thinking of how she would have to grovel before them and beg for forgiveness, that she didn't hear the man or even Mattie. But she stopped when Mattie grabbed the back of her sweater and gave it a tug. She turned.

"Ladies?" He offered a formal bow and gestured toward the seats.

"How?" Mattie chose the one closest to the aisle.

Edna slipped past her and settled in next to the window. She crooked her neck and stared up at the man. "Why?"

He didn't answer, offered only a brief smile, ensured that their seatbelts were fastened, and then glided up the aisle to attend to another passenger.

"Whatever has happened?" Edna whispered to Mattie.

Mattie shook her head. "No friggin idea," she said.

The captain banked first to port and then to starboard to give passengers on both sides of the plane a view of the iconic symbol of Sydney. "It does look like a ship," Edna said. "An enormous ship. Look at all those sails."

Mattie could not speak. Her heart stuck in her throat.

They were halfway through a dessert of date meringue pie and miniature cups of strong dark coffee, when a dignified man in a business suit approached them. A young girl followed him. Except for the scarf draped over her head and across her face, she dressed like any other teenage girl: blue jeans, long-sleeved T-shirt, running shoes with pink laces. Although only her eyes showed from behind the veil, her smile was tangible.

"Excuse me, ladies." The man bowed, then straightened with grace. "So sorry to disturb your meal. I shall be brief. My name is Youssef Samaha. In-house Counsel for Barclay's Bank, Egypt. I would like to introduce you to my daughter, A'ishah." The girl extended her hand. Mattie reached up and although she didn't know why, she squeezed rather than shook the girl's hand. A'ishah's eyes sparkled.

"My daughter has a passion for Facebook," he said. "She is good with computers." He laid his hand on the girl's shoulder. "I suppose it is foolishness, but harmless." He gazed at his child with obvious pride. "She has followed you ladies on your journey."

Edna's eyes widened, and she slapped her hand over her mouth.

"Oh! Oh, not in a bad way. Please. Do not fret." The man furrowed his brow. "We only mean good." He pressed the palms of his hands together and rushed on. "When my daughter saw you pass through the cabin she recognized you. She asked me, convinced me, to upgrade your seating. The flight is long, and you will be more comfortable here."

"Oh my." Edna stared up at the man. She glanced from him to his daughter.

The man appeared confused. "You are the . . . the . . ." He turned to the girl and leaned down. She rose up on her toes, cupped her mouth through the veil and whispered in his ear. "Ah, yes." He turned back to Mattie. "You *are* The Grannies. Yes?"

"I wish people would stop calling us that." Mattie leaned back in her seat and pulled a blanket up to her chin.

"Calling us what?"

"Grannies. We're women, not grannies. I'm not even a grandmother. And Katie is your adopted granddaughter."

"Oh, they don't mean anything by it." Edna picked a fleck of lint from the blanket. "But, since you bring it up, I wondered why your daughter didn't have children." She thought about what she'd said then added, "Or, maybe you did tell me, and it slipped my mind?"

Mattie shook her head. "No, she didn't have any children. Although I would have welcomed the sound of little ones in the house." The cabin lights dimmed. Edna reached out from under her blanket and touched Mattie's arm.

"Tell me more about your daughter," she said.

Mattie sighed. She didn't talk much about her daughter or even much about her own life. But, here she was—here they were, just her and her friend, her last friend, on a plane headed to some country with a strange name, and then on to Egypt to ride a camel. If they didn't get caught first. *Maybe it was time to remember the past.* She looked over at Edna.

Edna blinked and smiled at her. "Go on," she said. "Tell me."

Chapter Thirty-eight

Mattie's Story

"I guess I had a pretty normal childhood. I mean, for those times. Not much money, but a house full of love. My parents laughed a lot, with each other, and with me. We went to church picnics and Fourth of July parades, and we made presents for each other at Christmas; dad carved dolls out of wood, mom sewed dresses for them. I made clay ashtrays for my dad's Pall Malls and clay bowls for mom to put her wedding ring in at night.

"Now, thinking back, I don't think she ever took her ring off, but she kept all those little bowls on the nightstand for as long as I can remember. Even after I was grown, she kept those bowls by her bed.

"Mom and I baked cookies, and we popped corn and strung it on the tree. No brothers or sisters, but I had a cat named Mr. Muffels, and my father had two dogs. Hunting dogs. In the summers, my mother and I worked together in the garden. She used to take my hand in hers and squint at my fingers.

" 'I don't know why the rest of them are so pink when your thumb is so green.' That was our joke. But it was true. Flowers flourished under my care; columbines, Shasta daisies, and dahlias. Every year I entered the 4-H Club competition, and in my senior year of high school, I won a scholarship to the first two years of teachers' college. I wanted to be a science teacher. Wanted to teach children how things grew, how nature worked.

"The college was too far away for me to live at home so my dad made a trade with a woman who owned a boarding house by the school. He fixed her roof. It took him every free minute all summer long to do it. But in exchange, I had a place to stay during the school year.

"I'd never been away from my parents before, and at first, I was afraid. But pretty soon, I loved it. Loved learning. Loved reading science books. Loved all my teachers. My grades were perfect. Then I met Lance."

Mattie stopped. She closed her eyes and sorted through memories of the tall, handsome man who swaggered and called himself Lance, and Captain, and "The Man." Lance, a few years older and so much smarter. Lance, who swept her off her feet. Lance, the dashing man, afraid of nothing—the man who bought her ice cream sundaes and real satin ribbons for her hair. The man who could only visit her at odd times, sometimes in the afternoons, sometimes in the evenings, and never two days in a row. Lance, the man who showed her how to sneak into a barn loft without being noticed. She opened her eyes and exhaled, long and slow and continued.

"He said he was a sailor. He said he worked on a ship on the Bering Sea, in Alaska. He said he was waiting out the winter season until his ship could be repaired and then he was going back to sea. With me being from a small town in eastern Washington, a town where the only water was a creek that ran through our neighbor's farm . . . I was mesmerized. I asked him to tell me about ships and life on the sea.

"We spent long hours that winter wrapped together under a blanket in a hayloft. Lance would get all dreamy, and I swear he'd go a million miles away and then he'd talk about the sea. He told me about his ship, how big it was, how it was made of wood—wood that creaked and groaned during storms. He talked about how the sails filled with wind.

" 'Full and round,' he'd say, 'like a woman pregnant with girls.'

"He told me how his ship bounded over the waves and how he and the other sailors stood with their legs apart, how they shifted their weight, first on one leg, next on the other, balancing with the rhythms of the sea. Outside, the winter storms blew fierce, and the snow fell thick, but we were cozy under that blanket, in that sweet, clean hay.

"The first time we made love, he whispered about the waves, about how we were riding a ship of love, a ship of dreams, together. He said he would teach me to sail and that we'd make love all around the world. And that we would be free because a ship is freedom.

"When I discovered I was pregnant, I was so excited—could barely wait until the next time he came around. I could see us, the three of us, on a ship of our own with our little boy. Naturally, Lance would have a son. We'd sail around the world together, and I'd teach our son, so he didn't have to go to school, and when he grew up he'd join the Navy, and we'd be so proud. Oh, I was full of dreams, full of love. When I finally told Lance, he turned pale. Sort of gulped for air.

" 'You're happy, aren't you? Lance, tell me you're happy.'

" 'Yes, sweetheart. Yes. I'm happy. A baby. Oh wow. Wow. Oh wow.'

"We made love, but it was fast, and he didn't whisper about the sea or anything. When we were done he said he guessed he should give me a present. I hoped it would be a ring or a brooch or something that was his mother's. Something I would cherish and would pass down to our daughter. I figured, for certain, our second child would be a girl.

"We hurried out to his truck. Winter rain soaked through my coat. Lance kept his head down, didn't look at me, didn't say anything.

"A big metal box in the back of his truck overflowed with a jumble of tools: ropes, pulleys, wrenches, and a couple of hard hats. Tools, I guessed, that he needed on his boat.

"He pushed them around, and finally he pulled out a wooden box. It was too big for jewelry; I knew that. But he handed it to me.

" 'Here,' he said, 'take this.'

"It was a gun. I must have looked confused.

" 'It's a pistol,' Lance said. 'It's the best I can do.'

"He let me off a few blocks from the boarding house. I walked the rest of the way cradling that box against my chest to protect it from the freezing rain.

"I never saw Lance again. He didn't come when the 4-H Club took away my scholarship, or when the school made me quit because they couldn't have unwed mothers in teachers' college. He wasn't around when I had to tell my parents. They were hurt, bad. Crushed. I was afraid they would stop talking to me or make me move away, and I'd never see them again. But they fixed up my old room and let me stay. The hardest part for me was that *I believed* he would come back. I told myself he was busy getting our boat ready and that he would come back for our child and me. I was so sure he'd be there when our baby was born. So sure that he'd make it to the hospital in time. But he didn't make it to the hospital on time. He didn't come. Lance never came back."

Mattie stopped talking. She sighed and reached for her tea.

"Oh my," Edna patted Mattie's arm. "I'm so sorry."

Mattie shrugged. "Well, I wasn't the first foolish girl in the world."

The two friends remained quiet for a few moments, and then Edna turned slightly and spoke. "Tell me about your daughter. What did you name her?"

"I named her Cordelia because I read somewhere that it means Daughter of the Sea. She had his eyes. Eyes as blue as the sea he'd whispered about.

"She was a handful, that girl. As fearless and reckless as her father. Not a day went by when I didn't have to pull her out of a tree or look for her in some old shed, or grab something sharp from her before she cut herself. She never sat still for a minute. Like her father, she was restless; moving, moving all the time. I stayed at home until Cordelia turned three and then my mother took care of her, and I went to work at the nursery in town.

"I repotted plants, did all the weeding and carried sacks of fertilizer. And the plants! Like mom said, I had a green thumb. The owner of the nursery, Howard, took notice. He stood at the door of the greenhouse and watched me work. After a few months, he invited me out to dinner. Then to another and another. After a year of dinners, he asked my dad for my hand. He said he didn't care that Cordelia was born out of wedlock. He adopted her as his own.

"Howard, he was . . ." Mattie closed her eyes, breathed in slow. She could still smell the tonics and arthritis ointments and could still see the flakes of dry skin on his collar. Fifty seems ancient when you're twenty-five.

She sighed and continued. "He was good and kind, and he didn't bother me too much. After two years of marriage, I found out I was pregnant again. We, Howard and me, we were both surprised. But he was proud. Especially when we had a boy. We named him Jake.

"Jake was also a handful, but in a different way from his sister. Poor little guy, born too early and with a clubbed foot. Sickly most of the time. I spent all my time either at the doctor's with Jake or chasing after Cordelia. Howard was a good provider, but he wasn't able to help with the children even after he sold the nursery."

The flight attendant appeared from the shadows of the cabin. "May I get you ladies anything? Warm milk? Maybe a biscuit?"

"Oh that sounds good," Edna sat up. "I'd love milk and cookies."

"And for you?"

Mattie hesitated then shook her head no. The flight attendant turned.

"Wait." Mattie stretched out, touched the woman's sleeve. "On second thought, yes, warm milk. Yes. Thank you."

"So, tell me more about your daughter," Edna said. She pulled her tray table down, and then she reached for Mattie's.

Mattie went on with her story.

"Like I said, she was a handful. Ran with boys. Sent home from school more than once for mouthing off to the teacher. Took lipstick from my drawer and put it on when she got to school. Snuck money from my purse. And, no matter what Howard and I did or said, she seemed angry all the time.

Always wanted to argue. But she was so beautiful to look at. Everyone forgave her. Everyone let things slide.

"She got pregnant at seventeen. What could I do? Howard was disappointed, and he didn't want her around anymore. Especially since he was so frail and Jake was constantly sick. But I pleaded, was extra friendly to him, and finally, he gave in. Let her stay with us.

"I hoped that pregnancy would settle her down or at least when the baby came she'd mellow out some. But that didn't happen. She stopped being angry which, at first, we thought was a good thing. But she cried all the time. Or went into her room and shut the door and stayed in there. She sat on the floor by the side of the bed, in the dark, all the blinds pulled tight, for days on end. Didn't want to eat or even take a sip of water. I feared for the baby's health."

The flight attendant brought their snack, then morphed into the darkened aisle.

"Boy or girl?" Edna dunked a cookie in the milk.

Mattie lifted her glass, blew across the top, and set it down again. "Don't know."

Edna turned and scrunched her brow. "You don't know?"

Mattie shook her head no. She pushed the package of cookies to the back of her tray. "No," she repeated.

"The cobbler in our town passed away right about the time Jake turned twelve so we couldn't get his special shoes made anymore. But there was an orthotics doctor in the city who could fit Jake so I drove to Spokane.

"While we waited in the doctor's office, I picked up a copy of the local paper and happened to flip to the obituary page. There he was. Lance. Older, but definitely Lance. Same sexy grin, same dreamy look in those eyes. I was so taken in by that photo that at first, I skipped the name.

"After a few minutes, I read the words. As it turned out, his name wasn't Lance. It was Arney. Arney Chloper. He was survived by his wife, who'd been his high-school sweetheart, and their four children. I did the math. He already had three of those children when he was whispering to me.

"Seems funny now, but the worst part was that the paper said he'd been a lineman. A journeyman lineman for the county. Even during the war, he stayed in Washington—worked for the county. The paper said he lived his entire life in Spokane.

"I knew then that he'd never been a sailor. Never been on a ship. In fact, he'd never even seen the sea. I could barely breathe, sitting there, in that doctor's office with my poor crippled boy. I thought it was the worst moment in my life. But it wasn't.

"When we got home, there was a police car and a fire engine in front of our house. I told Jake to stay in the car. 'Howard! Howard!' I remember yelling his name as I ran to the front door. 'Oh my God! Howard.' I remember thinking for sure he was gone. I thought for sure it would just be me and Cordelia and Jake now. But I was wrong.

"Howard met me on the porch. He wouldn't let me pass. He wrapped his arms around me and turned me away from the door. 'You can't go in,' he said.

"Lights flashed on the police car, and our neighbors stood in their doorways and out on their lawns. They stared at me, shook their heads, and looked away. I remember that somebody put a blanket around my shoulders. I couldn't understand why.

"Howard never left my side, not for a second, not even when the policeman wanted to ask him questions. 'Later,' Howard said, 'I'll talk to you later. My wife needs me now.' That's what he told the policeman.

"Then they brought her out on a stretcher covered with something black, a plastic sheet, I think. They wouldn't let me see her. I screamed. I'm sure I screamed. I tried to go to her but Howard and the policeman, they wouldn't let me."

The two women sat still together. Edna struggled for something to say. Finally, she whispered, "How?"

Mattie swallowed. "Her father's gun. The one he gave me when he left. I didn't even know she knew I had it. But she knew. She knew."

Chapter Thirty-nine

Smarter than Dolphins
Doha International Airport, Qatar

The journey from Australia to Egypt took nineteen hours, including the three-hour layover in Qatar, a country neither of them had ever heard of and both had trouble pronouncing. They decided to have lunch while they waited for the final flight to Cairo.

Emboldened by her decision to continue onward, Edna insisted that she select the restaurant. She chose an open-air café inside Doha International Airport. The café featured glasses of cold sweet tea, olives, plates of dates, and something made with rice and lamb.

"I'm so excited, Mattie." Edna's eyes sparkled and darted about. She surveyed the crowd of men and women in smart, Western-style business suits who chatted, checked flight information, and hurried past. She wondered about the elegant women in designer outfits who covered their heads with silk scarves, and lunched or shopped together. She smiled at the young people, the ones who reminded her of Katie with their tattoos, and T-shirts, and cell phones.

Mattie propped her elbows on the table and rested her chin on her knuckles. Despite the comfortable seats and the excellent service, the plane ride left her drained and exhausted. She held groggy memories of tangled power lines, of dirty, swirling sea foam, and of boys with withered limbs who'd limped through her dreams. She vaguely remembered waking, several times, to watch Edna chew on the end of an Emirates airline pen as she struggled to find the right words to write on a single sheet of stationery.

Mattie considered an olive but decided she was too tired to deal with the pit. Instead, she followed Edna's gaze, first to a group of men dressed in flowing white gowns, and then on to several women in full black burkas: robes that concealed them completely. Even their eyes stayed hidden behind small rectangles of black mesh. She leaned over and whispered in Edna's ear. "Are there lots of nuns and priests in this country?"

"No," Edna said. She straightened and motioned toward the men in the robes and the women in the burkas. "They are not nuns or priests, Mattie. They are camel drivers."

Mattie furrowed her brow and squinted at the travelers. "All of them?"

Edna nodded. She didn't actually remember any women in long black gowns in that circus, but that was a long time ago, and besides, these people with their robes and scarves, these people *must* be camel drivers.

Too excited to rest on the flight to Cairo, Edna chattered continuously and read out loud from the guidebook she'd purchased at the airport. "Listen to this." She bumped Mattie's arm with her elbow. Tea splashed onto Mattie's lap. Edna didn't notice.

If it had been Dolores or even Helen, Mattie might have snapped at them, but she'd never seen Edna so animated or so happy. What was a little hot tea on her only clean dress?

"It says here that some people think camels are smarter than dolphins."

"Hmm . . ." Mattie dabbed at the stain with a napkin.

"And that camels are considered the ships of the desert."

"No kidding?" Mattie stopped her cleanup and turned to Edna. "Why?"

"It says they haul cargo like ships do. And they carry people across open deserts the way ships carry people across open seas."

"Interesting." Mattie went back to moping.

"There's a whole page of quotes about camels. Quotes from famous people." Edna poked Mattie's arm again. "Want me to read them to you?"

Mattie sighed. She dropped the soaked wad of napkin on her tray and turned to Edna. "Yes. Read me the quotes about camels."

As the plane made a sweeping turn into the wind and began its descent to the ancient city of Cairo, Edna read camel quotes to Mattie: a humorous anecdote from Jackie Kennedy, political thoughts of Adolph Hitler, a parable from Jesus Christ, and something they couldn't quite figure out by George W. Bush.

Chapter Forty

City of a Thousand Minarets
Cairo, Egypt

Grannies. Look for two archeology students at the airport in Cairo. The aunties are up to something. Don't know what so STAY LOW. Miss you! Miss you! Miss you! XXX Katie.

Edna and Mattie expected to connect with more young people sporting dreadlocks, nose rings and safety pins through their eyebrows. But instead, the young man and woman who waited for them at baggage claim dressed in pressed matching khaki slacks and long-sleeved shirts. An American flag and the seal of an American university embroidered on their breast pockets identified them. The man held an electronic tablet. White letters on a navy blue background spelled out:

Outrageous Women. Welcome.

"Finally," Mattie said. "They got it right."

"Hi!" The woman waved to them. She wore her thick blonde hair pulled into a neat ponytail. Her only makeup, coral lip gloss. Her companion wore his hair short, in a military-like cut. Both glowed with deep tans and looked pleasant in a no-nonsense sort of way. Mattie guessed early thirties.

Carl drove. Lindsey sat in the front of the late-model minivan. She stretched around to chat with Mattie and Edna. "We have to go to back to . . . to the dig, this morning," she said. "So we have to drop you off at your hotel now. But we know you must be tired from traveling. We thought you might get settled in and rest to-day, and tomorrow morning we'll come by and take you to the public market for a shopping trip. We'll give you a guided tour. You'll have such a good time. Then, tomorrow evening, before sunset, we'll take you out to where you can have that camel ride we've been reading about."

"It's so good of you dear," Edna said, "to organize everything for us."

Lindsey smiled.

Carl pulled the van to the front of a hotel hosting a massive glass and marble entryway. A uniformed doorman hurried over to the vehicle.

In the lobby, Mattie craned her neck and stared at the pool sized crystal chandelier overhead. "We can't afford this," she said.

Edna pressed her face into a fragrant bouquet and breathed deeply. The arrangement, mounted on a marble column, stood a foot taller than her, and held at least three-dozen lilies and as many roses, or more. Polished brass gleamed. The concierge's black walnut desk curved in a magnificent sweep along one wall. Heels of designer shoes clicked on the slick marble floor as women and men, some dressed in the height of Western fashion, others in traditional robes or full, blue satin burkas, hurried to official meetings or secret trysts.

"We really cannot afford this," Mattie repeated.

"Oh, don't worry," Lindsey said. "Here, why don't you both stand in front of those flowers. I'll take your picture. You look so pretty." She steered Mattie next to Edna. "Your granddaughter booked you in another place, a smaller place. But we didn't think it was safe enough. We got you the . . . ah, the university discount. This hotel is very comfortable. You'll like it here." She dismissed the issue with a single flip of her hand. "Now smile!"

Carl carried their satchels to the elevator, and they all rode, without speaking, to the twenty-eighth floor. Even though she'd heard Lindsey's explanation about the university discount, Mattie could not conceive of staying in a place like this.

Their suite featured two rooms; each with a king-sized bed, a large desk, a full sofa, and an overstuffed chair. Both rooms offered a panoramic view from the front of the hotel and of what looked like a sprawling public market a few blocks away. Vertical louvered shades filtered the already hot Egyptian sun. Mattie guessed that her room at Restful Palms could easily fit inside the bathroom.

"See? Comfortable." Lindsey smiled at them. She nodded to Carl to drop their satchels in the closet as she handed each of them a sheet of paper. "Keep these with you," she said. "We'll all be together outside of the hotel, but in case we get separated, you can show this to any policeman. It will help keep you safe." She thought for a few seconds and then added, "Because, you know, Cairo is such a dangerous city."

Edna folded the page and slipped it into her sweater pocket without question. Mattie examined the paper. Their names, passport numbers, the name and phone number of the hotel, and Lindsey's contact information were typed at the top of the sheet in English.

"What does this say?" She pointed to a string of words written in, she suspected, Arabic.

"Oh, nothing. Just the same stuff in the local language." As she had before, Lindsey flicked her hand and dismissed further discussion. She turned to Edna. "All right then, ladies, do you need anything else before we leave?"

Edna tilted her head, closed her eyes, and watched a thought float by—a thought she wanted to keep but couldn't. She opened her eyes, blinked, and then shook her head no.

"Good," Lindsey said. "Naturally, you can pick up the phone and call room service if you think of anything. Feel free to order whatever you want—food, drinks, whatever. Don't worry about cost; it's all covered."

Carl coughed.

"You know, the university's discount," Lindsey added.

Carl walked to the door and held it open.

"Questions?" Lindsey looked at Mattie.

Mattie puckered her lips, frowned, and touched her finger to her temple. "No, dear, not that I can think of. You seem to have everything under control."

"Super. If that's all, we'll see you ladies tomorrow."
Mattie and Edna nodded.

Chapter Forty-one

Easy Money

Carl tapped keys on his cell phone and hit Send. "Done," he said. "Money in the bank." They entered the elevator.

"That was the easiest trace we've ever done." Lindsey slipped her arm into his.

"Like shooting fish in a barrel." Carl looked down at her and grinned. "Thank you, Facebook." They watched the numbers—*twenty-seven, twenty-six, twenty-five* .

"You know, I almost feel guilty. We charged so much and the job was so easy." She bit her lower lip, frowned.

"No worries, babe. We did the job. They paid the money." He gave her arm a squeeze. "Besides, they'll be rolling once they get the old broad's money. This is nothing." He thought for a minute. "I know, let's go to the private bar in the Sheraton. Order champagne with breakfast. Take care of that guilt of yours." He leaned down and kissed her forehead.

Ping.

"Good plan." Lindsey smiled at him, released his arm, and stepped into the lobby.

Chapter Forty-two

A D a n g e r o u s P l a c e

"I don't trust her," Mattie said. She crumpled the paper Lindsey had given her and tossed it into a wastebasket by the desk. She walked to the window, pushed the louvered panels apart, looked down, and watched as the minivan pulled into heavy traffic. "I don't trust either one of them."

Edna crossed the room and stood next to her. "Oh, don't worry." She placed her hand on Mattie's arm. "They're graduate students. Katie says that all graduate students take life too seriously."

"Maybe." Mattie bit her lower lip and let the shade fall back into place. "Maybe."

Mattie sat on a bed and fiddled with the television remote. She wished she had a book or even a deck of cards.

Edna stood in the bathroom. She opened all the miniature bottles of shampoo and lotions and tried them out on the back of her hands. She managed to keep busy for fifteen minutes and then, with a sigh, she left the bathroom and crossed the room to Mattie.

"Would you do me a favor?"

"Of course."

"Will you keep a letter for me? I wrote it to Katie. I want to make sure she gets it and sometimes I . . ." Her voice caught. "Sometimes I forget things."

Mattie sighed. "We all forget things. I forget things all the time. But of course, I'll hold it for you, and I'll help make sure she gets it."

Edna rooted around in her handbag and pulled out an envelope. She handed it to Mattie. "Read it."

"You sure?"

Edna nodded. "Yes. I want to know if it makes sense and if you think it will work."

Mattie tilted her head. *Work*? She wondered but didn't say anything. She removed the single sheet from the envelope; heavy, cream-colored stationery, courtesy of the airline. She glanced at the letter and noticed a neatly printed name, a signature, an email address, and a phone number next to Edna's wobbly scrawl.

"Who is this?" Mattie pointed to the second signature.

"That man on the airplane. The bank lawyer, the one in the fancy suit—you remember him. The man with the lovely daughter." Edna gestured toward the paper. "Read. Read."

Mattie shook her head and then skimmed the words. When she'd finished, she lowered the paper to the bed and looked up at her friend. "This is really very good, Edna. He helped you with the words, didn't he?"

Edna nodded. "Yes. He was so kind. And smart. What do you think?"

Mattie hesitated a moment. She considered what she'd read. "Giving a power of attorney to Katie, and leaving all your money to her sounds right, but I don't think it will work."

"Why not?" Edna emptied her handbag onto the bed and reviewed the contents. "Oh, here it is." She picked up a business card. "From that nice man."

Mattie refolded the letter and slipped it back into the envelope. "I don't think it will work because I assumed your daughters already *have* power of attorney. I figured they would automatically get your money."

Edna reached for the envelope and dropped the card into it. She handed it back to Mattie. Then she tilted her head, raised her brows, and smiled. She shook her head, her eyes twinkled. "They *want* a power of attorney. They want to get all my money. *But they can't have it.*"

Mattie and Edna spent another half hour sorting through their bags, peeking into all the drawers and closets in the suite and staring out the window to the street scene below. Finally, Edna sighed. "I'm bored. There isn't anything to do in here, and they aren't coming back until tomorrow." She stood with her hands on her hips. "I want to go out now. We have my guidebook. We don't need them." She swayed a bit but held her stance.

Mattie grinned.

They left the hotel through a side entrance. Mattie's idea. Edna pointed to the photo of the market in her book, the taxi driver nodded. Five minutes later, he dropped them off at the main entrance to the Khan el-Khalili Bazaar.

At first, Edna clung to Mattie, gripped her arm, and walked so close that Mattie thought they both might take a tumble. But she understood. The market overwhelmed. For a few minutes, she thought that maybe they should have waited for Carl and Lindsey and the guided tour. However, the colors, sounds, smells, and even the jostle of the crowd, thrilled more than frightened them. Soon the two friends pointed, laughed, and wondered out loud to each other.

Ancient limestone arches stretched high in ornate architecture. Wooden stalls sandwiched between stairs led to indoor shops that peddled everything from blue jeans to crystal. One stand sold nothing but puppets dancing from thin black strings. Another offered music boxes inlaid with coral and mother of pearl. A jewelry store displayed hundreds of gold filigree bangles.

"Helen would go nuts in here," Mattie said.

The walls of tents, row upon row of canvas tents, breathed in and out with the wind that fluttered flags from a thousand different countries, towns, and territories. "Let's go to every one of those countries." Edna pointed to the flags.

Mattie feigned surprise, then chuckled. "That is such a *shocking* idea.*"

Enticed by the scent of bergamot and the sight of cakes spongy with honey, they stopped at a small café. "You're dripping." Mattie pointed to a splot of gold oozing down Edna's chin.

Edna scooped it up with her finger and laughed. "Remember that time in Ireland?" She popped her finger into her mouth and licked it clean.

Mattie laughed, too. "Yeah. Dolores and her fellow." She shook her head. "What a pair."

"How did she learn to dance?"

"That wasn't dancing, Edna. That was clomping around in circles. Dolores is way too fat to dance."

Edna stopped, cake midway to her mouth. Honey dripped between her fingers and slipped into her palm. "You shouldn't be so hard on her, Mattie. She can't help the way she is."

Mattie snorted. "Right."

"I'm serious." Edna lowered the cake to her plate and wiped her hand. Bits of paper napkin tore and clung to her sticky fingers. "She does the best she can. Considering."

Mattie rolled her eyes. "Considering what? That she is always too busy eating to . . ."

Edna stopped her. "Considering that nobody loved her. And she never had anyone to love. Except for Mr. William T. Broughton, and now, of course, Chuck."

Mattie closed her mouth. She stared at Edna. Helen had been Mattie's best friend, her closest confidant at Restful Palms. Helen was the smart one and the most genteel of all of them. She was the one who consistently had something wise or calming to say.

Helen was the woman Mattie sought out for advice or turned to when she wanted to confide in someone.

Edna, on the other hand, this little slip of a person with her confused looks and those ridiculous pom poms on the backs of her socks. Edna was as ditsy as they came. Most of the time Mattie felt a little protective of her but lately, she was . . . at least sometimes . . . Mattie couldn't put her finger on it, but something was different about Edna these past few days. Despite her forgetfulness and her spells of confusion, Edna seemed stronger, calmer, and just different somehow.

"Do you think she is happy, Mattie?" Edna searched her friend's face. "I mean, now, all alone in Ireland? Do you think Dolores is happy?"

Mattie blew across the top of her teacup. "Uh huh. I think so." She sipped the tea—too sweet for her taste. She took another sip and sat the cup down. "First of all, she's not alone. She has Chuck and Mrs. Doolin and all those other people. Second, yes, I think she's happy because, like you said, she finally found someone to love. She's falling in love. I think she thinks he's falling in love with her, too."

"I think he is," Edna said.

"Probably." Mattie nodded.

"Probably. Yes." Edna bobbed her head up and down. "But happy or not, she sure looked silly in that hat of hers." She giggled, made a face and pretended to be Dolores primping in her leprechaun hat.

Mattie's face crinkled into a smile. She reached over and gave Edna a quick, tight hug. "You're right," she said. "She *was* awfully funny in that hat."

When Mattie let go, Edna reached to her plate and broke off another gooey piece of cake. She squinted at the treat, appeared to examine it. "What about Helen? What do we even know about Helen?"

"We know she loved Roy." Mattie pulled another napkin from a basket and pushed it across the table toward Edna's plate.

"Do you think Helen was happy?" Edna said.

Mattie didn't have to think about that one. She answered immediately. "Absolutely. I'm positive she was happy." Mattie closed her eyes, allowed herself to drift back to Buttons Beach— a place she'd refused to think of since the day it happened. In her mind's eye she watched Helen standing in the swirling surf; her arms opened wide, her head tossed back. And Mattie could hear Helen's sweet, Southern voice calling out, *Lordy! Lordy! I am full of your praise today.*

"Yes," Mattie said, "I'm one hundred and one percent positive our Helen was happy on this trip." She opened her eyes and watched as Edna pressed the chunk of cake between her thumb and forefinger until honey oozed over her hand.

Edna looked up from the cake. "Well, then, what about Josephine? She didn't want to come on this trip. She didn't want to be outrageous, didn't even want to talk to us anymore." Edna licked across one sticky finger and swallowed. "Do you think Josephine is happy?"

Mattie narrowed her eyes, squinted at her friend. *Where is this leading? What brought all this up?* "I don't know. I suppose she probably is. Josephine is warm and safe and dry, and she actually likes the food at Restful Palms." Mattie paused for a brief moment—shuddered at the memory of congealed globs of grease floating on the surface of thin brown gravy. She hurried on. "And she has her husband to boss around. Yes." She nodded. "Yes, I think Josephine is happy at Restful Palms."

Edna looked up from the cake and leaned forward. Her sleeve dragged across the honey pooled on her plate. "Mattie," she said, "do you know anyone—anyone—who was ever happy at Restful Palms?"

Mattie looked away from Edna. She gazed through the open door and watched the swirl of colors, the smiles, and the movement on the street outside the café. She listened to happy chatter, to the call of merchants, to the music of a single flute. So much life, so much energy. But this trip, this journey . . . it was a quest. Restful Palms, for all its downsides, was home.

She started to speak, but Edna interrupted her. "Talk about hats . . ." she grinned. "Do you remember those corks on that hat of Helen's?"

They stayed in the café and revisited their adventures. They remembered, laughed, and remembered some more until when relaxed enough, and renewed enough, they prepared to venture out again.

"Here." Mattie set the cell phone on the table by Edna's tea-cup. "I'm going to the restroom, but Katie should be sending us an email today so watch for it. I'll right back."

Edna dipped her napkin into her water glass and wiped one hand. She glanced down at the cell phone and lost interest in the stray bits of paper still trapped on her other hand. She decided to work the phone by herself. At least, give it a try. *Mattie will be so proud.* She fished around in her handbag until she found the pencil. Engrossed in her task, Edna didn't see the scruffy teenager enter the teahouse.

He pulled up his hoodie, stepped inside, and scanned the diners. A few shopkeepers clustered together, no doubt on a break from work; he turned his face away from them. A couple, for sure on their honeymoon, held their phone out for a selfie, and kissed. A possibility. By the window, an old lady. Older than his gram for sure. She stabbed at her phone with a pencil. Kept stabbing and stabbing. She picked it up, peered at the surface, shook it, put it back down and stabbed at it again. Stupid old cow. Perfect. He kept his face partially concealed behind his hood and crossed the room.

"You need some help with that, granny?" He kept his voice low to muffle his British accent.

Edna looked up. The young man *seemed* familiar. "Are you one of Katie's friends? We're waiting for her email."

He chewed on his lower lip, his eyes darted around the room. No one paid attention. "Ah, yeah. Sure. Katie and me."

"Oh good." Edna held the cell phone out to him. "I'm trying to send her an email. Can you help me?"

The boy took the phone. He eyed Edna's handbag.

She stood up. "Do you want a little cake? Have a seat, young man. I'll go get you one." Edna picked up her purse and headed toward the glass counter filled with sugary treats.

The British teenager worked on blending in with tourists, on disappearing into the crowd. He didn't bother to read the email message on his most recent acquisition.

Grannies. Warning. The aunties hired some people to find you and bring you back. Don't go with anyone. Take a taxi to the youth hostel. It's in the guidebook. The kids, the REAL kids will find you. I'm soooo sorry. Tried to stop the aunties but they are too . . . you know. Love you to the moon and back, a zillion times. I will call on the phone. At lunch. Your time tomorrow. XXX Katie

The next day, at noon, Eastern European Time, the groggy teenager would wake from a drug-induced sleep to the sound of circus music. It would come from one of the stolen phones still stashed in the pocket of his jeans. He'd swear, roll over, and pass out again. The music would continue to play.

"He was right here." Edna pointed to the spot where the teen stood with their cell phone in his hand. "He said he could fix our phone for us. He said he was a friend of Katie's."

Mattie took a deep breath. *One thousand and one, one thousand and two . . .* She walked to the door and checked the crowd of shoppers, but she knew it was pointless. *It's not her fault. It's really not her fault.*

"Drugs." The café owner shook his head. "I tell my girls to watch out for those thieves, but they are too busy with customers." He shook his head again. "I call police."

"No. No," Mattie said, "they won't find him." She nodded back to the table where Edna sat with her hands in her lap, her eyes closed. "She doesn't even remember what he looked like except that he was a young man." She shook her head. "Don't worry. It's not your fault."

Chapter Forty-three

Old Friends, Like Bookends

"Oh, Mattie, he seemed like such a kind young man . . ."

"Stop." Mattie wrapped her arm around Edna's shoulders. They sat on a bench in a small, grassy park across from the market. "Don't worry. We'll manage." She turned her head and searched her friend's face, tried to read the lines of worry etched there. *She looks like a frightened child.* "It was just a cell phone. We can get another one."

"Really? Are you sure we can get another one?" Hope lit Edna's eyes.

"Yes. Yes, of course, I'm sure. In fact, I'll bet we can order one at the hotel through room service." This, Mattie knew, was an outright lie.

Edna threw her arms around Mattie and squeezed.

Mattie forced a smile. "Enough of this. We should be in that market shopping. Not sitting around chatting. Let's get going, sister. Let's roll."

Edna giggled. "Does your mother know you talk like that, Mattie Snorgenson?"

Together they wandered through the tight, twisting corridors of the market. They slowed to rub fabric between their fingers and to listen to the music of brass wind chimes, hundreds of them, dangling together from strands of twine tied to bamboo poles. They scurried away from the clock shop with its collection of frantic mechanisms ticking time away. At the spice shop, they lingered over woven baskets that spilled cinnamon, curry, turmeric, and several spices they couldn't identify. Edna purchased a bag of fennel powder. She wasn't sure what she'd do with it, but she loved the scent.

Mattie bought a full burka; the kind she'd seen the women wearing in the airport, the kind with a little window of black mesh over the face. She tried it on but decided she could only wear it for a few minutes at a time—much too hot. But what a perfect costume for the next Halloween party at Restful Palms!

At the bakery, they both over-sampled, delighting in piles of thick-crusted bread dusted with pale brown flour, dotted with seeds. Caraway and sesame.

Slabs of raw beef and lamb hung from sharpened hooks in the butcher's stall. Repulsed by the smell and the swarm of flies, Mattie held her nose.

Edna stood fixated in front of a stack of cages crammed with live rabbits. When the owner of the creatures smiled wide, two gold teeth glittered. He pulled a rabbit from a cage and handed it to Edna. She cradled it close, felt its heart beat—a timepiece truer than any in the clock shop. She rocked it and cooed to it and cuddled it until Mattie pried it away.

"Couldn't we have a pet, Mattie?"

"Oh, come on. Don't be silly." She took Edna's hand and gave a gentle tug.

Arm in arm, they meandered the length of the alley until Mattie noticed an elaborate display of rugs. "Look at those." She stopped and pointed to the carpets. Rugs woven in tight patterns of burgundy, gold, blue, and green fanned out in a star-shaped presentation. "One of those would make my room at home look like something out of a magazine," she said. "Let's go see."

Under the watchful eye of the dealer, Mattie pulled the exotic rugs back, carpet after carpet. She inspected each one and listened with care as the man explained weaves and patterns. This new knowledge, along with the visual and tactile beauty of the art, hypnotized her. But Edna grew bored.

"I want to go on," she said.

"Oh, just a little more time. I want to find one to take home." Mattie didn't turn away from the rugs. "Can't you stay with me a little longer?" She bent down, rolled another carpet aside, and scrutinized the rich brown and scarlet patterns on the rug beneath.

"You stay here," Edna said. "I want to go to the bread stand again, and back to the rabbits."

"No, Edna. We need to stick together."

Edna crossed her arms and looked directly at Mattie. "I've sure heard that before." She narrowed her eyes, swayed a little. "Why don't you tie us together with a rope?

Mattie straightened, wavered. She knew this was not a good idea; she knew they should stick together. But, she rationalized; Edna should be allowed to make her own decisions. And . . . she did move slow . . . plus, she did linger a long time in each spot. It wouldn't take much to catch up with her. "Alright then, just for a little while. But we need a plan."

"A plan." Edna nodded.

Mattie glanced around. The market teemed with shoppers and shopkeepers—bustled with people who smiled, people who laughed, and people who took photos of themselves with cell phones like theirs. Like the one they used to have. Armed guards stood at attention to ensure shopper safety. Sunlight warmed canvas and limestone structures. Cumin and cloves scented the breeze. Surely Edna would be all right for a short time on her own. "Promise me you'll stay in this section. Don't go to any other part of the market. I'll come and look for you, okay?"

"Okay," Edna repeated. Her gaze followed a young boy leading a donkey laden with woven baskets.

"If for some reason we don't find each other by. . . say. . ." Mattie glanced at her watch. "By one, we get in a taxi and go back to the hotel. We'll meet up and have lunch together. Got that?"

Edna nodded, but her attention remained with the donkey and its colorful load.

"Do you still have that paper with the hotel's name on it? The one Lindsey gave you?" Mattie touched Edna's sleeve. "Are you listening to me?"

Edna turned and faced her. Again she nodded. *Lunch. Hotel. Lunch.*

"Good." Mattie bit her lip. She wasn't sure. Truthfully, she *was* sure this was a poor decision. But Edna needed this, and besides, it wouldn't take long to select a carpet. Mattie stepped close and gave her friend a hug.

"Be careful," she said. But Edna, now distracted by thoughts of rabbits and donkeys, simply walked away.

Mattie bit her lip and furrowed her brow. She watched Edna wander off, sighed, and turned back to the dealer. He held two carpets out to her. Pristine, perfect rugs; one draped over each outstretched arm.

Edna forgot to stop by the rabbits. She passed the puppets and the bread but lingered at a fruit stand. A girl offered a wedge of juicy, ripe mango—a slice the color of sunset, the shape of a quarter moon. Edna smiled, thanked the girl, and absently slipped the dripping fruit into her purse. She continued on; wandered past china shops and shoe sellers, ambled by bakeries, and strolled near displays swathed in silk. Finally, she drifted beyond the alley where the rabbits and the carpets lived.

"Tired. I'm tired." Edna spoke to herself. "I should go." She thought she might have something to do, but she couldn't remember what, so she continued to roam until she found herself in an older, shabbier part of the market. She stopped in front of a tent where hundreds of oil lamps and lanterns hung from ropes and poles. *We could have one of those in our house, Louis*. She held the thought until it spiraled slow and drifted away like the smoke from the lamps.

Chapter Forty-four

Done Deal – Tampa, Florida

Suzanne called her sister. "The text came in from Cairo."

"And?"

"They found her. She's in the hotel. They'll put her on a flight in the morning."

"Photo?"

"Yup. And . . . she looks pretty good."

"I'll wire the funds."

Chapter Forty-five

Mattie made arrangements with the carpet dealer. He would send the rugs to her room at the Restful Palms Retirement Home. She couldn't choose between them, so she bought them both; one for herself, one for Edna. A surprise; let Edna decide which one she wanted. Something to remind them both of their adventures.

Edna stood in front of a wooden crate piled high with yellowed newspapers and old magazines. The papers smelled of mold and mildew. She wrinkled her nose and sneezed. She looked at the cover of a *Life Magazine*. A young woman in a pink pillbox hat sat in a convertible and smiled, her hand forever frozen in a parade wave. Edna remembered that smile, but she did not recall who wore it. *Such a lovely girl.*

Mattie checked with the rabbit seller and with the baker. She stopped at the café. Everyone remembered them; nodded, sympathetic, but no, they had not seen her friend a second time. After an hour, Mattie gave up and took a taxi back to the hotel. Edna is

okay, she thought. Probably got bored and left. Most likely taking
a nap.

Edna shuffled on and then she saw it. She'd missed it before;
maybe because of the crowd. A tent filled with animals just like a
circus tent. There were plush monkeys, teddy bears, toy elephants, lions, and even a parrot. And there, in the middle, right
there in that tent, hanging from a red silk cord—a small, stuffed
camel. Enchanted, Edna stopped and stared. A green brocade
cloth, fringed in gold, draped the hump. Fur, the color of melted
caramels, invited a touch. Black button eyes winked. Velvet lips
of purest white beckoned. Edna stepped closer and reached one
hand toward the camel.

"Oh Louis, *please*."

Their suite was empty. Mattie muttered to herself, "She'll be
along soon. She'll get hungry and come back for lunch." Mattie
dumped the contents of a paper bag on the dresser top: bread,
cheese, and spiced sausage. She arranged their meal, made it look
like a picnic; wished they had a couple of those miniature bottles
of wine from the airplane. She couldn't wait to tell Edna about
the carpets. Maybe she wouldn't keep them a secret. Maybe
they'd go back to the market together and look at the rugs one
more time.

A siren shattered Edna's thoughts. People around her yelled
and shoved and ran. She thought she smelled smoke. Hands

pushed at her. She breathed a strong body odor; familiar somehow, and not all that unpleasant. Something smashed into her.
She felt herself fall, felt air woosh from her lungs, felt a crush of
bodies against hers. She looked up, over the people, past the panic. A flag fluttered at the corner of a tent. She smiled.

Two hours went by, and then another, before Mattie heard the
knock on the door.

Chapter Forty-six

Tax Dollars at Work

Mattie sat on the edge of the hotel bed. The man from the American Embassy explained everything. A fire. Probably one of the lamps in a tent. Panic. The crowd crushed her. She didn't suffer, couldn't have suffered, it happened too fast. He said they found her passport and a sheet of paper with the name of the hotel and the room number. They notified her next of kin, her daughters. "Do you know them? Her daughters?" he asked.

Mattie didn't answer. She stared at her hands. Her fingers balled into fists on her lap. Her lips pressed tight

He continued. "They hired a couple of private detectives to find her."

She jerked her head up—searched his face.

"They didn't have permits here in Cairo. The detectives. They didn't have papers. They were working here illegally. They'll be charged and deported." Then, with a small smirk, he added, "Too bad those daughters of your friend spent so much money hiring them. That money is gone."

Mattie dropped her head back down.

The man was polite, organized, and firm. He said he was going to send her back home. Back to America, to Florida, to the Restful Palms Retirement Home. What else could he do for her?

She didn't raise her head.

He placed his business card on the dresser and said that his secretary would arrange a flight. He'd come by with a car in the morning to take her to the airport. Don't worry about anything. The United States government was there to help her.

He stopped talking and watched Mattie for a moment. Her shoulders slumped, her body bent, thin and frail. Her sparse white hair, frazzled, uncombed. She looked drained, defeated. Even so, *the old gal's got guts*. He almost smiled. "You ladies had a fair bit of air time, you know. Caused quite a stir back home."

Mattie remained silent; continued to stare at her hands.

He cleared his throat. "Do you want to see a doctor?"

She shook her head no.

"All right, then, get some rest." He waited for a beat. "I have to insist that you stay here. Don't leave the hotel." He paused and then added, "It's for your own good, of course."

She looked up. Blinked once. "Of course."

"Oh. Just one more thing." He opened his briefcase. "She was holding this when we found her. We thought she probably bought it for a gift. Maybe for a grandchild? Perhaps you could take it?"

On his way through the lobby, the man from the American Embassy stopped at the desk, spoke with the concierge and showed him a photograph. The concierge memorized the face in the photo and nodded. The two men shook hands and the man from the embassy left the hotel.

Mattie sat and held the stuffed camel for a long, long time. As the sun strolled over Cairo, it slipped between the louvered panels of the hotel's shades and sketched a pattern of bars on the carpeting; dark and light.

She tried to push her thoughts away; to forget where and even who she was. She tried especially hard to forget Edna and the others. After all, it was her fault, Mattie Lynn Snorgenson's fault, they had come on this trip. *She* was the one who wanted to be an outrageous woman, and she had convinced the others they did, too. *She* was the one who dragged them all away from the safety and security of their home. Now, it was her fault they were gone.

But no matter how hard Mattie tried to push them away, one by one they crept in close. She could almost feel a familiar touch on her shoulder, the press of a soft hand on her arm. She closed her eyes and sat still, just breathing, feeling. Without thinking, she reached down and absently brushed an imaginary crumb from her dress.

And then, she laughed. Laughed right out loud. Couldn't stop herself. There was Dolores—dancing. And Dolores, with her fellow, strolling along under that big, full, Irish moon.

"Don't you remember the look on her face when he told her she was beautiful?" Helen's soft, southern drawl whispered in Mattie's ear. "Don't you remember her joy?"

Mattie caught her breath and nodded. She kept her eyes shut tight.

"I expect there'll be a wedding before long." Helen's tease, so gentle.

"Dolores and Chuck? Married?" Mattie rolled the idea around for a moment. She wanted to ask more about that, but Helen continued.

"And Rose, bless her heart. She finally found the peace she needed. She was finally free."

"Really?" Mattie swallowed.

"Yes darlin', really."

"Oh, Helen," Mattie choked back a sob. "I got you killed on that beach. You were so happy, and I got you killed." Mattie pushed her fists against her eyes.

"Shush. Don't you know I'm with my boys? Don't you know I'm with my Roy? And, Lordy . . . there are kangaroos everywhere. Hundreds of 'em."

Mattie sat still, afraid to move, afraid to open her eyes.

"But Mattie-Girl." Helen so close now, Mattie could almost breathe the scent of lilacs. "I really gotta ask. What about Edna's camel? What about your ship? Are you just gonna forget them? Are you just gonna give up?"

Mattie shook her head. "It's over."

"Oh my." Helen's voice faded.

Mattie tilted her head slightly. Strained to hear.

Helen's voice, now a faint whisper. "I surely don't think it's over just yet. Not while there's still one outrageous woman on this good earth."

Mattie stayed still a while longer. When she finally opened her eyes, the room was cool and gray with shadows. She knew the sun had begun its downward dip. She stood.

Mattie gathered the stuffed animal and the letter Edna wrote to Katie and slipped them into the paper bag. She took a few moments to prepare, and just before turning to go, she noticed the heart-shaped stone she'd found on Buttons Beach. She dropped it in the bag and went down to the lobby. Mattie leaned against the gleaming walnut desk.

"I need to send a package to America," she said. "And I need you to call a taxi for me." She pointed to a page in Edna's tour book. "I want to go here."

If the concierge hadn't been so busy with a busload of new guests, he might have noticed that the woman in the full black burka, the one who sent a package to America, the one who climbed into a taxi in front of the hotel, wore combat boots.

Chapter Forty-seven

Edna's Camel

"Madam. Are you going to ride my camel or not?" He shifted from one foot to the other. She was his last customer of the day, and he wanted to go home to food, to his wife, to his young son. Still, he felt bad pushing her. She seemed so old and so frail. But the sun was low, the breeze was up, the day was ending. The camel driver sighed.

Mattie pulled her gaze from the animal and glanced toward the man. His white robes billowed full and round like sails pregnant with wind. Beyond his turbaned head, the desert sands rolled and shifted in shimmering golden waves. The bills in her hand—tiny flags—fluttered.

"Madam?" The driver cleared his throat.

Mattie took a step forward, hesitated, and turned back to the huge, caramel-colored beast. It was the biggest living creature she'd ever seen. It tugged at its line. She knew this was the most majestic, the most regal, and the smartest camel on earth. *This was Edna's camel.*

A camel is the ship of the desert. A desert is a sea of sand. Mattie smiled. She lifted her head. Confident. Strong. Nothing left to lose. She reached out, handed the bills to the man, and walked to the camel.

Thank You

I would like to thank each and every one of you who nudged me along on this journey. But I won't be able to do that—the list is too long. Still, please know that even if your name doesn't appear on this page, you are forever remembered, and appreciated, in my heart. My sincerest thanks to:

My teachers, Jack Remick, Laura Kalpakian, Priscilla Long, and Elizabeth Engstrom—tough task masters all. You've taught me that discipline is our obligation to the gift, that sentences do not begin with "it," the difference between real and pretend writers, and that novels require two pages, two pages, two pages…

James Lynch, a generous writer, and a darn nice guy. You told me to hang in there; you reminded me to watch the horizon.

The incredible artist and dear friend, Karen Francis. Your Wisdom added to this story, your Art adds to my life.

The members of my Friday Critique Group: Janet Oakley, Nancy Adair, Francis Howard-Snyder and Laura Rink—you guys are the lighthouse.

Bill Rink, your art, and skill is a wonder, and your grin is infectious. Jim Imhoff, your photography is stellar.

Words on paper need Kari Neumeyer, the Amazing Comma Queen, the incredible writing coaches Mindy Halleck and Cami Ostman, and the amazing team at Village Books, Bellingham.

Nancy, Joan and Sam Ging—nothing gets done without your support and friendship. I love you dearly.

The writers of Louisa's Café (the Spirit lives on), to the Red Wheelbarrow Writers, to the Washington Writers and Publishers, and to the Writers of Malta. I offer thanks for the hard work, the laughter, and the wine. Lots and lots of wine.

Andrew McBride, your skill is well, it's magical. Thank you.

The Outrageous Women of Sun City Center, and to George and Neva Getman—you are, of course, the inspiration.

Richard Bach, ever gentle, strong and steadfast. You are my Guiding Star.

Denise Cantrell Winkler—my sister, friend, partner in crime and so much more. You are the wind.

Finally, thanks to Malarkey, my Siamese cat, as no project begins or ends without his critical scrutiny.

Jessica H. Stone (Jes) enjoys putting words on paper and hulls in water. She is a long distance sailor and author of the best-seller, *Doggy on Deck – Life at Sea with a Salty Dog*. Her articles and columns are popular with travelers and dreamers alike. On a recent backpacking trip to Cuba, she fell in love with the gentle people of that beautiful island. When not traveling or sailing, Jes writes in a cottage by the sea. www.jessicahstone.com

CPSIA information can be obtained
at www.ICGtesting.com
Printed in the USA
FFOW03n0953011017
40529FF